Tangled
Allure

Contents

— **Prologue:** —

In the bustling city of New York, where fashion reigns supreme, Isabella Rivera, a talented and driven fashion designer, finds herself working for the renowned fashion house of Maxwell & Co. Known for her impeccable taste and innovative designs, Isabella is determined to make a name for herself in this competitive industry.

Enter Sebastian Maxwell, the charismatic and influential CEO of Maxwell & Co. From the moment they meet, Isabella and Sebastian clash fiercely. Their creative visions collide, and their conflicting personalities ignite a firestorm of tension. They become the epitome of enemies as they spar over designs, strategies, and the future of the company.

However, fate has a way of surprising even the most stubborn of hearts. When a prestigious fashion event looms on the horizon, Maxwell & Co. faces a crisis that threatens its reputation. In a desperate move, Sebastian reluctantly turns to Isabella for help, recognizing her unmatched talent and a keen eye for detail.

Isabella reluctantly agrees to assist Sebastian, driven by her unwavering dedication to her craft and a desire to prove her worth. As they work together behind the scenes, they begin to discover unexpected layers beneath their initial animosity. Isabella witnesses Sebastian's tireless devotion to the fashion house, his unwavering commitment to quality, and his vulnerability beneath his confident exterior. Sebastian, in turn, recognizes Isabella's passion, her raw talent, and her unwavering determination to succeed.

Amid the chaos of deadlines, demanding clients, and the tantalizing allure of the fashion world, Isabella and Sebastian's dynamic evolves. Their shared pursuit of perfection and their undeniable chemistry leads them on an unexpected journey from enemies to reluctant allies and, ultimately, to lovers.

As their professional relationship morphs into a clandestine romance, Isabella and Sebastian must navigate the treacherous waters of office politics, power dynamics, and the potential fallout if their secret is revealed. They face not only external judgment and societal expectations but also the risk of jeopardizing the very success they've both fought so hard to achieve.

Tangled Allure is an intoxicating tale of passion, self-discovery, and the journey from adversaries to lovers. It explores the complexities of finding love in unexpected places, the blurred lines between personal and professional lives, and the transformative power of embracing vulnerability. Against the backdrop of high fashion and fierce competition, Isabella and Sebastian must choose whether love is worth the risks and whether their shared passion can withstand the pressures of the world they inhabit.

— Chapter 1 —
The Day The History Began

The morning light filters through the curtains, painting soft hues across the walls of my spacious penthouse apartment. I blink, the weight of another busy day settling in my bones. With a sigh, I stretch my arms above my head, trying to shake off the remnants of sleep. The soft sheets cocooning me reluctantly release their hold as I swing my legs over the edge of the bed. As my feet hit the cold hardwood floor, I'm immediately reminded of the day's significance. It is when the highly anticipated Maxwell & Co. runway event takes place—the moment the fashion world has been waiting for. My pulse quickens at the thought, and a rush of excitement mixed with nerves surges through me.

I stroll into the sleek, modern bathroom, where the marble surfaces reflect my reflection. I splash water on my face, hoping to wash away any lingering traces of fatigue. The man staring back at me, with his chiseled features and tousled, dark hair, is the confident CEO the world knows. But beneath the facade, there's a flicker of doubt—the perpetual fear of not living up to the legacy my father built.

After a quick shower, I slip into a tailored black suit, perfectly accentuating my lean frame. As I button up my crisp, white shirt, my mind races with the details of the day ahead. I mentally run through the checklist, ensuring every last detail is in place for the event: the lighting, the music, the lineup of models, all carefully curated to showcase our latest collection in its best light.

My phone buzzes with a series of notifications, signaling that the world is already in motion outside my penthouse walls. Messages from my assistant, my PR team, and the media flood my screen, demanding my attention. I skim through them, answering where necessary, but my unwavering focus remains on the runway event.

As I make my way to the kitchen, the aroma of fresh coffee fills the air. My chef, Luis, greets me with a warm smile, a steaming cup of espresso waiting for me on the countertop.

"Good morning, Mr. Maxwell," Luis says with a bow, ever the picture of professionalism.

"Morning, Luis," I reply, taking a sip of the rich, invigorating brew. "Thank you."

With coffee in hand, I glance at the clock on the wall, realizing I need to get moving if I'm to make it to the venue in time. I bid Luis farewell, promise to be back for dinner, and head toward the elevator that will take me to the ground floor.

The ride down feels like an eternity, the anticipation building with each floor that passes by. When the elevator doors finally open, I step out into the bustling lobby of the building. My chauffeur, Michael, stands by the door, holding it open with practiced ease.

"Morning, sir," Michael greets me with a nod.

"Morning, Michael," I reply and slide into the backseat of the sleek, black limousine.

The cityscape rushes past the tinted windows as Michael expertly navigates through the bustling streets of New York City. My mind is a whirlwind of thoughts, focusing on the runway event and the expectations that weigh heavily on my shoulders.

As the limousine glides smoothly to a stop, the purr of its engine fades into the night. We've arrived at the venue—a majestic ballroom that stands as a beacon of sophistication in the heart of the city. The exterior of the building is a tapestry of grandeur, adorned with cascading banners that proudly display the Maxwell & Co. logo. The emblem, meticulously crafted, gleams under the strategically placed spotlights, a testament to our fashion empire's legacy.

Stepping out of the car, I'm greeted by an electric atmosphere that crackles with anticipation. The air is thick with excitement, a tangible energy that seems to hum around me. The night is alive with possibility, and I feel it in the very marrow of my bones.

The entrance is flanked by a sea of flashing lights and eager faces. Paparazzi lenses shimmer like stars against the night sky. The crowd is a vibrant mix of haute couture enthusiasts, industry insiders, and devoted fans, all drawn by the allure of the fashion elite gracing this event. The evening breeze carries snippets of animated conversations and the occasional whoosh of a couture gown sweeping the ground. Laughter mingles with the melodies of excitement, forming a harmonious crescendo that fills the air.

Inside, the energy is electric. The final preparations are underway, with models being fitted into their exquisite ensembles, makeup artists and hairstylists adding their magic touches. The air is filled with the hum of excitement and the scent of anticipation. I head toward the backstage area, where the design team is putting the finishing touches on the runway setup. My eyes search the room attentively before I make my way into the ballroom. I stand in the center of the grand ballroom, my heart pounding with anticipation as the lights dim and the music begins to fill the air. The runway stretches out before me, and the audience leans in, hungry for a glimpse of the latest creations from Maxwell & Co. The pressure is familiar, yet it never ceases to consume me. After all, I carry the weight of my family's legacy on my shoulders, a legacy built by my father, a legend in the fashion industry.

As I watch the models glide down the runway, showcasing our latest collection, I can't help but feel a surge of pride. Standing at the edge of the runway, I feel a mix of nerves and pride. The audience is buzzing with excitement. Models strut out, each one a unique canvas of style. Their outfits are a blend of textures and colors that catch the eye. Some designs hug curves, others flow with grace. Applause fills the room at the end. I exchange glances with Isabella, a mix of relief and accomplishment in her eyes.

These designs are the result of countless hours of hard work, dedication, and an unwavering commitment to excellence. But even in the midst of this success, there is a restlessness within me—a desire to push the boundaries of fashion, to create something truly extraordinary.

As the show comes to an end, the applause echoes through the ballroom. I take a moment to breathe. The models exit the runway, and the backstage area transforms into a whirlwind of activity. The design team rushes to dismantle the set, photographers clamor to capture the perfect shots, and journalists hover around, seeking interviews with the key players of the show. It's a controlled chaos that I've grown accustomed to over the years, but today, there's an undercurrent of excitement I can't quite shake.

Later in the day, with the excitement of the runway's success still in bloom, I head to the meeting room where the design team is already seated.

The meeting room is abuzz with creative energy as the design team gathers to brainstorm ideas for the next Maxwell & Co. fashion show. The walls are adorned with mood boards, sketches, and fabric swatches, all contributing to the vibrant tapestry of our design process. I take my seat at the head of the table, ready to guide the discussion and ensure that our vision for the new collection aligns with the brand's identity.

Amidst the flurry of voices, I observe the team closely, taking in each suggestion with equal consideration. And then, I notice a new face among the designers.

Her dark hair falls gracefully over her shoulders, and her eyes hold a certain fire—an intensity that sets her apart from the rest. I raise an eyebrow, intrigued by her presence, wondering what unique perspective she brings to the table.

"I think we should consider incorporating more bold and unconventional silhouettes," this newbie declares, her voice firm yet alluring. "Let's challenge the norms of fashion and create something that truly stands out."

The room falls silent for a moment, and then, a murmur of surprise ripples through the team. This woman's suggestion is unconventional, and it stirs something within me—an unyielding curiosity to see where her vision might lead us.

My voice smooth but laced with curiosity, I ask, "And who might you be?"

"I'm Isabella Rivera, the new designer on the team," she replies, her gaze meeting mine with refined confidence.

I nod, acknowledging her status, but my mind is still grappling with her idea. It veers away from the classic elegance that has thus far defined Maxwell & Co. I find myself hesitating to embrace such a radical departure.

With a polite smile, I respond, "Thank you for your input, Isabella. We appreciate fresh perspectives."

Seeking to explore other options, I turn to the rest of the team, asking for their input. As they share their ideas, Isabella remains poised, her eyes focused on me, waiting for a chance to defend her vision.

Amid the discussion, she leans forward, her voice steady but assertive. "I believe my suggestion has merit," she counters. "It's not professional to dismiss it without even considering its potential."

Her words catch me off guard, and a spark of irritation ignites within me. Who is this newbie to challenge my judgment?

"You must understand," I begin, trying to explain my reservations, "our brand is known for its classic elegance and timeless designs. Your suggestion is far from what we're known for."

Isabella doesn't back down. Her gaze remains steady, her tone defiant but respectful. "Maybe that's the problem," she argues. "Maybe it's time for the brand to evolve and strategize for the future and be more inclusive. We might have had a successful runway show with old ideas, but it won't be too long before people begin to get bored. Fashion is ever-changing, and what worked in the past may not continue to captivate our audience forever."

Her words strike a chord, and I find myself momentarily at a loss for a response. There's daring wisdom in her perspective. It challenges me to reconsider my stance. The tension in the room is palpable as the clash of creativity over the direction of the new collection fills the air. I can sense the eyes of the other designers on us, waiting to see how I'll respond. At that moment, I have a choice: to stick to tradition and play it safe, or to embrace the unexpected and take a chance on Isabella's vision.

— Chapter 2 —
Being An Artist

Every Sunday, year-round, 100 W 77th Street, Columbus Avenue becomes more than a fair at the Grand Bazaar; it becomes a cultural heaven for art, fashion, and culture nerds like myself.

This place on the Upper West Side is where I go to immerse myself in the world of art and fashion. The sights are a creative marvel of everyday people, casually alluring as a collective. But when I narrow down my scope to view each passerby through the lens of their fashion statements, I see more than my eyes could take util I catch myself with a small smile creasing the corners of my lips.

The Grand Bazaar is a vibrant kaleidoscope of colors, scents, and sounds, teeming with the DNA of talented artists, designers, and collectors. The atmosphere is contagious, and while I am not sure why I have come here today, I know for sure that by the time I take my leave, I will not be leaving empty-handed.

Coming here is how I find inspiration whenever I hit a creative block. Everything feels like a mosaic of many colors, a collection of tales where everyone seemed like the main characters in their stories. I love every bit of it. And while my new boss has a more conservative sentiment toward fashion, I believe it is meant to evolve. To be colorful like the bustling streets of New York, where everyone expresses themselves through their clothing and accessories.

Each person seems to be a living canvas, their outfits telling a unique story about their personality and taste. It's like witnessing a moving art gallery, with the city itself serving as the grand curator.

Amid the sea of style, I find myself subconsciously drawn to certain ensembles, colors, and patterns that resonate with me. I feel my mind ticking with fashion ideas. My subconscious pulls my inspiration from the array of street fashion on display.

As I observe passersby, I notice an eclectic mix of people from all walks of life. Hipsters rocking vintage pieces with modern twists. Business professionals exuding sophistication in their tailored suits. Carefree artists adorned in bohemian chic. The Grand Bazaar is a melting pot of cultures and lifestyles. This diversity is reflected in the fashion choices of traders, artists, and customers.

The arts are alive and well in this city. Buskers play soulful melodies on their instruments, dancers sway to the rhythm of their own beats, and graffiti adorns the walls like colorful murals. The city itself is a work of art, with its towering skyscrapers and gritty streets forming a perfect backdrop for the vibrant urban canvas.

As I wade through the lively sea of people, the recent memory of the clash between me and my boss, Mr. Maxwell, keeps flashing through my head. The encounter left a bitter taste in my mouth. But for now, at this moment, as I immerse myself in the heart of this place, he becomes a distant memory.

The city seems to embrace me, wrapping me in its eclectic embrace, and I feel like I belong at the forefront of it all. In this place, surrounded by the pulse of New York's street fashion and arts, I know that my subconscious is leading the way to a world of creativity, where my designs will bloom and flourish like the city itself.

Even when I try my best to not pay attention to the conversions in the background, my ears betray me. I can't help but eavesdrop on distant and not-so-distant murmurs and chatters of the market.

"...I can't believe she made that jewelry by hand..."

"...Did you hear they donate profits to local schools?"

I stop by a quaint, little, but vibrant, art gallery tucked away on the side of the street, adorned by captivating artworks—mostly paintings—hanging on makeshift walls and leaning on sturdy shelves. Passersby stop in awe, admiring the art's colors and stories. And then, fleeting moments later, they continue their journey through the lively isles of the marketplace.

There is an abstract painting that everyone else seems to have missed as they get caught in the most vibrant of them all. This one, almost as if the artist or the vendor had the intention to hide it away from the rest, as abstract as it is, it speaks to my soul. I watch the colors blend into each other, wondering what the artist must have been thinking when he made that.

Lost in my admiration, I haven't noticed anyone standing next to me, also gazing at the same piece.

"Beautiful, isn't it?" a deep, seasoned voice interjects my thoughts.

I turn to the source of the voice, smiling. It is a man in a brown, striped peacoat and a matching flat cap.

"Yes, it truly is," I say. "There's something captivating about the colors and shapes. It's like they have a language of their own."

The stranger nods, appreciating my observation. "Art has the power to communicate emotions and stories beyond words. And you, my dear, you're an artist, too, aren't you?"

Surprised by his keen perception, I hesitate before replying, "Yes, I am. I'm a fashion designer."

The man smiles warmly. "Fashion, an art form often underestimated in its ability to evoke feelings and narratives. Relegated to the back benches of mere cuts and stitches."

"To be fair," I started, "a lot of people just want to wear clothes. Sometimes the clothes fit the narratives, sometimes it doesn't." I laugh a little to further lighten the mood.

Ignoring my little remark, his eyes fixated on the piece up ahead, he asks, "What message do you want to convey through your designs?"

I ponder his question, and I realize I've never truly articulated my core motivation as a designer before. "I suppose I want people to feel confident and beautiful in what they wear." I feel shallow with my answer. As if there is more that I should have said. So, I add, "Maybe I just want to empower people through my creations." I remember my encounter with my boss a few days ago, and I realize I just echoed his thoughts and views.

There's an awkward pause between me and this stranger standing shoulder to shoulder with me.

Then, I figure what I said initially isn't what I really want. I want to challenge the status quo. I want to create unconventional beauty and innovative designs. But before I can speak, the stranger glances at me and nods.

Encouraging me, he says, "Empowerment, a noble pursuit, indeed. But let me share a different perspective with you. Fashion, like all art, reflects the times we live in. It mirrors society, culture, and values. Your designs have the potential to not only empower but to challenge and provoke thoughts."

I smile, thinking how this stranger doesn't know how badly I want my sentiments on fashion validated. Even when I do not know who he is, it feels good hearing this from someone different, someone totally removed from my reality.

My curiosity piques, and I lean in, eager for more of this man's wisdom.

"You see," he continues, "true art is not confined to comfort zones. It dares to question, push boundaries, and challenge the status quo. Fashion can be a vessel for social commentary and change, a visual narrative that speaks volumes about the world we inhabit."

A door to endless possibilities swings open within me as I hear him validate my sentiments. My designs don't have to conform to conventions; they can make a statement, inspire dialogue, and spark change. I badly want Mr. Maxwell to hear this man speak. Maybe, just maybe, he will listen to me.

Our conversation continues for a couple of hours, delving into the nuances of art and fashion, creativity, and purpose. I have heard this stranger whose name I do not know, and do not remember to ask, reference a lot of fashion designers, groups, trends, and cultures across different ages. He is seasoned with wisdom and knowledge, and he has an interesting perspective. He uses architectural designs and interior designs to drive home his points, mentioning cities like Barcelona and the history of its architecture. I listen as he gives me a whole lecture on culture and the need to be a rebel. Then, I tell him about my boss and my new workplace and how they want a more conservative, evolution-resistant style. He smiles and assures me it's expected.

As he brushes his peacoat, about to take his leave, I feel an overwhelming sense of gratitude for this chance encounter.

Before parting ways, the stranger offers one final piece of advice. "Do not forget, a true artist never stops evolving. Embrace your uniqueness, challenge yourself, and trust in your creative instincts. The world needs your voice, your perspective, and your daring spirit."

As I leave the vibrant art gallery and continue outside toward the market, a sense of purpose propels my every step as I swiftly whisk out my small sketchpad from my leather bag.

I find a perfect spot on a picnic table in a secluded corner of the market street. Sitting down, I look around, observing the colorful tapestry of people passing by. Their diverse styles and unique fashion choices intrigue me, and I know I have stumbled upon a well of inspiration.

There is an inner thirst coming along my throat. I get up and stop by a small drink kiosk with bright yellow bulbs hanging on the wooden walls. Right in front is an array of wooden benches and small tables for customers and passersby who just want to sit, read books or hold conversations.

I smile at the vendor behind the wooden counter, "I'll have the mango-orange pineapple, please," I say as I gesture toward the menu plastered on the wall.

After I receive my order, I throw my sketchpad on the table and whisk out my pen from my purse, and I begin to let my pen glide across the paper, capturing the abstract shapes and intricate patterns of the artwork from the art gallery. The stranger's words, along with those of my new boss, fill the space in my mind as I continue to sketch. But as I watch different people, each with their own simple but innovative styles, a fresh wave of creativity surges through me.

I shift my focus, and I sketch the people passing by, their authenticity, the way they wear their clothes with confidence, spark ideas within me. I start to envision the possibility of incorporating these genuine elements into my designs, breathing new life into the fashion industry through Maxwell & Co.

A young woman with an oversized denim jacket layered over a delicate floral dress catches my eye. The juxtaposition of edgy and feminine elements speaks volumes, and I quickly translate it into a potential design concept.

Across the street, a group of friends laugh and chat while dressed in an array of vintage and retro pieces.

I continue to sketch, even as the sun dips lower and lower till its golden glow begin to spill over the street. I feel a renewed sense of purpose and excitement for my work. The city hums with its vibrant energy, and I cannot help but smile, knowing that I have found the missing piece of my creative puzzle.

The sketches in my pad begin to take shape, and I see the threads of authenticity and innovation weaving together to form an embroidery of fashion ideas. With each stroke of my pen, I feel more certain that my designs will carry the spirit of anyone who walks in them.

I down my glass of fresh juice and close my sketch pad, knowing that I have found my artistic compass. The city has spoken to me through its people and art, guiding me to a deeper understanding of the impact fashion can have on individuals and society at large.

I cannot wait to present my ideas at the office tomorrow.

***

As I step into the presentation room at Maxwell & Co., excitement and anxiety take turns trying to squeeze me out of existence. The atmosphere is stiff and cold. There is a large mahogany table in the room, with chairs and people around it. As I take my place at the front, I can't help but notice Sebastian Maxwell, the stern and enigmatic CEO, seated among the other stakeholders.

The tension in the room is palpable, and I can't help but feel his eyes on me as I prepare to present my designs. Our glances meet at different intervals, and each time, he looks away, as if avoiding any form of connection with me. His shifty glances add to the unease I feel, leaving me with a gnawing sense that he disapproves of me, or perhaps dislikes me altogether.

As I begin to present, I can't shake the annoyance that subtly rises within me. It's as if Sebastian's presence alone has the power to unsettle me. The room's silence seems to amplify the sound of my heartbeat, and even the voice in my head, making me feel vulnerable and exposed under his watchful gaze, almost as if he could hear me think.

"Imagine a world where fashion is no longer confined by the shackles of imitation," I start, my voice unwavering. "Architecture and interior designs once had souls, unique characteristics that defined cities and spaces. But now, we see a trend of minimalistic designs, and thus, a loss of creativity; everything looks the same. From skyscrapers to phone booths, to even the dull gray of our living rooms."

I grip the remote in my hand, and the screen behind me comes alive, showcasing the visual journey of my ideas.

I maneuver around the room with purpose, making eye contact with each stakeholder as I speak. "I met someone yesterday at the Grand Bazaar, and he opened my eyes to the power of authenticity. I want us to reclaim fashion as an art form, as a medium of expression that speaks to our individuality."

I click to the next image which perfectly illustrates my pitch. "Barcelona serves as a shining example of how innovative ideas can create a unique city model. They've blended tradition with creativity, preserving their cultural identity while embracing modernity."

Pausing for effect, I let the idea linger before drawing parallels to the fashion industry. "We, too, can create a revolution in fashion by incorporating innovative ideas, celebrating diversity, and challenging norms. Let's breathe life into our designs, infusing them with the soul and essence they deserve."

As I shift the focus to my fashion designs on the screen, I describe how each piece is a reflection of this newfound perspective. "My designs embody the spirit of the Grand Bazaar, where I discovered authenticity in the everyday people I sketched. Each piece celebrates individuality, and I've drawn inspiration from various cultures and styles to create a harmonious fusion of uniqueness." My fashion ideas showcase outfits that blend bold prints with intricate details, juxtaposing vintage elements with modern twists. Each design tells a story, a narrative of liberation from conformity.

"These designs aren't just garments; they're statements that speak to our core values, that redefine fashion as a celebration of our individuality. Let's embrace the soul of fashion and create a collection that will revolutionize the industry."

I keep going and going, and by the time I am done talking, I feel a lot better than I did before I started. But when my gaze meets Sebastian's, there's no hint of approval or encouragement. It's as if my ideas clash with his vision for the company, and I can't help but feel a surge of frustration. At that moment, I know that he does not like my approach, and it fuels the unease that's been building inside me.

"Isabella," Mr. Johnson, the Head of Marketing interjects my thoughts. "Your designs are undeniably unique, but do you think they will appeal to our target market? How do you plan to strike a balance between creativity and commercial viability?"

I have imagined someone asking me a question like this, so I already have an answer waiting for this. "Thank you for your question, Mr. Johnson. While my designs may challenge some conventional norms, I believe they have the potential to resonate with our target audience in a refreshing and authentic way. By incorporating elements of creativity while keeping an eye on current market trends, we can strike a balance that appeals to both our loyal customers and those seeking something fresh and innovative."

Half of the room nods in agreement with my point. My eyes shift toward Sebastian, and I find him twirling a pen between his fingers. Still unimpressed with his attitude, I want to reach out and scream in his face. But instead, I just stand there, looking over everyone else's heads.

"Isabella," Sebastian's baritone voice reverberates and bounces off the walls of the room. It sends shivers down my spine a little as I struggle to keep my composure. "Creating innovative fashion often involves higher production costs." He continues, "How do you propose we manage expenses while still maintaining the integrity of your designs?"

A ripple of murmurs sweeps through the room as the board whispers amongst themselves, most nodding in agreement with Sebastian's question.

But I know Sebastian isn't asking to see how we will tackle that issue; his demeanor and gestures suggest he is only asking so he can watch me self-sabotage.

I smile a little. "I appreciate your concern, Mr. Maxwell." I stare straight into his eyes as he holds mine. "While it's true that innovation can come with increased costs, I've strategized to use sustainable and ethically-sourced materials whenever possible." Sebastian is unwavering in his subtle way of showing dominance. I cannot bear eye contact anymore, so my eyes subconsciously shift away to the rest of the room. "Additionally, I plan to work closely with our production team to optimize processes and find creative solutions that maintain the essence of my designs while keeping expenses in check."

Half of the board doesn't seem to buy my answer as I look around, subtly looking for approval on their faces. Sebastian, on the other hand, continues to ask question after question until he runs out of questions to ask. I answer his questions with so much conviction and confidence that it makes him concede and recline in his seat.

The other half of the room stares back at me with admiration and approval, and that is all that I need to place a huge bet on my proposal getting approved. And as for Sebastian, I still do not know how best to work around him, and the constant stern look on his face.

— Chapter 3 —
The Legacy

My father sits against the backdrop of the gentle hues of dusk. His salt-and-pepper hair frames a countenance that holds stories of an era gone by and eyes that harbor the wisdom of seasoned experience. He leans back, holding a teacup with hands that have tirelessly shaped exquisite masterpieces.

His presence exudes an air of authority and stoicism, reflected even in the glimmer of his Rolex watch. In his sixties, he started as a bespoke fashion designer and tailor in the vibrant heart of New York City during the eighties. It was at this time that his principles took root. It was what shaped his unwavering conservatism.

My father speaks with passion, recounting the glory days of his favorite baseball team in the seventies, eighties, and nineties. And though I've heard these stories countless times, I find myself hanging on to every word, admiring the way he clings to the golden threads of the past.

Everyone who meets him respects him. It's a sentiment that I've always yearned to echo, to possess even half of the respect and admiration he garners in the industry.

Yet, in my pursuit of making my mark, I find myself entangled in a constant struggle to balance tradition with innovation, principles with adaptation. It's as if I'm chasing the shadows of his enormous accomplishments. Yearning to fill the footsteps of a legacy that casts a long and unyielding shadow.

As the evening light fades, I listen to him ramble about how the advancement of technology has led to a decline in the quality of things. He holds this notion with unshakable conviction. My subconscious yearns to honor his principles, but the landscape of the industry beckons me to chart a different course.

In this moment, across the teacups and amidst the echoes of baseball tales, I find myself grappling with not just a decision but an identity. I'm caught between a crossroad: forging my own path and preserving the legacy that he built from threads of timeless tradition.

"Lovely tea, Father," I say as I drop my teacup on the table before the two of us.

My father nods in solemn agreement.

"You've always known how to pick the finest blends," I add, staring straight at him.

"Thank you, my boy," my father replies. "Just like how you've always known how to make intriguing decisions in your life."

I raise an eyebrow. "Oh, have I now?" My father is a man who reserves his compliments and never throws them around lightly. Unless, of course, he's being sarcastic.

"Indeed." He lifts his teacup to kiss his lips. "You've been quite the enigma lately, Sebastian. A man of your stature, with no love interests to speak of. Curious, isn't it?" He drops his teacup on the table between us and smirks.

I reach out to pour some tea into my teacup and some into his while thinking of the best way to deflect his fatherly concerns. "Ah, you know how it is, Father," I start. "Been busy with work, barely any time for such matters."

"Work, work, work. That's all I hear from you. But there's more to life than just the company, son. You have to find a balance for work and family. And family always comes first."

I lean back, waiting for him to go into his two-hour usual lecture on how a man should start a family early.

But instead, he says, "It's about making choices that define your legacy."

"I know, Father," I reply. "And I've been doing my best to uphold the family's legacy."

"Your best?" My Father arches his brows. "I'm not so sure about that, son." His tone changes from lukewarm to stone cold in a second. "You've been making decisions that I can't quite fathom. Changing the direction of the company, aligning with new investors."

My father is edging me closer to the wall, and I have no other option than to get defensive. So, I say, "I'm just exploring new avenues, trying to keep up with the changing times."

"Changing times? More like chasing shadows. You're lucky to inherit a legacy like mine, and yet, you squander it on whims and fancies."

I start to feel the frustration build as I struggle to hold my composure. "Whims and fancies?" I retort. "I assure you, Father, every decision I make is carefully considered."

"Considered, yes," My father's voice comes with an unwavering calmness. "But not with the wisdom that comes from experience. You've yet to comprehend the intricacies of this industry."

"I'm doing my best," I say. "But I won't be overshadowed by your enormous achievements."

My father leans forward, "Overshadowed?" He lets out a small, infuriating laugh. "Is that how you see it, Sebastian? I've worked my entire life to build this company, and you treat it like a mere stepping stone."

"It's not just yours, Father. It's mine, too, and I'm entitled to have a say in its future."

"Ah, yes, your say," My father says with a knowing glint in his eyes. "But do you truly understand what you are saying? Or are you just dancing to someone else's tune?"

"I assure you, I'm in control of my decisions."

"Are you? Then explain this recent partnership, this alliance with outsiders who might not have our best interests at heart."

"They bring fresh perspectives and opportunities."

"Opportunities? Or potential threats to our tradition and integrity? Your decisions, Sebastian, are like wild horses, untamed and unpredictable."

"Enough!" I snap. "I won't be questioned and belittled like a child."

"I'm not belittling you, son," My father leans forward calmly. "I'm challenging you to step up and truly understand the weight of your choices."

I take a deep sigh, and say, "I will prove myself, Father, in my own way."

"That's all I ask, Sebastian," he says with a knowing smile plastered to his face. "Prove yourself worthy, and you will truly find your place in this world."

I cannot argue further with him. He's quite dogmatic when it comes to matters that concern tradition. He will rather lose out an opportunity to make millions than shift away from his perceived values. My mother will say it is how he made so much fortune in the nineties and early 2000s. At a time when the world of fashion was moving too fast, my father stuck to a more traditional approach. In doing so, he attracted the attention of the city's wealthiest aristocrats, and his prices went up a notch.

My emotions simmer beneath the surface as I lean back, loosening my tie to enjoy the evening breeze. I can still feel the intensity in the air as my father unpacks a small pack of cigarettes.

I watch him search frantically for his lighter that he dropped earlier. I pick it up and help him light the cigarette. He lets out a half-hearted *thank you*. This moment of raw confrontation is nothing new to me. We both know that we are grappling not only with our roles as CEO and founder but also as father and son. The air is heavy with unspoken truths and unresolved expectations.

***

"Sebastian, there you are. Quite the event, isn't it?" A familiar voice breaks through the bustling crowd.

I turn to see Richard, a designer I've crossed paths with on several occasions. Despite the noise and excitement around us, there's a hint of camaraderie in his eyes that instantly puts me at ease

"It certainly is, Richard," I reply, a faint smile forming. "The energy is incredible, don't you think?"

Richard chuckles, adjusting his stylish glasses. "It always is at these gatherings. But you seem a bit tense, my friend. Everything alright?"

I take a moment to gauge my response, knowing Richard can read between the lines. "I suppose it's just the anticipation. The weight of the event, you know?"

He nods knowingly, his expression empathetic. "Ah, the pressure. We all feel it, especially when representing our brands. But let me tell you, Sebastian, your work is always exceptional. Don't let doubts cloud your talents, my friend. Let's wait for this year's collection. I'm sure it would be nothing short of brilliance." He taps my arm. "Enjoy your evening," he says before disappearing into the crowd.

There are three kinds of people you'll meet at the Fashion Extravaganza Gala here in Paris:

Fashion icons. They are the faces of these brands. They are who people think of when they hear "fashion." They are celebrities, renowned fashion influencers. Everyone talks about them. Everyone wants to be like them. The subtle and overly braggadocios whose mere presence set the tone for the event. They are who people come to look like. My father once told me that sometimes it is not the quality of the clothes that matter. It's the environment in which it's exhibited, the shoulders it sits on. The body it hangs on. People pay for sentiments. It's probably why my father is a very sentimental man.

Fashion enthusiasts. They are the students of the game. Their energy is infectious. Nerds, I like to call them. From bloggers to underground designers. They design some of the best, artistic offerings you'll ever see somewhere in their basements. They are usually fashion purists. They do not do it for the paparazzi, nor the cash, nor the glam. They are invested in the artistic sides of it. My father was one, still is.

The last people are *industry power players*. This sphere is where I belong, striding in my father's giant shoes, making the big decisions like the rest of other CEOs, founders, and investors. We make the industry go round. Nothing happens without us, I like to believe. But that lady, Isabella, the new designer at the company, seems to have a contrary view. I heard her speak to a coworker once about how people are fashionable and that fashion belongs to everyday people.

The Fashion Extravaganza Gala—the holy grail of haute couture gatherings. It's where the fashion world's A-listers converge from every corner. The grand runway dazzles with crystal chandeliers, casting a soft, mesmerizing glow over a sea of impeccably dressed attendees.

Anticipation crackles in the air, mingling with the heady fragrance of high-end perfumes and the constant hum of chatter and paparazzi cameras. The room is a sartorial carnival, and I'm smack in the middle of the attention, even when not a lot of people know who I am. But they sure do know my father.

Right before the show starts, I slip away from the crowd and all the buzz. I find my way to the backstage where the models, designers, and a few other kinds of people are cramped together like sardines in a can. Seeking a moment of solace, I slip into the restroom. The cacophony fades out as soon as I shut the door. I stand over the basin as I wash my face, as if to wash off the anxiety. My reflection stares back at me as my father's words still echo in my head. His words reverberate like an earworm.

With a resolute inhalation, I gather my strength. I'm Sebastian Maxwell: not just a son clinging to a legacy, but the force propelling Maxwell & Co.'s future.

I return to the fray, and the runway is set ablaze with bright, almost celestial-like lights. I find myself in the middle of two overly dressed attendees, executives from industry rivals. It doesn't take long before models start to saunter before everyone like ethereal creatures, adorned in the best of our collection this year. These designs are the best of our creations this window, I handpicked them myself. They are testaments of months of hard work and sleepless nights, a testament to our creative geniuses as the runway buzzes with electric energy, charged with creativity.

"Honestly, what is this?" The overly dressed woman to my right sneers, her eyes narrowing.

Her companion, a man with a superiority complex, scoffs, "I don't know, but it's certainly not haute couture. Looks like a mishmash of tacky trends."

They whisper, but I overhear their cutting words clearly. The smile dissolves on my face almost as quickly as I hear them talk. A flicker of annoyance and hurt flashes across my face.

"This color palette is a disaster!" the woman continues, her voice dripping with scorn.

"And those patterns? Ugh, they're an eyesore!" the man chimes in.

My heart sinks as I continue to hear them tear into the fabrics, the color choices, and the overall concept with so much contempt. They are oblivious of my presence as the CEO of Maxwell & Co. I struggle to keep my composure, clenching my jaw and rubbing my brow with a finger. But as I listen to their barbs, I steel myself. This is my moment, my vision brought to life, and I won't let their words shake me.

Despite the harsh criticism, I watch on as the models strut in the finest of our creations with poise and grace. And though the executives may not see it,

I know that this collection is a masterpiece in its own right.

After the show is done, the grand hall is abuzz with chatter and mingling. As I move through the crowd, a few, old industry veterans recognize me and offer brief, sincere praises for my collection. I nod and smile in response, offering a humble "thank you" and briefly shaking their hands.

As I weave my way through the crowd, I find myself before the two rival executives who did not hold back earlier.

"Quite the show, huh?" I say with a sly grin, extending my hand. "I'm Sebastian. What did you think of the first exhibition?"

They both share a knowing glance, as if relishing the opportunity to share their unfiltered opinions once more. Their laughter is condescending when they let it out, assuming I am just another spectator.

"Well, you know," the woman begins with a dismissive wave of her hand, "I wasn't too impressed. It lacked that wow factor, you know what I mean?"

Her companion nods, adding, "Absolutely. And the color choices, don't even get me started."

The smirk grows on my face. "Oh, I see," I say, feigning an air of nonchalance. "So, according to you, it was all just lackluster and uninspired? You must be true connoisseurs of fashion then. I'll definitely take your profound insights into consideration."

Their faces register surprise, unsure how to respond to my unexpected retort. But I know I now have them where I want them, and I relish in their discomfort.

"And the color choices," I continue, making sure my tone drips with sarcasm, "yes, because you two are renowned for your exquisite taste in colors. Truly unparalleled."

The executives exchange awkward glances, realizing that they may have just stepped into a trap. My biting wit and confident demeanor have caught them off guard.

"But hey," I add with a little smirk on my face, "everyone's entitled to their opinions, right? And I value yours. Really, I do."

With that, I offer a mockingly polite nod before turning to walk away, leaving the two executives stunned and speechless. I can feel the burns of their eyes as I wade through the traffic.

I do not want to reveal my identity as the CEO of Maxwell & Co. just yet, but I've had my fun. I'm sure they'll find out later somehow later. Putting them in their place is all that matters to me. As I continue through the sea of people, I know that my collection has spoken for itself. I'm more than determined to forge my way and make my mark in the industry. I'm more than capable of holding my own in the cutthroat world of fashion.

— Chapter 4 —
Confrontations

At my cluttered desk, I twirl a pen absentmindedly between my fingers, my mind drifting between the sketches scattered before me. The world of fashion design is both exhilarating and daunting, and today is no exception. Just as I'm lost in my thoughts, a subtle but insistent knock on my office door breaks the reverie.

"Come in," I call out, setting the pen down.

The door opens, and my assistant steps inside, holding an elegantly embossed envelope. "Isabella, this just arrived for you."

My curiosity piqued, I take the envelope from her and open it. Inside, there's an invitation to Elysian's Elegance– a private fashion exhibition hosted by Vogue Chronicles, a renowned fashion magazine, one that attracts influential editors and industry insiders. My heart skips a beat, and a mix of excitement and nervousness rushes through my veins. The opportunity to showcase my designs in such an esteemed company is both a dream and a challenge.

"Thank you," I say to my assistant as she finds her way out.

As the day of the exhibition approaches, I pour my heart and soul into perfecting every detail of my collection. I carefully select fabrics that caress the skin like whispers and hues that dance like watercolors. My fingers deftly sew, bringing life to my vision, while my mind is a whirlwind of hopes and aspirations.

When the day finally arrives, and with the invitation clutched in my hand, I make my way to the venue. The atmosphere buzzes with anticipation. The sounds of stilettos clicking on marble floors and whispered conversations filled with industry jargon fill the air.

Entering the venue feels like stepping into a realm of ethereal beauty. The space is transformed into a celestial gallery, the walls adorned with stunning fashion photography and avant-garde artworks. The colors, the textures, and the scents intermingle, creating an intoxicating atmosphere that leaves me both awestruck and humbled.

In a corner, a musician plays a hauntingly beautiful melody on a grand piano, its notes mingling with the soft chatter of the guests. The air carries the heady fragrance of exquisite perfumes, and as I navigate through the crowd, my heart flutters like a butterfly, torn between excitement and trepidation.

I spot a group of influential fashion editors, their presence exuding an aura of power and discernment. My hands tremble slightly as I approach them, and I take a deep breath to steady myself.

"Good evening," I say with a confident smile, extending my hand. "I'm Isabella, and I'm delighted to have the opportunity to showcase my collection tonight."

Their gazes fall upon me, and I can feel their keen eyes sizing me up. The tension in the air is palpable, but I stand tall, determined to make my mark.

"Oh, another aspiring designer, I presume?" one of them remarks, her tone veiled with skepticism.

I choose to brush off her cynicism and instead channel my passion and love for my craft into every word I say. "Yes, aspiring and passionate," I reply, my voice tinged with enthusiasm. "Fashion is an ever-evolving art form, and I'm excited to contribute to its tapestry."

Another editor smirks, looking amused. "And what makes your collection stand out from the sea of other aspiring designers out there?"

In that moment, I see my designs unfurling before my eyes, a kaleidoscope of colors and innovative silhouettes. "I believe my collection is a conversation between the past and the future," I explain. "It's a homage to timeless elegance blended with daring experimentation. Each piece tells a story of individuality and empowerment, and I'm committed to pushing the boundaries of traditional fashion."

I notice the initial skepticism in the editors' eyes slowly giving way to curiosity. One of them, a woman with a meticulously styled bob and a reputation for being the most discerning of the bunch, leans forward ever so slightly.

"So, Isabella," she begins, her tone carrying a hint of genuine interest, "you say your collection blends timeless elegance with daring experimentation. Could you give us an example?"

With a confident smile, I reach for a nearby portfolio, carefully unveiling a sketch that depicts a flowing gown with intricate lacework merging seamlessly with modern geometric patterns. "Take this design, for instance," I explain. "It's an ode to classic Victorian aesthetics, reimagined with contemporary asymmetry. The juxtaposition of delicate motifs against bold lines creates a harmonious clash of eras, symbolizing the constant interplay between tradition and innovation."

The editor's raised eyebrow softens into a look of intrigue as she studies the sketch. Her skeptical demeanor seems to be unraveling, replaced by a more open-minded contemplation. Across the group, the other editors exchange glances, seemingly intrigued by the unexpected fusion of elements.

As the conversation continues, I notice another editor, known for her discerning eye for color palettes, examining a vibrant display of fabric swatches. She holds one up to the light, her lips subtly curving into a contemplative smile.

"And these colors?" she inquires, her voice a gentle lilt. "They're certainly bold choices."

"Indeed," I reply, my voice carrying the excitement of discovery. "Each hue is carefully chosen to evoke emotion and resonance. This rich crimson, for instance, represents courage and determination, while the deep indigo signifies the enigmatic allure of the unknown. By harmonizing these intense shades with more subdued tones, I aim to create a visual symphony that resonates with diverse sensibilities."

As I elaborate, I see the editors leaning in closer, their expressions shifting from guarded skepticism to genuine engagement. The editor who had initially questioned me even nods appreciatively, acknowledging the depth of thought behind each design element.

As if destiny has plotted for this moment, I unfurl a life-size tapestry showcasing a striking ensemble from my collection. The intricate details, the interplay of fabrics, and the unexpected yet harmonious union of design elements seem to cast a spell over the room. The once-cynical editor who had spoken earlier stands before what she's seeing, her fingers tracing the contour of the fabric.

"This," she murmurs, her voice almost reverent, "is certainly unlike anything I've seen before."

As if on cue, the other editors gather around, their gazes fixed on the tapestry. The room is alive with whispered conversations and the rustling of papers as they discuss amongst themselves. In that moment, I realize that I've managed to not only capture their attention but also immerse them fully in the world I've woven through my words and designs.

The night progresses, and I find myself engaged in animated conversations with various industry insiders. I'm humbled by their praise and inspired by their insights. My nervousness has transformed into an electric energy that fuels my determination to carve a niche for myself in the elite world of high fashion.

Hours seem to pass like fleeting moments, and before I know it, the exhibition draws to a close. As the last guests bid their farewells, I find myself standing amidst the aftermath of my dreams coming true.

My heart swells with gratitude for the opportunity to showcase my designs among the fashion elite. I'm no longer the timid designer at her desk, twirling a pen in uncertainty. Tonight, I have been seen and heard, and I feel a renewed fire burning within me.

As I leave the venue, the echoes of inspiring conversations still reverberate in my mind. With each step, I feel the weight of responsibility and the thrill of possibilities. The world of high fashion may be relentless, but I know I'm ready to take on the challenge, to push the boundaries and to make my voice heard in this intoxicating symphony of beauty and innovation.

***

As I stand there, facing Jennifer's skeptical gaze, my heart pounds with a mixture of anxiety and determination. This is my chance to prove myself, to show everyone that I belong in this high-stakes game. I straighten my posture, refusing to let her doubt rattle me.

"You know, Isabella," Jennifer begins, leaning in closer, "this client isn't just difficult; they're notorious for driving designers like you to their breaking points. Are you sure you can handle the pressure?"

I wonder what she means by "designers like you." Her words sting like a slap across the face, but I'm not about to let her see the impact they have on me. I meet her gaze with unwavering resolve.

'I wouldn't be here if I wasn't confident in my abilities," I shoot back, my voice steady and strong. "I may be new to this company, but I have the talent, the passion, and the dedication to take on any challenge that comes my way."

Jennifer smirks, her eyes gleaming with a hint of mischief. "We'll see about that. Just don't come crying to me when things get tough."

I fight the urge to roll my eyes at her condescension. I don't need her approval or validation. I know what I'm capable of, and I'm determined to prove it to everyone in this office.

With a curt nod, I turn away from Jennifer and make my way to the conference room. My heart races with a mix of excitement and apprehension. This is it, the moment I've been waiting for—my chance to prove myself on the grandest stage.

I step into the room, and all eyes turn to me. I feel the weight of their scrutiny. But I refuse to let their doubts hold me back. I greet the celebrity client, Lily Harper, with a confident smile.

"Hello, Ms. Harper. I'm Isabella, your fashion designer for this project."

Lily eyes me curiously, her sharp gaze assessing me from head to toe. "Isabella, huh? They say you're the new talent around here."

"That's right," I reply, trying to suppress the nerves that threaten to betray my composure. "I'm here to bring fresh ideas and creativity to this collaboration."

Lily's lips curve into a faint smile. "We'll see if you can handle what I have in mind. I'm not one to settle for mediocrity."

I swallow hard, feeling the weight of her expectations bearing down on me. "I promise you, Ms. Harper, that I will give my all to meet your vision. You won't be disappointed."

As the days unfold, Lily's demands prove to be as challenging as I anticipated. We sit across from each other, the conference room table covered with sketches and fabric swatches. Her critical gaze lingers on each design, dissecting every detail as if she's searching for flaws.

"You're close, Isabella, but not quite there," Lily says, her voice a mixture of critique and challenge. Her fingers tap lightly on the paper, emphasizing the areas she wants me to revise. "I want this silhouette to be more pronounced, and the fabric needs to have a subtle sheen—something that catches the light just right."

I nod, trying to hide any sign of frustration. "I understand, Ms. Harper. I'll make the necessary adjustments."

Her expressions range from thoughtful contemplation to stern scrutiny. There are moments when I can see the wheels turning in her mind, envisioning the final outcome with a precision that leaves me in awe. Other times, her eyebrows furrow, and she leans in to scrutinize a particular detail, her lips pressed into a thin line.

"I need this neckline to be a bit lower, Isabella. It's crucial to the overall balance," she remarks, her tone firm but not without a hint of admiration.

With each request for refinement, a fresh wave of determination surges through me. I feel the pressure mounting, but I refuse to let it break me. There's something invigorating about the challenge, about pushing my creativity and skills beyond their limits.

Late nights turn into early mornings as I pour myself into my work. The dim light of my studio casts long shadows across the array of fabric samples and sketches strewn about. I experiment with different textures, drape fabrics over dress forms, and meticulously stitch intricate details. There are moments when doubt creeps in, when I question if I'm capable of meeting Lily's expectations. But then, I remember my resolve, the determination that has driven me to this point, and I press on.

The conference room meetings continue, and with each presentation, I can see the subtle changes in Lily's demeanor. Her critical gaze seems to soften at times, replaced by a more contemplative look. There are instances when a small smile tugs at the corner of her lips, almost imperceptible but undeniably present.

"You've really captured the essence of what I envisioned, Isabella," Lily admits, her voice holding a note of surprise. "The way you've played with these colors and textures—it's remarkable."

"You're not like the others," Lily remarks one day, her gaze softening as she studies my latest sketches. "You actually listen and understand what I want. It's refreshing."

A sense of pride swells within me, knowing that my hard work and dedication are earning me the respect of one of the industry's most demanding clients. I continue to push myself, surpassing even my own expectations.

When the final pieces come together, the moment of truth arrives: the unveiling of Lily Harper's collection. I stand backstage, my heart pounding with anticipation. This event is the culmination of everything I've worked for, the moment where I will either rise to the occasion or falter under the pressure.

The lights dim, and the runway comes alive with the energy of the crowd. I watch as each model showcases my designs, each piece a reflection of Lily's unique style and my unwavering dedication. The audience gasps, their eyes transfixed on the striking creations before them.

As the show comes to an end, the applause thunders through the room, and I feel tears welling up in my eyes. I've done it. I've proven myself to everyone who doubted me, including Sarah.

I make my way back to the office, and I can see the looks of admiration and respect in the eyes of my colleagues. No longer are they skeptical of my abilities; they now see me as a force to be reckoned with in the world of high-profile clients.

I walk past Sarah, her jaw slightly agape as she watches me pass. With a satisfied smile, I say nothing, knowing that my actions speak louder than any words ever could. I've silenced the doubts and proven that I belong in this world of fashion and creativity.

— Chapter 5 —
A Backlash

Tension hangs thick in the air as I walk into the meeting room. My eyes are immediately drawn to the large screen at the front, displaying an array of social media posts, hashtags, and comments accusing our brand of cultural appropriation. The accusations are glaring, and my heart sinks with the weight of the situation.

The room is dimly lit, and the screen's glow casts an eerie hue on the faces of my team members, who are huddled around the table. Their expressions range from worry to anxiety, all waiting for my response.

"Sebastian," Emma, my head of PR begins, her voice strained. "We have a serious issue on our hands. The backlash is spreading rapidly, and the public perception is turning against us."

I nod solemnly, taking in the gravity of the situation. "Alright, let's address this head-on. Show me the key posts and comments."

The screen changes to display the specific posts in question, and I can feel the weight of the responsibility intensify. Each word and accusation stings, and I can't help but clench my fists, feeling the urge to protect the brand I hold so dear.

My head of marketing chimes in, her voice urgent. "We need a strategy, Sebastian. How do we respond? What can we do to salvage our reputation?"

I take a deep breath, my mind racing with possible solutions. "First, we need to issue a public statement acknowledging the concerns raised. We'll express our regret for any unintentional offense caused and commit to conducting a thorough review of our designs and processes."

The room remains quiet as they absorb my words. But I can see the uncertainty in their eyes, the doubt lingering like a shadow.

"We'll also reach out to the communities affected and engage in open dialogue to understand their perspectives better," I continue, my voice steady. "We must be transparent and demonstrate our commitment to cultural sensitivity."

"But what about our upcoming campaign?" my creative director interjects, clearly concerned. "It's scheduled to launch in a week, and we've invested so much into it."

I take a moment to consider the implications, realizing the potential risks. "We'll put the campaign on hold for now," I say firmly. "We can't proceed without addressing these concerns first. It's vital that we prioritize respect and empathy."

The room falls into silence again, the weight of the situation unmistakable. I can feel their eyes on me, waiting for my guidance.

"We're not alone in this," I say, trying to instill some reassurance. "We have a talented team and loyal customers. Together, we'll navigate through this storm, learn from it, and emerge stronger."

My father never taught me to run away and hide in the middle of a crisis. Or to push the blame on someone else. Standing strong against any oncoming challenges is what a man does, especially a leader like myself. But in the face of this public backlash that seems to be growing by the day, I know I have to tackle this head on. People have to hear me speak, and maybe it will put their minds at ease.

My phone has been ringing nonstop since the beginning of the backlash. I haven't visited my father, either, because I know what he will say.

So, when I'm invited to speak on air to address these concerns, Emma says she should go. It's her profession, it's what she knows how to handle. But I feel like when people hear the CEO himself speak that it would have more weight. I have Emma give me a rundown on what to expect.

When the day comes, it isn't until the clapperboard slams that I fully realize that I'm sitting under the harsh spotlight of the public gaze. The heat of it amplifies the pressure surrounding me. The room is filled with the low hum of voices, cameras flashing, and the distinct scent of fresh ink on notepads. The questions are sharp, relentless, forcing me to think on my feet and address the accusations head-on.

The journalist's piercing gaze fixates on me, ready to dissect my every word. "Mr. Maxwell, your latest collection has faced criticism for cultural appropriation. How do you respond to those who accuse you of exploiting other cultures for your own gain?"

I take a deep breath, steadying my nerves. "Firstly, I want to clarify that cultural appreciation, not appropriation, is at the heart of our designs at Maxwell & Co. My collection is a tribute to the beauty and richness of diverse cultures around the world. It's about celebrating their artistry, their craftsmanship, and their stories."

"But many argue that you're commodifying cultural symbols and turning them into mere trends," the journalist presses on, her pen poised to capture my response.

I glance around the room, feeling the weight of the scrutiny from all directions. "I understand those concerns, and I take them seriously. That's why my team and I have engaged in extensive research and collaborations with experts from the cultures we're drawing inspiration from. We've worked closely with artisans and craftsmen to ensure that our designs are respectful, authentic, and done with the utmost care."

The journalist's brow furrows, skepticism evident in her eyes. "But what about the criticism that you're perpetuating harmful stereotypes?"

My heart pounds, and I lean forward to meet her gaze directly. "I assure you, that's not our intention at all. We're striving to create designs that bridge gaps and foster appreciation for different cultures. Our goal is to unite, not divide."

A murmur of voices rises in the room, and I can sense the tension mounting. I must choose my words carefully to convey my sincerity.

"Every design we put forth is a labor of love. It's a celebration of the stories, art, and heritage that each culture brings to the table. We believe in empowering individuals to embrace and celebrate their cultural identities through fashion."

The journalist's expression softens slightly, but she continues to press me, "What steps are you taking to ensure that your collection doesn't perpetuate cultural harm?"

"We're continually educating ourselves, learning from feedback, and holding ourselves accountable," I reply, my voice unwavering. "We're committed to fostering dialogue and understanding, both within our team and with the wider community. It's a journey of growth, and we're willing to take it."

As I speak, I can feel the room's intensity fluctuating, emotions running high. I'm navigating a tightrope of defending my vision while acknowledging the valid concerns.

The journalist nods, absorbing my words. "It's clear that this is an issue you're deeply invested in. But how do you plan to prevent similar controversies in the future?"

I lean back, exhaling slowly. "Moving forward, we will be even more proactive in collaborating with cultural experts and ensuring that our designs are rooted in genuine appreciation. We'll continue to embrace diversity within our team, bringing in voices that represent the cultures we draw inspiration from. Ultimately, our aim is to create an inclusive, respectful space within the fashion industry."

The room falls into momentary silence, the weight of the conversation settling around us. I take a moment to collect my thoughts, aware of the significance of this moment in shaping the narrative surrounding my work.

At the end of the interview, a lady walks up to me to introduce herself, then asks for an autograph with a small smile on her face. I oblige with my heart still heavy and my mind still troubled. I know the crisis is far from over, but this little interview is like putting bandage over a bleeding wound. It won't take the pain away, but it will sure stop the bleeding and also stop the damage from expanding. There's still a lot more work to be done.

And there's only one person I can bring on to help me fix this mess.

***

I hesitate outside Isabella's office door, my heart pounding as I take a deep breath to steady myself. She isn't my first choice, but I've exhausted all other options. The sense of urgency weighs heavily on me as I knock, hoping against hope that she'll be willing to put our differences aside, just this once.

The door creaks open, and there she stands, looking as stunning as ever. Her eyes widen in surprise at the sight of me, and she immediately straightens up, mustering a professional demeanor. I can't help but notice how she carries herself with grace, even in the face of our mutual animosity.

I take a step into her office with my hands pocketed trying to feign nonchalance. My eyes catch a glimpse of a design sketch on her desk. Despite everything, I can't deny that she has a unique eye for fashion.

Without breaking the silence, I reach for the sketch and inspect it with curiosity. It's a beautiful piece. My respect for her talent can't be denied, but I can't let it overshadow the purpose of my visit.

Finally, I break the silence, my voice tinged with a hint of arrogance. "You can shut the door," I say curtly. "I need your help."

Her eyes flicker with surprise, her guarded expression never faltering. "My help?" she echoes, clearly taken aback by my unexpected request.

"Yes," I reply, trying to keep my emotions in check. "I've exhausted all other avenues, and I'm left with no choice but to turn to you."

A mix of confusion and curiosity plays across her features. "Why come to me?" she asks, a hint of defiance in her voice.

I sit in one of Isabella's office chairs, adjusting my suit jacket while she stands across from me. The atmosphere feels charged with tension, an invisible force that crackles in the air between us. Reminding myself to keep my emotions in check, I take a deep breath.

"You're aware of the recent troubles at Maxwell & Co.," I begin, choosing my words carefully.

"Of course," she replies, and her brow furrows with confusion.

I continue, my voice measured but laden with gravity, "It's about the cultural appropriation accusations in our designs."

Isabella's eyes widen slightly, and I can see the cogs turning in her mind as she processes the information. "Yes, I've been following," she says.

"Good. Now I need your help," I state firmly, meeting her gaze.

Her confusion deepens, and she stammers, "But... how could I be of any use in this situation? It requires someone with more experience."

I shoot up from the armchair, my frustration momentarily getting the better of me as I head to the window. I peer out into the bustling streets, gathering my thoughts. "I saw how well you handled Lily," I say, my voice softer now. "The celebrity client that everyone avoids because of her difficult nature. I was impressed by how you handled the situation."

Isabella's skepticism remains evident as she responds, "But this is a different scenario altogether. It's much more complicated."

I turn back to face her, my eyes locking with hers. "That's precisely why I need you," I explain. "Your fresh perspective, your unique ideas. I believe you have something valuable to contribute."

Reluctantly, she concedes, setting aside our personal differences for the moment. "Alright," she says, "I'll assist you."

I nod, a sense of relief washing over me. "Good. Wait for me after work. We'll discuss how to tackle this. I have somewhere to be right now," I reply, my tone a mixture of urgency and anticipation.

I stride out of the room, leaving her door ajar, and I feel a mix of emotions coursing through me. The animosity between us may be passive, but it's always there, simmering beneath the surface. But today, despite everything, I see her in a new light—and that she has eyes that glimmer like a Tuscan sunset.

— Chapter 6 —
Stitches In Time

My workspace is a dimly lit sanctuary of creativity, adorned with sheets of paper covered in intricate sketches, a mosaic of colorful fabrics, and a collection of fashion magazines that serve as my wellspring of inspiration. The soft glow of my desk lamp illuminates my intense expression as I sketch with unwavering determination.

But amidst my focus, thoughts of earlier this evening swirl in my mind like a gentle breeze on a summer night. Sebastian Maxwell, the critiquing CEO who disagreed with me, had come to me for help in navigating a crisis at the company. Surprising even myself, I find amusement in the unexpected turn of events. The man I've clashed with since my first day at Maxwell & Co., seeking my assistance— what an ironic twist of fate.

His office feels as if the air is charged with a mix of tension and anticipation. Sebastian leads me in, his tall figure towering over me. The dim light casts a warm glow on his features, and for a moment, I can't help but notice the slight crinkle at the corner of his eyes as he smiles, as though he is genuinely glad that I am here.

"So, Isabella," he begins, his voice smooth and composed, "let's tackle the issue once and for all."

I nod, feeling the weight of the conversation settling upon my shoulders. I can feel his frustration mounting, and it is evident that he is used to having all the answers, but this time, they elude him.

Sebastian's brow furrows, his fingers tapping restlessly against the polished surface of his desk. "Isabella, I appreciate your insights so far, but we need to find a way to address this PR crisis without further escalation. We can't afford to downplay the concerns, but we also can't admit fault."

I lean forward, my fingers tented as I meet his gaze with unwavering determination. "Sebastian, I believe the key lies in demonstrating cultural sensitivity and a commitment to education. We could organize workshops or events that showcase the cultures we've drawn inspiration from. This would allow us to share the beauty of these traditions while acknowledging their origins."

Sebastian's lips quirk up into a half-smile, the corner of his eyes crinkling once more. "Ah, so you're suggesting we turn this crisis into an opportunity for cultural exchange?"

"Exactly," I reply, my own lips curling into a thoughtful smile. "By engaging with the communities we've inadvertently impacted, we can foster understanding and bridge the gap. It's not just about the designs; it's about the stories behind them."

He nods.

I glance at him, surprised by his reaction. "You're actually considering that?" I ask, my skepticism evident in my raised eyebrow.

He chuckles, a rich sound that I never thought I'd hear from him. "Well, desperate times call for desperate measures, don't they?"

I can't help but laugh at the unexpected humor in his voice. It's a sound that feels like a revelation, a chink in his armor. The lines on his forehead, which were once etched deep in frustration, now seem to soften, and his eyes crinkle in a way that adds years of character to his face.

"Let's not rule anything out," he adds with a playful glint in his eyes.

As the ideas continue to flow, his jokes become more frequent. Some are quick and clever, others are delightfully cheesy. Despite my initial resistance, I find myself slipping into the rhythm of our banter. It's as if a door to a hidden side of him has been unlocked, revealing a person I never knew existed.

"You know, Isabella," he says with mock seriousness, "if this brilliant plan of ours fails, we can always start a new career in stand-up comedy."

I roll my eyes, but there's a smile playing on my lips. "I think the world might not be ready for that."

Sebastian leans back in his chair, his eyes fixed on me. "Oh, I beg to differ. I believe our comedic genius would be unmatched."

In the midst of the serious conversation, we somehow find ourselves teasing each other, bantering playfully. It's a delicate dance of wit and charm, and I savor every moment, my heart pounding in my chest.

As we wrap up the discussion, I can't help but admire Sebastian's intelligence and tenacity. There's a fire in his eyes, a determination to do right by the company and its designers.

"Isabella," he says, his tone softer now, "I appreciate your honesty and passion. We'll find a way to navigate this together."

The words are unexpected, but they wash over me like a wave of reassurance. I realize that beneath his stern exterior, he genuinely values my input, and it makes me feel seen, acknowledged, and respected.

As we walk out of his office, the tension that once gripped us has faded, replaced with an unspoken understanding. Our paths have been rocky, but this evening, something shifts, and it leaves me curious to see where this newfound camaraderie might lead.

Later that day, I struggle to return my focus to the sketch before me. The night's encounter with Sebastian has stirred a myriad of emotions and thoughts, leaving me curious yet cautious about the enigmatic man who stands as both my adversary and an unexpected ally.

Throughout the evening, I had accorded him the respect befitting a CEO, despite our passive animosity. But now, beneath the surface, a new dynamic is at play—an intriguing push-and-pull of energy.

***

Down the dimly lit archives of Maxwell & Co., I find myself surrounded by a treasure trove of fashion history. Dusty boxes line the shelves, each containing pieces of the brand's past waiting to be rediscovered. My heart races with anticipation as I delve deeper into the forgotten world of design.

Amongst the vintage dresses and accessories, my eyes lock onto a dress that seems to emit a soft, nostalgic glow. It's a breathtaking sight, a testament to the timeless elegance that once graced the halls of the company. I carefully lift the garment, feeling the weight of history in my hands.

The dress is a mesh of delicate lace and intricate embroidery, each stitching a whisper from the past. The color, a rich crimson that still retains its vibrancy, evokes emotions I can't quite put into words. The fabric seems to breathe, telling a story of its own, one that beckons me to listen.

As I hold the dress closer, the room around me fades away, and I'm transported to an era of grace and sophistication. I imagine the women who once wore this masterpiece, their elegance and confidence as they graced the dance floors and society soirées.

My excitement bubbles over, and I can't help but smile. This discovery is a gift, an opportunity to breathe new life into the legacy of Maxwell & Co. The dress serves as a bridge between the past and the future, offering me a chance to create a collection that pays homage to the brand's roots while forging a new path forward.

I feel a surge of emotions within me—pride, honor, and a sense of responsibility. As the newest addition to the Maxwell & Co. team, I'm determined to make my mark, to honor the brand's heritage while pushing the boundaries of creativity.

With the vintage dress as my muse, I imagine a collection that embraces cultural sensitivity, one that weaves threads of diversity and inclusivity into each design. A collection that appreciates the beauty of various cultures without appropriating or erasing their significance.

The idea excites me, igniting a passion for fashion that burns brighter than ever. I'm determined to create designs that celebrate the world's rich tapestry of traditions, to showcase that fashion can be a bridge that unites, rather than a wall that divides.

As I set the vintage dress back in its place, my mind swirls with inspiration and ideas. I'm ready to embark on this creative journey, to design a collection that will not only leave a mark on the fashion industry but also in the hearts of those who wear it.

With a newfound sense of purpose, I walk out of the archives, my heart full of dreams and aspirations. The legacy of Maxwell & Co. pulses through my veins, guiding me to create something extraordinary, something that will change the perception of fashion, one stitch at a time.

As I step out of the archives, a familiar figure stands in the distance. It's Sebastian Maxwell.

— Chapter 7 —
Resonating

Fashion exhibitions are a whirlwind of colors, lights, and bustling activity. The venue buzzes with a vibrant energy as journalists and media folks surround me, eager to capture every detail of Maxwell & Co.'s new vintage-inspired collection. The air is perfumed with a hint of excitement, and the low hum of chatter fills the room.

A journalist approaches, her camera ready to capture the essence of the event. "Mr. Maxwell, tell us about the inspiration behind this collection," she prompts, her eyes alight with curiosity.

I lean in, offering a warm smile. "Our vision was to pay homage to the timeless elegance of bygone eras while infusing it with a modern edge. Isabella, our brilliant fashion designer, brought this vision to life with her creative genius."

Isabella stands a few feet away, and as her eyes meet mine, I can see a glimmer of surprise and gratitude. I continue, "She meticulously crafted each piece, drawing inspiration from the glamor of the past and weaving it seamlessly into the present."

The journalist seems eager to know more. "And how would you describe the overarching theme of the collection?"

I pause for a moment, choosing my words carefully. "It's an ode to individuality and self-expression. Each ensemble is a story of its own, designed to empower our wearers and evoke a sense of nostalgia while embracing the possibilities of the future."

The room nods in appreciation, and the conversation flows effortlessly from one topic to another. As I engage with the media, my heart swells with pride, knowing that Isabella's talent is finally getting the recognition it deserves.

Amidst the conversations, my eyes catch Isabella's radiant smile. I can't resist the urge to put her in the spotlight, to give credit where credit is due. "Excuse me," I interject, "Isabella, why don't you join us for a moment?"

She looks a tad coy but gracefully joins the circle, her presence radiating charm and modesty. "It's all thanks to Isabella's ingenuity," I say, "that this collection came to life. Her vision and dedication have made this event a triumph for Maxwell & Co."

The journalists eagerly shift their attention towards Isabella, intrigued by the woman behind the exquisite designs. As she speaks, her passion for her craft becomes evident, and her eloquence captivates everyone around her. I watch with pride as she delves into the creative journey that led to the collection, her eyes lighting up with enthusiasm.

With a grin, I can't help but interject playfully, "Isabella, tell them about the countless nights you spent sketching and perfecting each design. I've never seen anyone so committed to their craft."

Isabella blushes, but her smile remains contagious. "It's true," she admits, her voice tinged with humility. "Fashion is my life, and every garment in this collection holds a piece of my heart. I wanted to create pieces that tell a story, that inspire confidence and self-expression."

The journalists nod appreciatively, clearly taken by Isabella's sincerity and artistic vision. They ask more questions, and Isabella expertly navigates each inquiry, leaving no doubt in their minds about the depth of her talent.

As the interviews wind down, Isabella and I share a knowing look, grateful for the opportunity to showcase our collaboration to the world. The exhibition hall continues to buzz with excitement, as industry insiders and fashion enthusiasts alike explore the collection. The vibrant hum of conversations fills the air, and the clicking of camera shutters becomes a symphony of its own.

Throughout the evening, I make a point to praise Isabella's work whenever the opportunity arises, ensuring that her name is synonymous with the success of the vintage-inspired collection. I can see the impact of her designs on the attendees as they marvel at the exquisite craftsmanship and unique blend of eras.

We find ourselves at the center of attention as the night progresses, celebrated for a collection that surpasses expectations. I never imagined that our partnership would lead to such a profound creative alliance. Isabella's unique approach to fashion has breathed new life into the brand, and I couldn't be prouder to stand alongside her.

With the exhibition drawing to a close, I steal a moment alone with Isabella amidst the whirlwind of congratulations and accolades. "You were incredible," I whisper, admiration coating my words.

She smiles, her eyes reflecting gratitude and happiness. "And you were fantastic, too. Thank you for giving me the opportunity to showcase my work."

"It was my pleasure," I respond sincerely. "You've elevated the brand to new heights. Our collaboration has been a game-changer, and I can't wait to see what the future holds for Maxwell & Co."

We spend the rest of the month flying across cities, running exhibitions. Isabella and I, and some other company employees. Exhibitions are one of the most daunting aspects of this job, and also the most exciting.

From interviews to interviews. Critics to critics. Runways to runways. It is during one of these days that we meet Elizabeth Kensington, a renowned British fashion critic.

"Isabella, I must say, these unique silhouettes of yours are rather perplexing," Elizabeth Kensington states with a raised eyebrow.

Before Isabella can respond, my voice cuts through the tension like a warm ray of sunlight, "Perplexing? That's precisely what makes them brilliant."

As the critic's eyes narrow, I feel the weight of her skepticism lingering in the air. My heart pounds in my chest, and I know I have to continue to defend Isabella's craft.

"Think about it," I say, my voice unwavering. "The fashion industry thrives on innovation. It's not about playing it safe and sticking to the same tired formulas. It's about pushing boundaries, breaking free from the ordinary, and creating something that resonates with people on a deeper level."

Isabella's eyes meet mine, and for a moment, I cannot tell if what I see is a flutter of affection or gratitude and relief in her gaze. She has poured her heart and soul into these designs, and I won't let anyone belittle her passion and dedication.

"These silhouettes," I say and gesture to them vaguely, "they are a breath of fresh air. They challenge conventions, provoke thought, and evoke emotions. Isn't that what true art should do?"

The critic seems taken aback by my fervent defense. I can almost see the gears turning in her mind, contemplating the essence of creativity and originality.

"It's easy to fall into the trap of playing it safe," I add, my voice lowering slightly but maintaining its intensity. "But what sets true visionaries apart is their willingness to embrace risk and forge new paths. Isabella has done just that."

I glance back at Isabella, and a smile tugs at the corners of my lips. She is more than just a fashion designer; she is an artist, a trailblazer, and she deserves to be recognized for her boldness.

The room seems to hold its breath, the air heavy with anticipation. And then, slowly, the critic's expression softens, and she nods thoughtfully.

"You make a compelling argument," she admits, her tone less confrontational. "Perhaps I was too quick to judge."

Grateful that my words have resonated with her, I nod in acknowledgment. "It's easy to be critical," I say, "but it takes true discernment to appreciate the nuances of artistry."

The tension in the room seems to dissipate, replaced by an air of understanding and respect. Isabella's designs have withstood the scrutiny and emerged victorious again, their uniqueness and creativity applauded.

As the conversation continues, I find myself drawn into debates about art, fashion, and the interplay of creativity and commerce. The atmosphere buzzes with the passion of like-minded individuals, each contributing their perspective to the tapestry of the fashion world.

As the evening wears on, Isabella and I find ourselves amidst a group of fellow artists and industry mavens, sharing stories and laughter. The doubts and insecurities that had shadowed me earlier now feel like distant memories, replaced by a sense of purpose and camaraderie.

At this moment, I know that defending Isabella's designs isn't just about protecting her reputation; to me, it's an explicable feeling towards her that I can't yet grasp.

While we stand side by side, her warm hand brushes mine. I'm caught off momentarily. I glance at her, and our eyes meet.

She looks away in awkward hurriedness.

A small smile creases the corners of my lips as I struggle to keep my mind away from Isabella. Voices become distant. Laughter sounds like it's coming from a mile away. Conversations fade, until all I can hear are my thoughts running into each other. However, one name keeps popping up: Isabella.

— Chapter 8 —
A Dance Of Butterflies

Amidst the dazzling chaos of The New York Fashion Week, I stand in the spotlight, fielding questions from eager journalists. Cameras flash, voices buzz, and I feel a surge of exhilaration. As I respond to their inquiries, my name rings through the air, called by a familiar voice from behind me.

"Isabella Rivera!" The voice cuts through the clamor like a melodic note, and I turn around, my heart racing with anticipation.

And there he stands, my greatest fashion idol, a name fitting his unparalleled status in the industry— Adrian Hartley. Awestruck, I feel a surge of excitement coursing through me, and before I know it, I'm engulfing him in a tight embrace.

"Oh, my goodness, Adrian! I can't believe it's you!" I gush, trying to contain my giddy smile. "I've admired your work for years."

Adrian chuckles, his warm eyes gazing at me with genuine admiration. "Isabella, I've been following your work since your latest collection. It's truly remarkable. When I heard you were here, I just had to come and meet you. You're an absolute talent."

The words send a thrill down my spine, validating every late night and challenging moment that went into creating my designs. "Thank you so much, Adrian. Your praise means the world to me."

Adrian Hartley isn't an easy man to find, as I have tried my hardest to meet him on several occasions until I felt I had no choice but to give up. But seeing him here, in the flesh, is a dream come true. And not only am I seeing him, he just mentioned that he's a big fan of my works.

Adrian pulls me close into a casual side embrace as we pose for the cameras in front of us. I wonder what the photos look like. I know they'd be out there later today, frozen in time with the one man who single-handedly inspired me to be a fashion designer.

Adrian bids his farewell, leaving me with an infectious smile.

"Isabella!" I hear Sebastian's voice from a distance, and my heart flutters. Turning, I see him striding towards me with that characteristic air of confidence and charm that never fails to make me smile.

"Sebastian!" I exclaim, unable to hide my excitement. "You won't believe who I just met—Adrian Hartley! He's been following my work!"

Sebastian grins, pleased with my elation. "I'm not surprised at all. Your talent deserves recognition on a global stage."

As we continue to chat, the crowd around us fades into the background. It's just the two of us, connected by fashion, fueled by dreams and fleeting desires that keep me up late into the night. In that moment, The New York Fashion Week becomes a backdrop to our shared chemistry, where passion and creativity intertwine.

***

Amid the quiet hum of the studio's soft lighting, I find myself working late into the night, accompanied only by the rhythmic tapping of my pencil against the sketchpad. The faint scent of fabric and ink fills the air. I glance up from my designs, startled by a soft knock on the door. It swings open, and there stands Sebastian, his silhouette framed against the warm glow of the hallway lights.

"Isabella, still here?" he asks, his voice smooth as silk.

Feeling a rush of excitement mixed with a hint of nervousness, I nod. Working alongside Sebastian is both thrilling and intimidating.

"I couldn't resist the pull of inspiration," I reply, offering a small smile.

"Oh, wow." He stands by the doorway, glances around for a bit, and continues, "I thought I was the only one here until I saw the little light." Before I can say anything, he turns briefly and says, "Give me a second."

I stand there, a little confused, wondering where he has disappeared to. I hear the sound of his shoes fade away in the distance.

A few minutes later, Sebastian returns with two wine glasses, a bottle of red wine, and a wide smile on his face. He steps into the room, and I can't help but notice the way the dim light accentuates the sharp angles of his face, the way his dark hair falls gracefully over his forehead. The tension between us is heavy. I wonder if he feels it, too.

As he rolls up his sleeves, I catch a glimpse of the veins in his forearm, tracing the lines beneath his skin like an intricate map of hidden stories. I force my gaze back to my sketches, trying to ignore his presence so close to mine.

I struggle to keep my composure as he walks towards my desk, the drink in his hand. I watch him squeeze the cap off after placing the wine glasses on the table. He pours into both glasses and hands me one.

I mutter a half-hearted *thank you* as I take the glass from him.

"Your designs are truly captivating," he remarks, his eyes lingering on my work.

The compliment from such a discerning eye sends warmth surging through me. "Thank you," I reply, my heart fluttering. "Coming from you, it means a lot."

Sebastian leans back in his chair, the subtle play of candlelight casting a warm glow on his face. "You know, Isabella, I've always been fascinated by the interplay between fashion and art," he muses, his eyes locking onto mine.

I nod, captivated by the depth of his gaze. "Oh, absolutely," I respond, my heart pounding in my chest. "They're like two sides of the same coin, each influencing and inspiring the other."

He chuckles softly, the sound like a gentle caress. "Exactly! It's like they share this symbiotic relationship, drawing from one another to create something entirely unique and extraordinary."

As the conversation flows, we delve deeper into our shared passions, our voices intertwining like a delicate dance of words. We speak of fashion designers who blur the lines between clothing and art, their runway shows becoming ethereal performances that leave the audience spellbound.

"And the art world," I add, my eyes lighting up with excitement. "It's incredible how artists can use their work to make a statement, to challenge conventions and provoke thought."

Sebastian nods, his gaze never leaving mine. "Yes, art has this uncanny ability to speak to the soul, to evoke emotions and spark conversations. It's truly transformative."

The warmth of his words washes over me, and for a moment, it feels like we're the only two people in the world. The studio fades away, and all that remains is the magnetic pull between us.

"Speaking of transformative," he continues, his voice dropping to a softer tone, "how do you approach your designs, Isabella? What drives your creativity?"

I take a moment to gather my thoughts, feeling the weight of his attention on me. "I've always believed that fashion should be an expression of individuality," I say, my voice tinged with passion. "It's about empowering people to embrace their uniqueness, to wear something that makes them feel confident and beautiful."

Sebastian leans forward, and his eyes lock onto mine with an intensity that leaves me breathless. "Empowerment," he murmurs, his voice barely above a whisper. "I believe you."

A jolt of electricity shoots through me at his close proximity, the air between us charged with unspoken desires. I catch myself stealing glances at his lips, wondering what it would be like to taste the words that hang between us.

But I quickly shake off those thoughts, reminding myself that this is a professional setting, and we're here to discuss fashion and art. Still, the romantic tension remains, simmering just beneath the surface.

We continue to talk for what feels like hours, our conversation flowing effortlessly from one topic to another. From fashion, we delve into art, and from art, we venture into music. Each shared interest brings us closer, and the walls between us crumble with every exchange.

"Can you dance?" he asks suddenly, catching me off guard.

I chuckle. My cheeks flush with embarrassment. "Not at all," I confess, shaking my head. "I've always been a bit clumsy when it comes to dancing."

A playful glint sparks in his eyes. "Well, I could give you a lesson sometime," he offers, the suggestion lingering in the air like a gentle caress.

I laugh again, feeling the intoxicating pull of his presence. "I might take you up on that offer," I reply, and my heart races at the mere thought of it.

The tension between us is undeniable, hanging in the air like a delicate dance of butterflies. But we both pretend not to notice, the unspoken words heavy with unfulfilled desires.

We talk about mundane things as if the world outside the studio doesn't exist. The night wears on, and the darkness outside seems to mirror the secret emotions simmering within us.

Yet, as the minutes tick by, I catch myself stealing glances at him, mesmerized by the play of shadows on his features. He's magnetic, his every movement captivating, and I find myself drawn to him in a way I can't fully comprehend.

With every brief graze of our hands, my heart skips a beat, the electricity between us sending shivers down my spine. I'm torn between wanting to lean closer and feeling the weight of the unspoken words holding me back.

We both sense the growing intensity, the unspoken truth simmering beneath the surface. But we're locked in a delicate dance of restraint, neither daring to make the first move.

The air around us is thick with unspoken desire, the tension so tangible I can almost reach out and touch it. Yet, we keep it hidden, the weight of unspoken words heavy on our hearts.

As the night wears on, I catch myself lost in a sea of thoughts and emotions, my internal monologue betraying the calm facade I wear on the outside. I'm entranced by his presence, by the way he sees me and my work, and I can't help but wonder if he feels the same pull I do.

But we remain in the realm of unspoken truths, navigating the waters of temptation and restraint, the magnetic pull between us somehow growing stronger with every passing moment.

— Chapter 9 —
The Missing Piece

I can't help but steal glances at Isabella, my eyes drawn to her like a moth to a flame. As she moves around the studio, every gesture she makes captivates me, and her presence feels magnetic, pulling me closer with each passing moment.

Her eyes are like pools of warm amber, reflecting a depth of emotion that intrigues me. There's a spark of intelligence, curiosity, and a hint of mischief in her gaze. It's both comforting and alluring, and it draws me in like a beacon.

Her hair cascades in soft waves, a rich chestnut hue that catches the light, making it shimmer with a mesmerizing glow. I can't help but imagine the feel of her hair between my fingers, its softness a stark contrast to my own rough hands.

Her skin is a canvas of porcelain perfection, smooth and radiant, and I notice a flush of color on her cheeks that betrays her emotions. I wonder what it would be like to trace the contours of her face with my fingertips, to feel her warmth against my skin.

Isabella's style is effortless and chic, a reflection of her artistic soul. Her outfit hugs her figure in all the right places, accentuating her grace and poise. Each piece she wears seems to be carefully chosen, expressing her individuality and impeccable taste.

But beyond her physical beauty, what captivates me the most is the way she carries herself. There's a quiet strength about her, a sense of self-assurance that I find both intriguing and alluring. She's not afraid to speak her mind, to challenge me and push me to be better.

As I continue to stare at Isabella, I realize that her beauty is not just skin deep. It emanates from within, from her soul. Her passion for fashion, her creativity, her kindness—all of these qualities combine to create a captivating aura that draws me in.

At this moment, I can't deny the magnetic pull I feel towards her. Isabella is more than just a beautiful woman; she's an enigma, a puzzle I want to solve, and a force that ignites something within me.

"Do you ever feel the weight of the world on your shoulders?" I finally break the silence, trying to veer the conversation toward a less dangerous territory.

Isabella looks at me, her eyes filled with understanding. "Every day," she responds, her voice soft yet resolute.

I take a deep breath, opening up to her like I haven't with anyone else. "Being the CEO of Maxwell & Co. is both an honor and a tremendous responsibility. I have to live up to my father's legacy, carry the torch of this prestigious fashion house, and steer it toward a bright future."

She nods, her empathy putting me at ease. "It must be daunting, having such high expectations placed upon you."

"It is," I admit, feeling the weight of vulnerability lifting slightly as I confide in her. "I try to exude confidence, but deep down, I sometimes doubt if I'm truly capable."

Isabella reaches out and places her hand on mine. The reassuring gesture sends a jolt of electricity through me. "Sebastian, you've accomplished so much already. The fact that you acknowledge your doubts shows your strength, not weakness. You're human, after all."

Her words warm my heart, and for a moment, I forget the chaos of the outside world. "Thank you," I whisper.

"The pressure to preserve your family's legacy must be overwhelming," she says, her eyes mirroring the compassion in her voice.

"It is," I reply. I can feel the weight of the past generations pressing down on me. "I feel like I'm chasing shadows sometimes, trying to live up to their enormous achievements."

Isabella's gaze never wavers, her presence a soothing balm to my restless soul. "But remember, Sebastian, you are not them. You are uniquely you, with your own strengths and vision. You have the power to create a legacy that's entirely your own."

I smile, touched by her wisdom. "You always have a way of making things seem clearer," I tell her.

She chuckles softly. "It's just the truth. Sometimes, we get so caught up in the past that we forget to live in the present and shape our own future."

Her words resonate with me, and for a moment, the weight on my shoulders feels lighter. With Isabella by my side, I find myself hoping that together, we can navigate the tumultuous waters of the fashion industry, embracing tradition while also encouraging change.

As we continue to talk, the tension still lingers between us, heavy and unacknowledged. But for now, we pretend it isn't there, keeping the professional facade intact. Yet, every now and then, our eyes meet, and I see a glimmer of something more, a connection that goes beyond words.

In this intimate moment, I feel a kinship with Isabella, a shared understanding that goes beyond the walls of the studio. With her by my side, I know that together, we can face whatever challenges lie ahead, and perhaps, just perhaps, turn the tension into something beautiful, both in our personal lives and in the world of fashion.

***

Isabella and I are worlds away from our comfort zones. In the city of Paris, where the Eclat Couture runway dazzles with its enchanting display of couture, we find ourselves united by a common purpose— to promote our new collection. Yet, tonight, as I steal a glance at Isabella, her eyes shimmering with excitement and awe, I realize that this trip is far from just ordinary business.

Stepping out of the venue, the Parisian night welcomes us with its alluring charm. The majestic

Eiffel Tower, adorned in a sparkling glow, stands tall in the distance, setting the perfect backdrop for our venture. Unable to resist the magnetic pull between us, I suggest we take a little tour around the city together. Along the cobblestone streets, amidst the romantic beauty of Paris, our connection deepens with each step.

Laughter and genuine conversations flow effortlessly as we explore quaint cafes and hidden gems scattered throughout the city. Isabella's passion for fashion and life mirrors my own, and every shared moment feels invigorating and profound. The magic of Paris intertwines with the enchantment of our partnership.

As we savor each passing moment, I can't help but notice how Isabella's eyes sparkle with excitement, finding joy in every new discovery. I admit, to myself at least, that I like her more with every passing minute. Breaking free from the confines of professionalism, I embrace this possibility of something tangible happening between us, and the feeling is liberating.

With every glance and every touch, I see Isabella in a different light—she's a captivating, exquisite soul I want to know even more intimately.

The evening air in Paris wraps around us like a soft embrace as Isabella and I stroll arm in arm through the charming streets. The city's lights twinkle like stars above, and the aroma of freshly baked pastries drifts from a nearby patisserie, teasing our senses.

Time seems to have lost its meaning as we chat and laugh, sharing stories from our pasts. Isabella's voice, like sweet music, fills the air as she opens up to me in a way I never expected. She talks about her university days, the dreams she once chased, and even her moments of anxiety. I listen intently, mesmerized by the honesty and vulnerability in her words.

She brushes a loose strand of hair behind her ear, and her smile illuminates the darkening Parisian sky. "You know, sometimes life can be a whirlwind, and I used to feel lost in it all," she confides, her gaze fixed on the moon above. "But then, moments like this, with you, make me feel like I've found my anchor."

Her words resonate within me, and I can't help but feel a surge of emotion. Isabella has a way of unraveling my defenses, and so, I find myself opening up, too. I share tales of my own moments of triumphs and failures.

As we continue walking, our connection deepens. We discover shared interests outside the realms of fashion and arts, laughing over our mutual love for obscure indie films and our bizarre fascination with vintage vinyl records.

Paris seems to fade into the background as we become engrossed in each other's stories, entwined in the magic of this deepening connection. The city becomes a canvas, painting a backdrop for our budding romance.

With every word exchanged, the tension between us becomes more palpable. It's a delicate dance of hearts and emotions. We both feel it. Our gazes lock, and for a moment, time stands still. I see the sparkle in her eyes.

The city bustles around us, but in this intimate moment, it's as if we are the only two people in the world. A warm breeze rustles through the leaves of the trees, carrying with it the promise of something beautiful, something that holds the potential to change everything.

As the evening draws to a close, we find ourselves lingering on a quaint bridge, overlooking the Seine. The city lights shimmer on the water, mirroring the spark between us.

Isabella takes a step closer, her hand finding mine. "Sebastian," she whispers, her voice barely audible above the gentle lapping of the river. "Thank you for tonight. It's been magical."

A smile plays on my lips, and I draw her close, feeling her heartbeat against my chest. "The pleasure is all mine," I say, my voice filled with sincerity. "Tonight has been nothing short of enchanting."

In this moment, beneath the moonlit sky and the watchful eyes of Paris, I know that something special has begun. Isabella has become more than just a talented designer; she's become the missing piece in the puzzle of my heart.

As we stand on that bridge, the world around us fades away, and it's just Isabella and me, together in this moment of undeniable connection.

— Chapter 10 —
In The Spotlight

It's Taco Tuesday, and as usual, I find myself in the office lunchroom, contemplating my recent encounters with Sebastian. Lately, he's been making subtle comments about me that are eerily accurate. I wonder if he's that attentive, observant, or has he been prying into my personal life. I can't help feeling a little vulnerable, realizing how little I know about him in return. As I sit with my colleagues, laughter fills the air as we exchange jokes and stories about our work escapades. But beneath their playful banter, I sense a subtle shift in their tone whenever Sebastian's name comes up. They feign lightheartedness, but I see the envy and jealousy simmering just beneath the surface.

"He's been quite chummy with you lately, Isabella," one of them says with a sly grin, nudging me playfully.

Another one chimes in, "Yeah, it's like you two are joined at the hip. Should we start calling you 'Sebabella?'"

The rest of the group chuckles, but I feel a knot tightening in my stomach. They're teasing, but a tinge of envy lurks beneath their words.

"Oh, you know how it is," I reply with a forced smile, trying to deflect their attention.

"He's not a heartthrob like everyone thinks," someone adds, trying to add some humor to the conversation.

I laugh along, trying to play it cool, but inside, I'm squirming with discomfort. I know my growing closeness with Sebastian is raising eyebrows around the office, and it's not a position I feel entirely comfortable in.

Attempting to maintain a sense of mystery, I say, "He might be more than he lets on."

"Oooh, do tell!" they chorus, and I shake my head, feigning coyness.

As lunch draws to a close, the teasing subsides, and I heave a silent sigh of relief. Alone at my desk, I let my face return to its usual neutral expression. It's hard to shake off the unease their words have stirred in me.

"Absolutely pathetic," I mutter under my breath, wishing I could just brush off their comments.

I overhear a coworker gossiping with another. "Isabella flirting with the boss, huh?"

I am taken aback a little. My head tells me to shoot out of my desk and confront them, to shout and tell them to mind the business that pays them. But that's too edgy and defensive. It will certainly give me away. So, I face the computer on my desk and manage a tight smile, unwilling to entertain any further discussions on the matter. I don't want to be the center of office gossip, especially when my heart and career are at stake.

As the workday continues, I do my best to focus on my tasks, but the lingering discomfort from lunch remains. I've always been friendly to everyone, but this newfound closeness with Sebastian is uncharted territory for me. I can only hope that the office chatter will eventually die down, and I can navigate this delicate dance with grace and professionalism.

But they won't give me a break. Everything seems to go by fast, but the small bubble around me takes slow turns. Twirling around me, letting the gravity of things sink me further down with each passing day.

It is on one of those days that Jennifer, our head of design, catches a small blunder.

The blunder – a dress blending modern style with vintage vibes. I decide on a lace pattern for the bodice, one that's subtle but special. Hours later, I step back and see it: a lace motif off-kilter, like a secret I missed.

It's a tiny thing, maybe only another designer would spot. The pattern's not symmetrical – one side's different. It's not a disaster, but it stings. I should've stuck with my gut. Fashion's about details, and I messed up a small but crucial one.

But Jennifer doesn't let things like that slide.

"Isabella, do you have any idea how crucial that attention to detail is in this department?" she scolds, her tone cutting through the air like a knife. "This is simply unacceptable!"

I feel the weight of her words crushing me struggle to maintain my composure. Jennifer has a reputation for being strict and no-nonsense, and

I'm all too aware of her high expectations. I try to explain, but she's relentless, berating me for letting my focus slip due to "extracurricular activities" at work.

Her words strike a nerve, and I'm taken aback by the personal jab. My cheeks flush with embarrassment as our other colleagues glance in our direction, their curious eyes adding to the awkwardness in the room. I want to defend myself, to explain that I'm doing my best, but the words catch in my throat.

"It was just a small mistake," I try to explain, but my voice wavers, and I know it's not enough to placate her.

"Small mistake? Isabella, we're not in kindergarten here," she snaps. "This is a professional environment, and we can't afford these kinds of errors."

Jennifer's words hit me like a punch to the gut, and I can't help but wonder if she's right. Have I been letting my personal distractions affect my work?

Her tirade continues, and with every word, I feel more and more like a failure. The room feels stifling. I long for a lifeline, a way to escape this uncomfortable situation.

No one dares to intervene. Instead, they go about their work as if nothing happened, leaving me to bear the brunt of Ms. Williams' disapproval. I take a deep breath, determined not to let this setback define me, and try to focus on my tasks despite the lingering sense of unease.

But it doesn't stop there.

Later in the day, I'm in the conference room, surrounded by my colleagues. The tension from earlier still lingers, but I try to put it behind me and focus on the meeting. As the moderator speaks, I exchange a knowing glance with Sebastian. His smile offers a hint of comfort, but it also stirs something within me—an inexplicable tug at my heart.

Suddenly, the moderator's words cut through my thoughts, calling me out in front of everyone. "Isabella, are you lost? Is there something you'd like to share with the group?"

The sudden attention startles me. I straighten up in my chair, trying to hide my discomfort. The room falls silent as all eyes turn towards me, waiting for my response. I open my mouth to speak, but the words stick in my throat.

Before I can gather my thoughts, Jennifer interjects, seizing the opportunity to criticize me once more. I feel the heat rise to my cheeks as she continues, and I wish I could disappear into thin air. The murmurs in the room grow louder, and I can sense the judgmental glances directed my way.

Sebastian steps in, his voice firm yet gentle. "Let's continue, please," he says, diffusing the tension. But the damage is done, and the whispers and glances continue.

I try to focus on the meeting, but it's hard to shake off the weight of judgment and the lingering awkwardness. I can't help but wonder if there's any truth to Jennifer's insinuations. Is my heart betraying me, threatening to distract me from my work? As the meeting carries on, I silently vow to prove them wrong and regain my focus, even if it means battling the conflicting emotions swirling within me.

Later that evening, I am hunched over my desk after office hours, trying to fix the mistake I made earlier on. It's a real headache, and I'm starting to feel at my wit's end. Just when I think I'm making progress, the frustration creeps back in. I'm so focused on my iPad screen that I don't even notice when Sebastian strolls in.

"Hey, Isabella. Still here?" His voice startles me, and I quickly minimize the window.

"Yeah, just trying to fix this before Jennifer comes back tomorrow and gives me a hard time," I reply, trying to sound nonchalant.

Sebastian leans on my desk, a smirk playing on his lips. "You know, you look worn out. You should take a break."

I shake my head, determined to get this assignment done. "I can't. I need to correct this before Jennifer gets a chance to reprimand me again."

He steps closer, his presence making it hard for me to focus. "You worry too much about work, Isabella. Come with me; let's get some drinks downtown. It'll do you good."

Before I can protest, he gently pulls me out of my seat. I'm grateful for the distraction, but I don't say it. Instead, I manage a smile and follow him out of the office. Walking along, I'm already a bit relieved from the stress.

We end up at a cozy bar, sitting across from each other. We ordered wine. He tells his stories. I laugh at his jokes, feeling the tension in my shoulders ease with every passing moment. I'm enjoying his company, and it feels like a breath of fresh air amidst all the heavy headedness. Now I tell my stories. He pays attention to my feelings and emotions, and deeply empathizes with them. He softly hugs me. Feeling his warm hands and cologne fragrance, I burst into crying. I might have been waiting for someone who could truly understand me. And here is he, embracing her weakness against all the odds.

After chatting for hours, we suddenly realize that it is a morning. We need to go back to our places. When getting out of the bar, we ran into one of our clients, although he seemed not to recognize that we have spent the whole night together. Now I think about the potential consequences of this growing office flirtation. Sebastian reads my concerns, and tells me, "Are you afraid of being exposed?" I nod. He just smiles, reaching out to put his hand over mine reassuringly. "Isabella, I'd do anything to protect you, to protect us. Don't worry about the rest."

His words calm the storm inside me, and for a moment, I forget about work and the world outside my growing affection. There's something about him that makes me want to let go of my worries and just be in the present.

I know I should be more cautious, that mixing business with personal emotion is risky, but right now, I just savor this stolen moment of happiness with him.

— Chapter 11 —
A Token Of Gratitude

Somewhere on 47th Street, I step into this small, unassuming jewelry shop nestled on a quiet side. It's very easy to miss shop. The owner, Ezra Goldstein, has been my father's friend for years. Long before I was even born. He often jokes about how he practically watched me grow into the man I am now.

The bell above the door chimes, and Ezra, an elderly man with kind eyes, glances up from his workbench. Recognition lights up his face. He stands somewhere between five foot five and six.

"Sebastian, my boy! It's been a while. What brings you here?"

I return the smile, feeling at ease in the familiarity of this place. "Just dropping by to see an old friend," I say as Ezra pulls me into an embrace. "And, well, maybe to find something special."

He nods knowingly, gesturing towards the bracelets displayed on the glass counter. "I see. Looking for the perfect piece, then?"

"I'd love to see your best bracelet designs," I reply, my eyes scanning the delicate crafts of this man. Diamonds and gold shine through the glasses.

He leads me around the shop, showcasing vintage and modern pieces, but one particular bracelet catches my attention. It has a design that seems to resonate with me, reminding me of Isabella.

As my fingers trace the curves of the bracelet, a soft smile plays on my lips, and memories with Isabella swirl in my mind like a sweet melody—the laughter we've shared, the secrets we've exchanged. Lost in thoughts of her, I'm brought back to reality when the shop owner speaks.

"Looks like you've found the one," he says, his eyes twinkling with understanding.

I chuckle, grateful for his insight. "Yes, I think I have."

Curiosity sparks in his eyes, and he gently prods, "And who's the lucky lady?"

"She's an incredible woman," I reply, a hint of admiration in my voice. "She has a way of holding my heart hostage, and I'm perfectly okay with it."

The man smiles knowingly, patting my shoulder. "Ah, love's a beautiful thing, my boy."

I nod, knowing he's right. "I want to engrave a date on this bracelet," I share, excitement and anticipation bubbling within me.

"Oh, a special date, I presume?" he asks.

"Yes," I answer without explaining further. It's the date Isabella launched her new collections that redeemed our public image and shot our stocks through the ranks. But it isn't the image of the company that matters to me at this moment. It's a date that marks a significant shift for Isabella's career.

Understanding dawns on the shop owner's face. "A significant moment indeed. I'll get it engraved for you."

I sit there and watch him under the lights, a master craftsman in his element. My mind wanders off to Isabella and wonders if she'll like the bracelet. It's the least I can do. I think of the best way to deliver it to her. Should I add a note? Should I deliver it myself or have it sent through someone?

So, I pick up a piece of paper and a pen from a table in Ezra's corner. I begin to scribble into it:

Dear Isabella,

I keep thinking about you. You are so beautiful. You evoke an emotion in me that I never thought I was capable of feeling. You deserve the world. And if I cannot buy you the world, I would steal it for you.

Love,

S

***

Jacob Banks' "Chainsmoking" is playing in the background, slowly wafting through the speakers of the Rolls Royce. My heart pounds almost in a rhythmic dance to the beat of the song as we approach the venue of the fashion gala. Isabella is seated right beside me, and we haven't said much to each other throughout the journey.

The air is tense, and I can almost feel my blood course through my veins. I glance over at Isabella, who's looking out through the window as the city shoots right past her eyes. I look down to find her hand trembling a little. Her anxiety is obviously kicking in. The anticipation hangs in the air like a charged current, and time seems to slow down. Without thinking, I reach for her moist hand and clasp it gently. She looks at me, and relief washes over her face, replaced by a grateful smile.

"I'm here," I say softly, my thumb caressing her hand as I lean in closer.

Isabella glances at me, then at my gentle clasp over her hand. I can see a flutter of relief, and maybe gratitude, in her eyes for a moment. So, I lean in closer and closer, staring straight into her eyes as I do so. I am irresistibly drawn to her. The distance between us closes until there's nothing left but the faintest breath of space. Our mouths meet in a soft, sweet, yet intense kiss. My free hand instinctively reaches for her thigh, and I gently grip it, feeling the softness of her skin underneath my touch.

The song's soulful melody continues to fill the air; the guitar chords resonate in my head, adding to the intensity of the moment.

A small, involuntary moan escapes her lips into my mouth, a delicate sound that sends of a jolt of desire through me. The intimacy of the moment is overwhelming, and yet, it feels right, as if we've been building up to this moment all along.

But just as the tension reaches its peak, I pull away slightly, giving us both a chance to catch our breath. I can feel the heat between us, the longing in her eyes mirroring my own. We're teetering on the edge of something powerful, and it's both thrilling and terrifying.

As I pull back, I see the desire and uncertainty in her eyes, and it only fuels my own yearning for her. The charged atmosphere lingers in the air, leaving us both suspended in that fleeting moment, aware of the depth of emotions we're exploring together.

My hand remains on hers, even when the car comes to a stop, and we step out. With her hand in mine, I feel ready to face the bustling venue of the fashion gala. The colossal portico has lights illuminating the massive pillars, as a long, dusty red carpet unfolded up to the large flight of stairs to the venue.

I hear Isabella's heels click against the carpeted stairs as she struts confidently behind me. Her dazzling, silver dress catches the camera flashes from the paparazzi. The glitter on her dress shines like stars, lighting up the night. There's buzz. Chatter. Chaos. Those with cameras run over themselves to find good spots as celebrities and top members of society strut in.

We stop for a quick interview, with seemingly hundreds of cameras flashing in our direction. I haven't let go of Isabella's hand, and I know the pictures will cause a ruckus at the office next week. I don't mind. Isabella is all that matters. I watch her pose for the fashion magazines cameras just before the host asks her who designed her dress. She locks her brows and answers with her own name before letting out a small laugh. Despite her anxiety, she fits here perfectly. By my side, in front of these cameras, getting recognition for her work.

Amidst all the glam and beauty, the lights and cameras flashing, I cannot help but think about the taste of Isabella's lips in the car. I long for more as we weave through the crowd. I wonder if she feels the same way, too. If she looks at me and desperately wants to peel my clothes off my skin and kiss me all over like I want to do to her.

"Look who we have here!" A familiar voice shoots through the cluster of people.

I turn to see Richard. My face stretches into a smile. He seems to be everywhere I go these days. But tonight, he's waking side by side with his wife, who seems to be a walking exhibition of one of his avantgarde designs.

"Who's that?" Isabella asks and locks her brows, a small smile creasing her face as she sees the way I beam.

"An industry friend," I mutter under my breath without taking my eyes off Richard, who is now making his way towards me.

"I always seem to run into you everywhere these days," I say to him and laugh.

"Oh, come on, big man!" Richard says as he reaches out for a hug. "One would think you are an engineer and I a carpenter." He pulls away from me with a smile.

I laugh at his sarcasm.

"Meet my wife," Richard says as he gestures to the woman beside him. "Sebastian, this is Elena. Elena, this is Sebastian, the CEO of Maxwell & Co."

"Of course, I know him." Elena smiles as she extends her hand toward me for a kiss.

Before I can introduce Isabella, Richard reaches for her hand. "Sebastian, you didn't tell me you are married now." He holds a laughing Isabella's hand to his lips as he locks eyes with her. "Knowing the kind of man you are, you probably went to the Caribbeans, somewhere on a private beach, to wed in secret."

I throw my head back and laugh a little. "Isabella, meet Richard, my industry friend," I say as I turn to her. "Richard, meet my girlfriend, Isabella." I keep my eyes on hers for a second longer than necessary, taking in the glimmer of surprise in them.

Isabella is clearly taken aback by my introduction.

— Chapter 12 —
Crossroads

I'm sitting at my cluttered desk in this cramped office, trying so hard to shake off the thoughts of Sebastian's kiss. It's like a movie in my mind, making me restless. Ever since he introduced me as his girlfriend, things between us have shifted. The intensity has skyrocketed, and now, we can't seem to stay away from each other.

I glance out of the small window from my office that opens into the hallway, and spot Sebastian rushing down the corridor. Our eyes meet, and he shoots me that silly expression he's so good at. Just as quickly, he disappears from view, his voice blending with the bustling noise of New York.

Sighing, I get up from my chair, holding my steaming mug of coffee, hoping some fresh air will help. I walk over to the window, watching the city's vibrant rhythm down below. But before I can get lost in my thoughts, my iPhone rings, showing an unknown number.

Curiosity takes over, and I answer, only to be greeted by an overly excited voice on the other end.

"Isabella, oh my gosh, it's been ages! It's me, Sarah!"

My eyes widen in surprise. "Sarah? Wow, I can't believe you found me! How have you been?"

Her voice is full of energy. "Life's been crazy, but I'm doing great."

I can't help but smile genuinely. "Sarah, that's incredible!"

The conversation flows effortlessly, and we decide to meet up later at a nearby bar to catch up properly. It is at this bar, sitting opposite each other, that she tells me she works for Alexandre Beaumont, a rival fashion brand since last year She had been working at their French Headquarters before she was transferred here to New York.

"So, tell me all about your gig at Maxwell & Co.," Sarah urges, her eyes glinting mischievously.

"Oh, you know, just a regular designing job," I reply, trying to downplay it.

She raises an eyebrow, not buying my words at all. "Come on, regular jobs don't involve being introduced as the CEO's girlfriend."

Blushing, I take a sip of my drink, needing a moment to gather my thoughts. "Well, it's not as serious as people make it seem. We're just dating, you know."

She grins, pushing further. "Come on, Isa! I need the juicy details. How did you two even get together?"

I hesitate, feeling a bit uncomfortable. "It's a long story, but let's just say we had our moments of bickering before things changed."

Switching gears, Sarah brings up our childhood days. "Remember when I moved to the UK when I was 11? Those were wild times, right?"

Laughing, I'm relieved for the distraction. "Absolutely! And you've got a hint of a British accent now, don't you?"

Sarah bursts into laughter, playfully denying it. "No way! You're just making that up!"

As the evening continues, Sarah's questions start to get more personal, veering into territory that makes me a bit uncomfortable. She seems genuinely curious, but her probing feels relentless, and I'm not sure if I want to share everything with her.

"Isabella, you know I'm dying to know more about Maxwell & Co. What's it really like working there?" Sarah asks, her eyes sparkling with intrigue.

I hesitate, not sure how much to reveal. "Well, it's a big company, lots of pressure and competition. But it's also exciting and challenging."

Her smile widens. "And what about Sebastian? Tell me about him. Is he as charming behind closed doors as he is in public?"

I try to choose my words carefully. "Sebastian is...well, he's charismatic and ambitious. He knows how to command a room."

Sarah leans in, her voice dropping to a conspiratorial tone. " Are the rumors true about him being a bit of a playboy? I mean, before he started dating you, obviously."

My discomfort grows, and I decide to be honest. "There have been rumors, but I don't know the truth behind all of them."

She doesn't let up. "But you're his girlfriend. You must know something. Is he a heartbreaker or just misunderstood?"

I shift uncomfortably in my seat, not wanting to feed any gossip. "Sarah, I really don't think it's fair to judge him based on rumors. People can change, you know?"

Sarah doesn't seem satisfied with my answer and pushes further. "You're right, people can change. But are you sure he's changed? I mean, he's never been in a public relationship before."

I feel my cheeks flush, feeling the weight of the situation. "Sarah, it's not fair to judge him or me based on his past. We're taking things one step at a time."

She seems to sense my unease and softens her tone. "I'm sorry, Isa. I don't mean to pry. It's just all so intriguing, you know? A CEO dating an employee— it's like something out of a scandalous movie!"

I try to lighten the mood with a small smile. "Well, let's hope our story doesn't end up on the front page of a tabloid."

Noticing my discomfort, she changes the subject with a gentle smile. "You're lucky, Isa. Don't take it for granted."

I nod, acknowledging the weight of it all. "You're right, I won't."

As the evening continues, there's an awkward silence between us as I try to glance around to keep my mind occupied. Sarah, on the hand, stares at me from time to time. Eventually, she excuses herself with a knowing smile.

"I've got to run, but let's catch up again soon, alright?"

I agree warmly, grateful for the reunion. I pay for our drinks before leaving. The encounter was genuine, capturing the ups and downs of reconnecting with an old friend: the laughter, the memories, and those moments of unease as you get to know one another again.

But there is something off about her energy. Something amiss. Perhaps it's the years playing tricks on me. My mother says even when you watch people play around as kids, you never know who they'll become later down the line.

For the next two weeks, Sarah and I try to rekindle that friendship we lost several years ago when she moved to the UK. And since I don't know who my friend really is anymore, I've been trying to find the lost answers in her eyes. They seem like they have stories to tell.

It's on one of those evenings of me trying to find answers that Sarah and I are sitting out by the water, throwing stuff into the river and watching ripples roll through it until they fade out. Something's still off with her. Every time we talk, I catch this sadness lingering in her eyes. So, I figure tonight's the night to find out what's going on.

The sun's going down, painting the sky orange and pink. I glance at Sarah, and she looks lost in her thoughts. "Hey, you okay?" I ask

She sighs and fiddles with a pebble. "Honestly, not really. Work's been a mess," she confesses, her voice soft.

I scoot a little closer, feeling worried for her. "What's happening at work?"

"There are problems, and if I don't fix them, my whole career as a designer is in jeopardy," she admits, her voice shaky.

Now I understand why she's been so down. "Is there anything I can do to help?" I ask.

At first, she brushes it off, saying it's nothing I need to worry about. But I won't let her shut me out. "You can talk to me, Sarah. You know that, right?" I tell her.

She looks like she's struggling with something, and finally, she blurts it out. "I need something, Isabella. I need some design concepts and prototypes. Just a little secret that might give me a chance to save my career. It won't hurt you, I promise."

I can't believe what I'm hearing. She wants me to betray not only Sebastian's trust but that of the whole company by sharing confidential information? "No way, Sarah. I can't do that," I say firmly, shaking my head.

But she's not giving up that easily. She starts pleading, using emotional blackmail, making me feel torn inside. "Please, Isabella, I'm desperate. You don't know how much this means to me," she says.

I walk away, trying to process it all. The sound of waves crashing against the rocks matches the turmoil in my head. This isn't some fairy tale with clear-cut choices. It's real life, and I have to decide between my loyalty to Sarah and doing what I know is right. And right now, I'm not sure which way to go.

The air is thick with tension as I walk a few more steps away from Sarah, needing some space to think. The distant hum of city life surrounds us, but in this moment, it's like we're the only two people in the world.

I take a deep breath, trying to sort through my conflicting emotions. Sarah is my friend, and I want to support her, but her request goes against everything I believe in. Betraying someone's trust, even if it seems harmless, is not something I can easily justify.

She follows me, her steps hesitant. "Isabella, please don't be mad," she says, her voice tinged with regret.

I turn to face her, trying to keep my voice steady. "Sarah, you know I care about you, but what you're asking is a big deal. It's not right to use someone else's secrets for personal gain."

She looks down at her feet, her shoulders slumping. "I know, and I hate myself for even considering it, but I'm desperate," she admits, vulnerability seeping into her words.

I reach out and gently touch her arm, trying to offer some comfort. "I get that you're going through a tough time, but compromising your integrity won't make things better in the long run," I say, hoping my words can get through to her.

She looks up at me with pleading eyes. "Isabella, you're my last hope. If I don't turn things around, I could lose everything," she says, her voice cracking.

I can see the fear in her eyes, and my heart aches for her. "Sarah, I wish there was an easy solution, but this isn't it."

She takes a step back, a mix of frustration and resignation in her expression. "I guess I can't force you to help me," she says, her voice barely above a whisper.

I hate seeing her like this, but I can't give in. "I want to help you, but not like this," I say, trying to convey my sincerity.

Silence settles between us, the weight of the situation heavy on both our shoulders. The waves continue their rhythmic dance against the shore, as if echoing the ebb and flow of our emotions.

Finally, Sarah lets out a sigh and looks away. "I should go," she says quietly, her tone defeated.

I nod, understanding that she needs space to process everything, too. "Take some time to think about what's really important to you, Sarah." I hope she'll find the strength to make the right choice.

As she walks away, I feel conflicted. I hate seeing her hurting, but I know I can't compromise my principles. It's a tough situation, and I'm left with the weight of a difficult decision.

The evening sun dips below the horizon, and the world around me darkens. I stay by the water, feeling a mix of emotions swirling inside me. I don't know what the future holds for Sarah and me, but I know that in this moment, I need to stay true to myself and what I believe in. And maybe, just maybe, that's the best way to help my friend, too.

But Sarah doesn't relent. She calls me nonstop for days, leaving voice messages and texts, asking me to reconsider my stance. I am too ashamed to face her now. And even speaking to her feels like betraying Sebastian's trust in me.

So, when Sarah calls again, I pick up and before she can speak, I ask her to never contact me again.

— Chapter 13 —
The Scandals

I have spent the last couple of weeks in different cities in Europe, from London to Paris to Lisbon to Milan. And it's been the longest two weeks of my life, being away from Isabella.

So, when I arrive home this weekend, I stop by Isabella's apartment holding a bouquet of flowers I handpicked in Milan. She jumps on me the minute her apartment door slides open, almost ruining the flowers I hold in one hand. I have a bottle of red wine in the other and a smile plastered to my face.

It's not the first time I have been to her apartment. But I hope surely that it's going to be the first time she lets me in. So, I stand there as she plants kisses all over my face until I am giggling like a child.

"Are these for me?" She reaches out to grab the flowers before I get the chance to even respond to her question.

"I've missed you," my voice rasps from the mild autumn cold.

"I've missed you, too." She leans forward for a kiss.

And when our lips meet and sink together, I feel the passion course through me. I pull away and ask, "Can I come in?"

Isabella says "sure" as she opens the door wide for me to step in. As I walk into Isabella's apartment, it feels like entering a romantic dream. The cozy living room has dim lights and comfy, plush couches. The sweet scent from a vanilla-scented candle fills the air, and soft jazz music plays in the background. It's nothing like the cold, minimalistic atmosphere of my home. The view from the floor-to-ceiling windows is stunning, with the city lights twinkling outside. Lace curtains sway gently, giving the place a touch of charm. In a corner, there's a cozy reading nook with cushions and clearly beloved books. The open plan kitchen has a homey feel, and the air smells of freshly-baked pastries. It all screams that Isabella lives here.

"Lovely space," I say, watching her scamper around nervously before sinking into her couch with my legs crossed.

"Forgive me," she says as she stands over me, looking a little confused. "My house is a mess right now…"

"Your home is beautiful, Isabella," I interrupt her.

But she doesn't let up, "… I don't usually get guests. I didn't know you were coming."

With a smile on my face, I interrupt her again, "I love what you have done with the place." I glance around again, taking it all in.

Isabella is restless, as she disappears into a corner again, fixing one or two things that really do not need fixing.

As I watch her bounce around, I notice that she's wearing an oversized t-shirt that hangs loosely on her slender frame. Her hair cascades gracefully down the side of her face, creating an effortlessly beautiful look. The low lights in the living room accentuate her radiant features, making her look even more captivating.

She moves with a carefree saunter, wearing flip flops and knee-high socks that add a touch of playfulness to her style. I can't help but notice how her perfectly shaped butt rolls gently under the loose fabric of her t-shirt, giving her a relaxed and alluring charm.

The moment I settle into the cozy couch, my eyes catch sight of a vintage vinyl record player with a collection of records by its side. Intrigued, I move off the couch and walk over to it, my curiosity piqued. I reach out and touch the record player while asking Isabella if it works.

She smiles and responds with a soft "yes." The scent of her fragrance envelops me, just as intense as when we hugged and kissed at the door. My fingers glide over the retro record player as I observe its timeless charm.

Beside the record player, I notice a classic Teddy Pendergrass' "Life Is a Song Worth Singing" record lying on the floor. With a flutter of excitement, I pick it up and place it on the turntable. As the needle touches the vinyl, the room fills with the mesmerizing melody of the music. The soft, dim lights from her lamps and scented candles create a magical ambience that perfectly reflects Isabella's energy.

Feeling the rhythm, I look up at Isabella and playfully say, "I want to watch you dance."

Throwing her head back, she chuckles and replies, "Only if you'll dance with me."

The slow, beautiful song wraps around us, and I move smoothly towards her, placing my hand on the small of her back. Our eyes lock, and a small smile escapes me as we begin swaying together in perfect harmony. The music seamlessly transitions from one song to another, and time seems to slow down as we dance together.

The atmosphere is electrifying. There's a nagging voice in my head, urging me to kiss her now. Without hesitation, my hand moves up her waist, and the other gently holds the nape of her neck. And in that moment, our lips meet, and the world fades away, leaving only the intoxicating connection between us.

The world around us dissolves into a blissful haze. Each gentle caress feels like a whispered promise of desire and devotion. The boundaries between us begin to blur, and our hearts start to beat in unison.

The nagging voice in my head intensifies as sparks of energy shoot through my whole being. It's as if someone pulls a plug in my head as my hand travels farther down her back, then to her waist. It doesn't take long before my hands find the perfect lobes of her butt. I can feel the texture of her skin, and I know the only thing between us is the thin t-shirt she's wearing.

I deepen the kiss as my hands continue to wander into uncharted territories: underneath her shirt, just a little above her waist.

"I've always wondered what you taste like…" I pause, feeling the hotness of my breath. "…everywhere." I throw caution to the wind and prepare to make my next move.

As if my words have added fuel to the fire raging in her head, she pulls me closer, like she wants to taste the remaining words out of my mouth before I speak to them. She moans into my mouth as I carry her straight to the couch.

We both sink into it with our lips still locked in shared chemistry. The silky voice of Teddy Pendergrass rolls through the living room, hugs the walls, and whispers in my ears. Nothing else matters as Isabella raises her left leg and wraps it around my waist to pull me closer. My weight is heavy on top of her. Her moans get louder and louder as I pull away from her lips, and I begin to plant kisses on her body.

Her neck.

Her collarbone.

"Do you like that?" I ask, breathing down her ear, making sure it steams down on her.

"Yeah, don't fucking stop," she cusses under her breath. Her eyes burn with so much desire as I watch her body wriggle with pleasure.

Her reaction sends sparks of electricity through my body to my brain as my bulge continues to grow larger and larger. Her hands soon find my zipper, and she fiddles with it for a second, partially distracted by the things I'm doing to her.

My hand grazes her already taut breasts, then I raise the shirt up her body as I continue to kiss her torso, down to her belly button. Her loud moan escapes her, and her thighs cage me as the two of us are intertwined in each other's passionate embrace.

"Yes…more…yes…"

And as soon as I lower my head to find her inner thighs, the doorbell rings, jolting us back to reality. Isabella hurriedly untangles herself from me, adjusting her shirt and running her fingers through her hair with a playful urgency.

I smile back as I sit up on the couch.

The doorbell rings again.

She glances at me, and I'm already on my feet, trying to pretend that I haven't been caught off guard.

As Isabella approaches the door, I feel a slight pang of disappointment. It's a delivery man at the door, and Isabella signs on a paper with a casual flick of her wrist, bringing in a small parcel. She turns around, brandishing the box, explaining that it's something she ordered a few days ago that's just now arriving. I smile and nod at her obvious enthusiasm.

This is enough for today and I have to leave for a client meeting.

"I guess it's time for me to head out. It's getting late, you should get some rest." I say, glancing around the cozy room once more. "Your place is lovely and has such a cozy vibe. Mine is, well, a little too minimalistic. It could use a romantic touch, honestly. Sometimes, it feels like an asylum in there."

Isabella laughs. Her laughter is infectious, but she says nothing, just walks over and wraps her arms around me in a tight hug, resting her head against my chest. I gently pull her head up and kiss her softly on the lips before heading out into the chill of the evening.

***

The next Monday, as I step into the boardroom, the scent of freshly-polished wood mixed with a hint of nervous anticipation greets me. My heart beats faster, memories of the weekend with Isabella still dancing in my mind. I try to shake off the distraction, knowing that today, I must face the board of directors.

The board, a mix of seasoned executives and long-time partners, sit around the polished table. I find my spot, one hand resting on the cool surface, projecting an air of confidence. The chairman of the board, an old friend of my father's, Robert Sinclair, occupies the head of the table.

Silence hangs heavy in the air, like a thick fog settling over the room. I can feel the weight of their eyes on me. Robert clears his throat, breaking the silence.

"Sebastian, we've been discussing concerns about the office romance policy," he begins, his voice firm but cautious. "Your relationship with Isabella Rivera has raised some eyebrows."

I maintain my composure, my eyes meeting Robert's unwaveringly. I wait for him to continue, even though my pulse quickens with each passing moment.

"Some of the board members have raised concerns about favoritism," Robert continues, his gaze penetrating my soul. "And there are whispers about Isabella's focus being affected."

I take a deep breath, trying to keep my emotions in check. This is not the first time I've faced scrutiny, but it still feels like walking through a minefield.

"And what do you have to say about these concerns?" one board member interjects, his voice carrying a hint of skepticism, like he's not sure how seriously I'll take the matter.

I lean back slightly, my hands gesturing subtly as I respond, "I won't deny that I've shielded Isabella from malicious attacks, but I've done the same for anyone facing bullying. There's a difference between criticism and personal attacks."

The room remains tense, the air charged with unease. I continue to defend my actions, my voice unwavering as I speak.

"But we can't ignore the success we've achieved during this period," I add, my eyes sweeping across the room. "Sales have skyrocketed, and our PR has never been stronger—all thanks to Isabella Rivera."

A murmur ripples through the boardroom, but I stand my ground, my resolve unyielding.

"Isn't it possible that your judgment might be clouded?" another board member challenges, leaning forward with a furrowed brow.

I give a faint smile, and my eyes lock with his. "I assure you that my decisions are based on what's best for the company. Isabella's contributions are invaluable, and as long as her relationship with me doesn't affect operations, there shouldn't be a problem."

Robert's silence is deafening, but I don't back down. I can't afford to falter, not in this moment of uncertainty.

"Besides," I continue, my tone unwavering, "my mother served as the chief accounting officer for years before her retirement. My father appointed her, and her presence was never questioned."

A few board members shift in their seats, their expressions thoughtful. I see a flicker of realization in some eyes.

"But you know why that policy was made in the first place," Robert speaks up again, his voice carrying a mix of frustration and concern.

I shake my head, my smirk playing at the corner of my lips. "And you know that we're experiencing unprecedented success right now. All because of Isabella Rivera."

The room falls silent once more, my words hanging in the air like a challenge. I know I've hit a nerve, and the weight of their judgment is tangible.

"Maybe you don't fully grasp the gravity of your actions," Robert finally says, his tone stern. "Perhaps it's time to reconsider your position as CEO."

His words strike me like a blow, and for a moment, I'm taken aback. But I don't falter. I refuse to be shaken.

"I stand by my decisions," I retort firmly. "As long as our company continues to flourish under my leadership, I won't let personal prejudices undermine our progress."

— Chapter 14 —
Steadfast

Amidst the pulsating energy of the fashion show, I find myself in the company of industry insiders, their laughter and chatter filling the air like confetti. I take a moment to enjoy my drink, feeling the cool glass in my hand and the fizz tickling my senses.

Suddenly, a figure catches my eye—a man with salt-and-pepper hair, exuding confidence and influence. He approaches me with a magnetic presence, a warm British accent dancing in the air as he introduces himself. "Ms. Rivera, a pleasure to meet you. You can call me Daniel." His eyes lock onto mine, and I can feel the weight of his presence in the room.

"Nice to meet you, Daniel," I reply with a grin, curious about this intriguing man.

He compliments my dress, and I can't help but feel a surge of pride. "Thank you," I respond, "I designed it myself."

As if drawn by an invisible force, I lean in as he begins to talk. He's a man full of stories. He tells me about how his grandfather started their family's company. But Daniel never mentions the name of the company. I don't ask, either. I am too engrossed in his accent, his charisma, and the mystery of his person. But one thing is certain: he's a very influential man.

"Ah, let me tell ya a little story, Ms. Rivera, 'bout this Italian automobile brand, aye?" Daniel starts another round of stories. "See, they had this rival car company, right? And there was this bloke, a genius of an engineer, workin' for 'em. He was givin' 'em sleepless nights, he was, settin' trends that no one else could match."

His eyes twinkle mischievously as he leans in, pulling me deeper into the story.

"But here's the twist, Isabella. Despite all his talents, he was underpaid, aye? Bloody ridiculous, if ya ask me. So, this Italian car brand, they see the opportunity, and they snap this fella right out from under their rival's nose. And you know what they do? They give 'im creative freedom like no other, mate."

His hands move with the rhythm of the story, emphasizing the turning points of the tale.

"With this newfound freedom, the engineer starts buildin' cars like a bloody artist. No one could stop 'im. He rises through the ranks, showin' 'em what he's truly capable of. And before ya know it, he's buildin' his own subsidiary of the company, becomin' equal partners with these Italians."

I chuckle heartily, thoroughly engrossed in Daniel's captivating storytelling.

"Isn't that something?" I reply, entertained and intrigued. "So, what's the moral of this tale, Daniel?"

A wry smile tugs at the corners of his lips as he slips a business card into my hand. "Well, my dear, let's just say I've got an offer you might not want to refuse. Whatever you're gettin' now, you'll get double of it with me, and you'll have the creative freedom you deserve. You'd be head of design, and together, we'll set the fashion world ablaze."

I feel a surge of excitement rush through me at his offer, and he shakes my hand as if we are already sealing the deal. There's an air of intrigue and possibility that surrounds Daniel, and I can't help but be drawn to his charisma.

As he walks away, I watch him go, not knowing what to make of what just happened. I slip the card into my purse and continue to immerse myself in the show.

**

I sit at my office desk, the weight of Daniel Stanton's business card in my hands. Fingers fiddling with the edges, I can't help but be intrigued by the offer he presented at the fashion show. Curiosity gets the best of me, and I do a little background check on Daniel. I find out he's the CEO of Craig Stanton's—a large British fashion brand establishing a satellite network across the world. It doesn't seem like a bad move at all.

The company's origin story is captivating, too. Named after Daniel's grandfather, an army tailor who sewed military uniforms in the Great War, the company spans generations, and now, Daniel stands at the helm of this renowned brand.

Furthermore, the position is based in Paris, the place which every designer intends to live in at least once in their lifetime. And he even promised a much higher salary. This is, absolutely, an attractive opportunity.

Trying to forget the charismatic businessman and his offer, at least for a moment, I search for another topic to occupy my time. My thoughts drift to my budding relationship with Sebastian. A smile tugs at my lips as I get flashbacks from our last time together. The laughs. The kisses. The way he groped me and the little flames inside me that just the thought of him continues to fan. But with Daniel's offer now tangible and tempting, my mind is divided between the excitement of new possibilities and the uncertainty of what it could mean for my current path with Sebastian.

I think, if Sebastian really loves me, he should be able to still support me, even if I leave Maxwell & Co. I'm in love with *him*, not the company. But the issue is, knowing how indecisive I am when it comes to making big decisions, I need a lot of self-conviction to take Daniel's offer.

I glance at the phone on my desk, the card beside it, devoid of any indication that Daniel is the CEO and board chairman. It seems he prefers to keep his identity discreet, though it's not difficult to find the truth with a bit of research.

Summoning the courage, I reach for the phone and dial the number on the card. The phone rings, and as someone on the other end is about to answer, I panic and quickly hang up. My heart races, and I can feel the weight of the decision I'm about to make.

I take a deep breath, realizing that I need to make a choice. The allure of being in control of Craig Stanton's affairs in the US is hard to resist. It would be a step towards new horizons and possibilities I've always dreamt of. I can climb up the ladders really quickly, most likely quicker than I can in my current position.

As I pick up the phone again, my mind races with thoughts of Sebastian and the future I have always imagined at Maxwell & Co. A sense of indecision grips me, and I hesitate before dialing the number once more.

The phone rings, and Daniel's voice breaks through the static, his hoarse accent filling the line. "Hello, Isabella."

My heart skips a beat.

***

Falling for someone feels remarkably similar to discovering a whole new world. I know the whole of New York inside out—well, I always thought I did. But then, I realized I hadn't even seen a quarter of it when I met Sebastian. He's taken me to places I never knew existed, both in the city and in my heart.

Every time I look at him, I'm hit by an avalanche of emotions. It's not just love, as one would expect. There's also guilt tugging at me, reminding me of Daniel Stanton's invitation to join Craig Stanton's. I wonder if Sebastian somehow knows what's been going on in my mind, if he can see the turmoil within me.

When he looks into my eyes, I can't help but look away hurriedly, hoping to hide the secrets that lie within them. Maybe if he stares long enough, he'll find something I don't want him to know.

It's a couple of hours after our Big Bus Tour, and I find myself seated on the rooftop of an apartment building in Central Park South, with Sebastian right across from me. From this vantage point, we can see the city below, bathed in the shimmering glow of night lights. Sebastian occasionally points at something in the far distance, and his laughter echoes through the air as he cracks hearty jokes.

The air is alive with romance as I sit opposite Sebastian at the rooftop table. The soft glow of city lights frames the edges of our world, and the faint rustling of Central Park's bushes and trees provides a soothing backdrop. An array of delicious Italian dishes adorns the table, their tempting aroma mingling with the fragrance of both our perfumes.

I can't stop myself from smiling as I take in the sight before me—the breathtaking view of the city skyline and the man who has opened my eyes to a whole new world. I run my fingers gently over the smooth tablecloth. A mix of excitement and nerves flutter within me.

Sebastian pours champagne into our glasses, and as I raise mine to my lips, I glance at him, seeing that his eyes are filled with warmth and affection.

"You know, I never thought I'd experience New York like this," I admit, my voice laced with wonder. "It's like seeing the city for the first time."

Sebastian grins, his eyes sparkling with happiness. "I'm glad I could show you a different side of it. There's so much more to explore together."

As we sit there, gazing at the city below and enjoying the evening's beauty, I comment on the weather. "Isn't it a perfect night?" I ask with a soft smile, sipping my champagne. "The city looks breathtaking."

Sebastian nods in agreement. "Absolutely. It's like the city is putting on a show just for us," he replies.

I laugh softly. "Well, we did have our show earlier, and it was a huge success," I say, referring to the event we just attended together. "Remember that guy who thought you were the designer and kept praising your 'vision?'"

Sebastian chuckles, shaking his head. "Oh, that was hilarious! I didn't have the heart to correct him. The poor man was so enthusiastic," he says, amusement evident in his voice.

As the laughter subsides, the conversation takes a more serious turn. Sebastian hesitates for a moment before opening up with, "Isabella, I need to tell you something, even though I know I shouldn't be sharing this."

I nod, encouraging him to continue.

"They are frowning on us being together," he says with a touch of frustration both in his voice and on his face.

"I wasn't expecting them to be thrilled about it," I reply. "But, Sebastian, I believe that love can conquer all obstacles. We'll find a way through this together."

Sebastian's expression softens, and he looks at me with deep affection. "You always have a way of seeing the positive side of things."

I smile gently and take a moment to sip my champagne, giving him the space to continue if he wishes. He takes a deep breath before delving into a heartfelt story about his parents.

"My father met my mother when she was in university, studying accounting," he begins. "He had already founded what would become Maxwell & Co., but it was just Maxwell's Apparels at the time."

I lean in, captivated by his tale, and he goes on to explain how after his mother graduated, his father made her the company's accountant. "The company was just a floor in a building somewhere in New York back then."

Sebastian's eyes glimmer with pride as he shares how his parents built the company from the ground up, long before any board members joined. "They laid the foundation for everything we have now," he says with admiration.

"But now, the board is disapproving of us." His voice is back to being tinged with frustration and uncertainty.

I reach out and place my hand on his, giving it a reassuring squeeze. "Love, true love, is steadfast," I say earnestly. "Just like your parents' love and dedication to each other and the company. We'll navigate this, together."

A moment of tender silence envelops us, and I take a deep breath, finally finding the courage to confess my feelings. "Sebastian," I say softly, "I love you."

His eyes light up with joy and affection, and a radiant smile spreads across his face. It's at this moment I know that even though I have always fantasized about building my own fashion brand, my heart belongs to Sebastian. I wasn't sure what to make of Daniel Stanton's proposition, if I should take it and leave Maxwell & Co., but hearing of how Sebastian's parents built this enterprise together makes me want to build a future with him also.

Without a single iota of doubt in my mind, I call Daniel the next morning, and my exact words are: "Thanks for the offer, Daniel. But I'm staying at Maxwell & Co."

— Chapter 15 —
Old Flames

Before Isabella came into my life, I was chasing after one supermodel after another, engaging in what my father termed as, "excessive behavior." I collected this long line of exes who could strut down runways, and it was all fun and games until it wasn't.

Victoria, she is one of those exes. Stunning, no doubt, but she had her own drama to bring to the table. I fell hard for her charms, but like every other drama queen, she came with a baggage carousel I couldn't keep up with. And as much as I tried, our relationship eventually hit a dead end, leaving me feeling older, wiser, and ready to leave that chapter behind.

Victoria is well behind me now. At least, that is what I thought. But seeing her in the middle of all this glam in that black sequin dress that rides up a little too high, I lose the control I thought I had for a moment.

The laughter and chatter echo in the silent room up in my mind as I am temporarily detached from the events happening all around me. As a certain kind of first-class elegance permeates the air, the guests are dressed in their finest attire—women in flowing gowns adorned with sequins and jewels, and men in tailored tuxedos. The sound of lively chatter and clinking champagne glasses fills the room. A live band plays enchanting melodies, their smooth jazz tunes adding a touch of class to the event.

Isabella's laughter pulls me back to the present, and I find myself smiling as I watch her interact with others, effortlessly lighting up the room with her warmth. There's something about her that makes me want to be a better person, to leave the baggage of my past behind and embrace the future with open arms.

But here's the thing; there's a part of me that wonders if I'm ready for something real. Maybe I've been so used to the whirlwind romances and the superficial allure of the fashion world that I don't know how to handle a connection that runs so deep. Isabella's got me feeling things I've never felt before, and it's both exhilarating and terrifying at the same time.

I find myself standing amidst the grandeur of the opulent ballroom, the soft glow of crystal chandeliers casting warm shadows over the elegantly dressed guests. The scent of exotic flowers and expensive perfumes fills the air, creating an intoxicating atmosphere that swirls around me, adding to the anticipation of the high-profile event. I hold a glass of champagne, the delicate bubbles tingling on my lips, but my focus is on Isabella, who stands beside me in a stunning, vintage gown.

Out of the corner of my eye, I watch Victoria glide through the ballroom. The spotlight seems to follow her every step. She's wearing an alluring, yet elegant dress that accentuates her curves, leaving a trail of admiration in her wake. My heart tightens at the sight of her, memories of our past relationship and unresolved emotions resurfacing.

As Victoria approaches, her mischievous smile hints at the subtle jabs and sarcasm to come. "Hello, Isabella," she says with a feigned sweetness that barely conceals her condescension. "It's been a while."

I'm confused. They've never met, at least not to my knowledge.

Isabella's cheeks flush with embarrassment, but she maintains her composure. "Victoria," she replies, her voice steady yet guarded. "We've never met."

"Oh, yeah," Victoria starts, the mischief still creasing her face in a smile. "Then how come you know my name? I see Sebastian here has been talking a lot about me to his new sweetheart."

I shift my weight from foot to foot, glancing around, searching for something. Anything. Anyone that can save me, perhaps drag her out of my sight, until I regain control of myself.

Isabella locks her brows, her face asking all the questions.

But before Isabella can retort, Victoria's gaze then shifts to me, and I feel her scrutinizing me, trying to gauge my reaction. "Sebastian, darling," she coos, her tone dripping with familiarity. "You're looking quite dashing tonight. I see success suits you."

I take a breath, steadying myself. Her words sting since I know they hold more than just a compliment.

"Thank you, Victoria," I respond, trying to keep my emotions in check. "You look stunning, as always."

Victoria chuckles softly, the sound sending a shiver down my spine. "Oh, I know," she says, her eyes locking with mine. "I've been seeing your name in the headlines quite often. The women must be all over you now."

Isabella shifts slightly beside me, and I can sense her discomfort. I feel the weight of Victoria's gaze, her unspoken challenge lingering in the air. "Well, I'm here with Isabella tonight," I reply, my voice steady. I try not to show the effect Victoria's words have on me.

Victoria smirks, her confidence unyielding. "Of course," she says, her gaze shifting between Isabella and me. "I can see that." Her words are laced with insinuation, and I know I need to address the tension between us, but I'm at a loss for words.

Isabella clears her throat, breaking the silence. "Excuse me," she says, her voice calm but her unease evident. "I need to freshen up."

As Isabella leaves, I'm left alone with Victoria, the unresolved feelings and power dynamics between us creating an undeniable tension. I take a moment to collect my thoughts before speaking again. "Victoria," I say, my voice steady yet filled with emotion. "Don't do this right now. Tonight, I'm here with Isabella, and I'd appreciate it if you respected that."

Her amusement never faltering, Victoria raises an eyebrow. "Oh, I'm just having a little fun. But if you insist, darling, I'll be seeing you around."

As Victoria walks away, a whirlwind of emotions envelops me. A little flutter of excitement as she gently touches my arm before melting away into the crowd. I shut my eyes for a second to catch my breath.

I know I need to confront my past and the impact it has on my present with Isabella. My heart yearns to share my feelings and fears with her, to let her know that she is the one I want to be with. The allure of the past and the possibilities of the future collide within me, leaving me uncertain and vulnerable.

***

As I stumble out of the show with Isabella by my side, the night air slaps my face like a wake-up call. We're both giggling and a little drunk from the champagne, trying to shake off the buzz of the flashing cameras that followed us out.

Damn paparazzi never gives up.

Isabella's laugh is like music, and I can't help but grin as we dodge through the maze of desperate photographers. Her heels click-clack on the pavement, and she clings to my arm, leaning in close. My Rolls Royce is parked a distance away from the venue. Once we find the car, the driver eases up conveniently to let us both slip into the back seats.

I nod along to the music playing from the radio, my heart racing, and I lead us down a quieter side street. We spot the neon sign with the word "MOON" of a hidden-not-so-hidden speakeasy above a door that looks like it's from a 1920s movie. We exchange glances, and without saying a word, we both know we're going in.

We step inside, and the atmosphere wraps around us like a warm, comforting blanket. The air is thick with the smell of cigar smoke, and the jazz band in the corner adds a smooth vibe to the place. It's dimly lit, and the shadows create a mysterious, almost surreal ambiance. This is exactly what we need right now. Away from the glaring eyes of the public.

Isabella and I find a secluded booth in the back, and we slide in with a sigh of relief. I can still taste the champagne on my lips. I take a deep breath, trying to shake off the adrenaline from the chase. The drive.

"I've never seen you move so fast," Isabella says, her voice still breathless and full of excitement.

I chuckle. "Well, you know, escaping from the paparazzi is one of my special skills."

She laughs, and it's like magic. In that moment, it feels like it's just the two of us, no cameras, no fame, just us. It's like we're in our own little world.

As we exchange glances, the lights suddenly flicker and go out, plunging the room into darkness. The jazz music stops, and all I can hear is the sound of our breathing. The air feels charged with something electric, and for a moment, we're just suspended in time.

"Are you okay?" I ask, my voice low and close to her ear.

Isabella nods, and I can feel her hand trembling slightly in mine. "Yeah, just a little shaken, I guess."

I squeeze her hand gently. "Me too. But hey, at least we're safe now, right?"

In the darkness, I can smell the mix of cigar smoke and her perfume, and it's intoxicating. Our closeness feels both nerve-wracking and thrilling. It's like we're in a movie scene or something.

And then, just as suddenly as it went out, the lights flicker back on, and the jazz music starts up again, like nothing happened. But this time, something has changed. There's a connection between us that wasn't there before.

Our eyes meet again, and there's a vulnerability there, a mutual understanding. It's like we've seen each other in a different light, beyond the facade of fame and parties.

In the hushed intimacy of the speakeasy, I find myself drawn to Isabella in a way I can't explain.

She looks stunning tonight, even with a bit of a tipsy sway to her step. Her Tuscan sunset eyes are glassy, reflecting the low yellow light of this speakeasy, almost blending into the warm ambiance of the room. She's talking, and I'm trying my best to follow her stories, but it's getting harder to concentrate. Not because she's not making sense—it's just that I can't take my eyes off her. And, yeah, maybe the alcohol is playing a part in that, too.

I mean, how can I not be mesmerized by her? This speakeasy is filled with celebrities and high-caliber people, but right now, it feels like it's just the two of us in our little world. It's like we've managed to escape all the glam and noise of the outside for a while.

We're sitting on this curved velvet seat, and Isabella's leaning into me, her words softly mingling with our breaths. It's intimate, and I can feel the electric charge in the air. I can see the lust building up in her eyes, and I know it's mirrored in mine.

As she speaks, her words are like music, and I find myself just listening, getting lost in the way she tells her stories. Even when I can't quite keep up with everything she's saying, it doesn't matter. It's the way her eyes hold mine, the way her lips move, that has me captivated.

And then, there's a moment—a pause—and it's like time slows down. We're so close that I can feel her warmth against me, and our mouths are just inches apart. It's as if the world around us fades away, and all that's left is her and me.

I can't hold back anymore. I lean in, and our lips meet in a kiss that's like an explosion of sensations. The alcohol is swirling through my veins, adding to the intensity of the moment. I can feel the kiss imploding through my body, and it's like I'm floating and grounded all at once.

The speakeasy may be filled with famous faces and buzzing with excitement, but right here, right now, it's just Isabella and me. And in this stolen moment, I know that I want more of this, more of her. The world outside may be chaotic, but with her, it feels like everything is falling into place.

So, yeah, maybe it's the alcohol talking, but it's also the truth. I want to be with Isabella, to get lost in her eyes, her stories, and her laughter. I want to savor these stolen moments and see where they lead us. And if it means escaping the glitz and noise for a while longer, buried in hushed conversations with her, then I'm all in.

— Chapter 16 —
A Lone Sailer

I watch them all, my family, gathered around the dinner table, and it's been too damn long since I've seen them like this. You know, the whole gang sharing a meal, laughing, and joking like there's no tomorrow. I've been so busy with work lately that these moments have become a rare treat, like a gourmet dessert after a long day of salads.

There's Dad, a retired engineer who's built half of New York's skyline with his bare hands, or so he likes to say. But honestly, the man's got a knack for turning blueprints into towering behemoths that scrape the heavens. He's always been a man of few words, preferring to let his buildings do the talking. But even in his silence, he's got this way of making you feel safe, like nothing in the world can touch you when he's around.

Then there's Mom, running that little grocery store down the street like a boss lady. She's got that no-nonsense attitude, the kind that keeps customers coming back for more. She can be a bit overbearing at times, and God forbid you forget to call her at least once a day; she'll unleash the wrath of a thousand hurricanes. But beneath that tough exterior, she's got a heart of gold and would move mountains to protect her family.

And let's not forget Emily, the baby of the family, studying business administration at Columbia University. She's the brainiac, the one who's got all these plans and strategies for conquering the world. Watching her, I can't help but feel like the underachiever of the group. But hey, someone's gotta keep the world entertained with their clumsy misadventures in the fashion world, right?

As I watch them, my mind drifts from one to the other, trying to soak up every detail, every quirk that makes them who they are. It's like I'm trying to capture their essence in a mental snapshot, to hold onto these moments forever.

But amidst the joy and laughter, there's a gnawing feeling inside me, like a tiny pebble in my shoe that I can't shake off. It's that internal struggle, that conflict between love and ambition, between what's expected of me and what I truly desire. I feel like a lone sailor caught between the crashing waves and the distant horizon, not knowing which way to sail.

"Pass me the salad, please," I say with a mouth full of Pollo alla Cacciatora. The dinner table is almost filled to the edges. For appetizers, we have garlic bread and stuffed mushrooms. For the main course, we are having breaded and fried chicken cutlets topped with marinara sauce and melted mozzarella cheese with Caesar salad. My mother is always extravagant with food.

"You won't believe what I'm writing about in my paper," Emily says excitedly as she passes the salad. And before we can answer, she goes: "Craig Stanton's expansion strategy from the UK and Europe to the US."

With a mouthful of food, I can't help but interject, "Oh, yeah? Daniel Stanton actually approached me to lead that expansion."

Their attention turns to me instantly, curiosity filling their faces as they ask in unison, "What did you say?"

A confused smile plays on my lips, and I reply, "Well, I turned it down, of course."

Silence falls over the dining room as my father chews silently, pondering my response. My mother, ever calm, speaks up, "Is this about your romance with Sebastian, dear?"

I protest immediately, "No, it's not!"

Emily chimes in, "If I were you, I'd work for Craig Stanton and still date Sebastian. Office romance can be tricky."

I've thought about that, I admit to myself.

My mother agrees, saying, "Exactly! Relationships with too many eyes on them are bound to fail."

I glance at my father, hoping for his approval or support. "I'm worried that you're putting romance before your career, Isabella," he expresses with concern.

Before my emotions can get the better of me, I stand up abruptly, leaving my food unfinished. Storming out of the dining room, the atmosphere turns tense, and uncertainty lingers in the air, both for me and my family.

Frankly, I'm torn between my personal life and my career aspirations. It feels like I'm being pulled in two different directions, and there's no easy answer. Why does this have to be so complicated? I love Sebastian, but I also want to excel in my career. Is it possible to have both? Or will I have to sacrifice one for the other?

As I pace the dimly lit hallway outside, the echo of our discussion still resonating in my mind, I can't help but wonder how I ended up in this bewildering situation.

Why can't things be simple? Why does life have to throw such tough choices my way? I feel like I'm stuck in a maze, and there's no clear path to take.

The conversation in the dining room replays in my mind. "Work for Craig Stanton and date Sebastian," my sister had said. It sounds like a plausible solution, but I can't shake off the feeling that it might not work out as smoothly as she thinks.

By the time I return to the dining room, my father raises his head from his plate. His voice sounding so concerned, he asks, "Isabella, aren't you going to finish your dinner?"

I slide my jacket on, and my response is brief, "Not hungry. Sorry, Dad."

"Isabella, where are you going?" My mother's soft mother's voice softens even more with concern.

"I have to leave immediately. I have some things to work on," I lie. "Goodnight, everyone."

"But it's raining right now, Isabella," Emily says.

I hesitate a little, hearing raindrops splattering outside. Then, without any more words, I yank the door open and rush out into the mild rain.

Stepping outside, I flag down a taxi and climb in. "511 East 80th Street, please," I tell the driver while lost in my thoughts. The city lights blur past me as the rain continues to fall, almost in tandem with the jumble of emotions in my mind.

"It's drizzling out there, so stay dry," the friendly driver advises, trying to make conversation. But I'm not in the mood.

"I just need some time to think, please," I respond, my voice a bit harsher than intended.

The driver understands and nods. "Of course, miss. Take your time."

As the car glides through the rain-soaked streets, guilt fills me for snapping at him. "I'm sorry for snapping. It's just been a tough night."

"No worries. We all have our bad days. Just had a rough one myself." The driver glances at the rear-view mirror, revealing a swollen and bruised nose. "My last passenger decided to punch me in the face. But hey, it happens," he says casually, as if such incidents are part of his daily routine.

My shock is evident. "That's terrible! I'm so sorry you had to go through that."

He chuckles softly, trying to brush it off. "Well, it's all part of the job, I guess. But enough about me. You take your time to sort things out, miss. I'll get you to 511 East 80th Street safe and sound."

Still feeling guilty for my earlier rudeness, I reply, "Thank you, really."

I return to looking out the window, the city lights blending into a foggy, blurry mess. In many ways, it reflects the confusion and turmoil inside me. The taxi's gentle movements ease my racing thoughts, allowing me to delve into the depths of my emotions.

Why do I feel torn between my career and my love life? My family's concerns resonate with me, and yet, I can't help but think of what my heart desires. Working with Craig Stanton or staying with Sebastian, both choices seem to lead to their own set of challenges.

Is love worth sacrificing a promising career opportunity? Can I find a balance between the two?

As I ponder these questions, I realize that the path ahead is unclear. But at least I have the night to think it over and figure it out.

The taxi driver's calm presence and my brief conversation with him offer an unexpected solace. Sometimes, the most candid conversations can come from the most unexpected sources. We're all just trying to navigate through our own struggles, and in this fleeting encounter, I find a moment of connection.

Soon, the taxi eases through the streets of New York, approaching my destination. "Here we are, miss. 511 East 80th Street," the driver announces, breaking my reverie.

"Thank you," I say softly, handing him the fare as I step out into the night.

As I make my way inside, the rain begins to fade, leaving behind a sense of renewal in the air. I may not have all the answers right now, but the darkness outside is replaced by the promise of a new day—a new chance to find my way amidst the uncertainties.

It's a few minutes past 5 on a Friday, and I'm still seated at my cluttered desk, the glow of the desk lamp casting a soft halo around my desk.

I sigh, rubbing my temples. It's been a long week. But the deadline keeps me anchored to my seat, even as the week draws to a close. My office door is wide open.

As I immerse myself in my computer screen, the rhythmic tapping of keys fills the air. Time seems to blur, and I lose track of the minutes slipping away. But then, a playful knock breaks my focus. I turn my swivel chair toward the door, and my eyes widen in surprise as I see Sebastian standing there with a sly grin on his lips.

Sebastian leans casually against the doorway, his shirt sleeves rolled up so I can see his strong forearms. I can't help noticing the veins gently popping on his arms. It's a sight that sends my pulse racing, and I try to compose myself as he walks further into the room.

"Working late again, Isabella?" he asks, his voice smooth and teasing.

I nod, trying to hide the blush creeping onto my cheeks. "You know me, always committed to finishing what I start."

He chuckles, the light in his eyes pulling me in, sucking me in like a gravitational force. "Well, I have something that might make your weekend more exciting," he says, reaching into his pocket.

My heart quickens with a mix of surprise and excitement as he pulls out two plane tickets. "I've booked us a trip to California for the weekend," he announces, holding them up with a flourish.

My jaw drops, and I struggle to find the right words. "Wait, what? California?"

Sebastian grins, clearly enjoying my reaction. "Yes! A weekend getaway. Just you and me." The mischievous tone in his voice adds to my intrigue.

I can feel the butterflies fluttering in my stomach. We've been on a lot of business trips together. But a weekend getaway? It's unexpected, to say the least. But before I can respond, he adds, "I'll pick you up at 7. Be ready!"

His confidence leaves little room for refusal, and I find myself nodding, a smile tugging at the corners of my lips. "Okay, I'll be ready," I say, my heart pounding in my chest.

With a playful wink, Sebastian turns and walks away, leaving my doorway and my heart aflutter. As the office door swings shut behind him, I sit back in my chair, trying to process the whirlwind of emotions that have taken over.

***

The night before a weekend getaway is always the best.

We spend six hours of that night on a plane to California. Me and Sebastian, holding hands and exchanging sloppy kisses from time to time.

The next evening, Saturday night, is the second best. The excitement of the weekend is wearing off, but the magic still lingers. We're on a private beach in California, far from New York's hustle, surrounded by the serene beauty of nature.

The setting sun paints the sky in brilliant hues of orange and pink, casting a romantic glow behind, around, and ahead us. As we stroll along the water's edge, the waves gently lap at our feet. Occasionally, Sebastian points at the seagulls gliding gracefully above us, their cries adding to the idyllic ambiance.

Sebastian exudes a carefree charm that makes me fall in love with him all over again. As we walk, we come across a collection of seashells scattered on the shore. Sebastian bends down to pick one up, and he hands it to me.

"Look at these," Sebastian says, grinning as he holds the seashells in a fragile clasp. "Nature's little souvenirs, huh?"

"Yeah, it's like Mother Nature's way of giving us a warm welcome," I reply, smiling back at him.

In the distance, the sound of laughter and faint music carries from a nearby beach bar. The occasional clinking of glasses and the murmur of conversations blend harmoniously with the gentle crashing of waves. We exchange knowing smiles as we continue down the beach.

There's a hidden cove nestled between two rocky cliffs. The water here is a shade deeper, as if inviting us for a swim. The sea breeze carries a hint of salt and adventure, and I'm tempted to explore the hidden beauty of this private spot.

With the setting sun now painting the horizon in brilliant oranges and purples, we decide to sit on a large piece of driftwood that has been washed ashore. The wood is weathered and rough to the touch, but it provides the perfect seat to witness the sun's descent.

I can't help but be drawn to the beauty of the night sky above us. With a gentle point, I direct Sebastian's attention to a group of stars that form a distinctive pattern.

"See that group of stars over there? That's Orion's Belt," I say, my voice filled with excitement. "It's one of the most recognizable constellations in the night sky."

Sebastian squints, trying to follow my gaze. "Ah, yeah, I think I see it now. It's like a row of three stars. Pretty cool!"

"Exactly!" I beam. "And right next to it is the bright star, Sirius. It's also known as the Dog Star."

Sebastian smirks. "Dog Star, huh? So, is it supposed to be a star shaped like a dog or something?"

I chuckle. "Not exactly. It's just a really bright star, and it's part of the constellation Canis Major, which means 'Greater Dog' in Latin."

"Got it. Greater Dog, not a dog-shaped star. Makes sense." He nods in understanding.

"You're catching on! Astronomy can be full of quirky names and fascinating stories behind each constellation," I explain.

"Tell me more! I'm hooked," Sebastian says, genuinely interested.

"Well, over there is Cassiopeia, the W-shaped constellation," I continue. "According to Greek mythology, she was a queen who boasted about her beauty and got punished for it."

"Ouch, I guess being too proud isn't a good thing, even for queens," he muses.

"Exactly. And that bright star there is Vega, which is part of the Lyra constellation. It's one of the brightest stars in the summer sky," I add.

"Vega, the superstar of the summer. I'll remember that," he says with a smile.

I playfully warn him, "You better, there might be a quiz later.'

Sebastian smirks. "I'll be prepared, Professor Isabella."

As our cosmic tour continues, I point out various constellations, each with its own unique story and significance. Sebastian is a willing student, absorbing every detail with genuine interest and occasional humorous remarks.

"Oh, and there's the Big Dipper, a famous part of Ursa Major, the Great Bear constellation," I say, directing his attention to the iconic pattern of stars.

Sebastian raises an eyebrow. "Wait, the Big Dipper is part of a bear?"

I grin, delighted by his reaction. "Yup! Those seven stars form the shape of a ladle or a dipper, and they are part of a bigger bear constellation."

"Well, that's one fancy bear with a cosmic spoon!" he quips, making me burst into laughter.

"You have a way with words, Sebastian," I say, still chuckling. "But it's amazing how ancient civilizations saw patterns in the stars and created stories to explain them."

"Definitely. It's like connecting the dots in the sky and turning them into epic tales," he agrees.

"It makes me wonder about the vastness of the universe and our place in it." My voice softens when I say, "There are billions of stars out there, each with its own story to tell."

Sebastian's reply is equally soft. "And yet, we're here, stargazing together, sharing this moment."

His words strike a chord within me, and I turn to him with a smile. "Yeah, it's a pretty magical experience, isn't it?"

Sebastian's gaze holds mine. "It is, especially with you."

A blush creeps onto my cheeks, and I playfully tease him, "You're such a charmer."

He grins. "Hey, I can't help it. When I'm with you, even the stars seem to shine brighter."

"Keep it up, and you might earn extra credit in 'Romantic Astronomy,'" I tease, trying to hide my growing affection for him.

"I'll take that challenge. What's next on our celestial tour?" he asks, his eyes sparkling with curiosity.

I look up at the night sky, feeling a surge of happiness. "Well, there's so much more to see. Let's explore the wonders of the cosmos together, one star at a time."

Sebastian nods, a warm smile on his face. "Lead the way, Professor Isabella. I'm all ears."

And as we continue our stargazing adventure, I realize that this moment, under the twinkling stars and with Sebastian by my side, is a chapter in my life that I will treasure forever. The universe has brought us together, and in its infinite vastness, I find a love that feels as boundless as the cosmos itself.

"Wow, I never knew you were into all this star stuff," Sebastian says, raising an eyebrow playfully.

"Yeah, it's a hidden talent," I reply with a chuckle. "I've always been fascinated by the mysteries of the universe."

Sebastian looks up at the sky, his gaze softening. "You know, it's like those stars are our little witnesses, watching over us tonight."

"Are you getting all poetic on me now?" I tease.

"Just saying," he says with a grin. "It's like they're shining just for us, adding some cosmic magic to our little adventure."

His words make my heart skip a beat. There's something about the way he says it, like he's hinting at something more profound, something that goes beyond this moment.

. The distant sound of crashing waves and the soft rustle of palm leaves create a soothing backdrop. We sit side by side, our fingers intertwined, as we watch shooting stars streak across the sky.

"Make a wish," Sebastian whispers.

I close my eyes for a moment, feeling the weight of his words. Then, I turn to him, my heart pouring into the confession I'm about to make.

"I don't need to make a wish," I say softly. "Because being here with you, under this magical night sky, is more than I could ever ask for."

Sebastian leans in and kisses me, his lips sink into mine until they become a melting, wet mesh of emotions.

"Do you believe we are all alone in the Milky Way?" I ask, turning to him, his fragrance lingering, floating around my nose.

"No," he answers. "I don't believe that." Then, he turns to me. We are sharing the same breath again. "But right now, you and I, we are alone, on this beach together, and that's all that matters."

— Chapter 17 —
The Old Boys

Love was an alien concept to me, at least before I met Isabella. Before her, I didn't know what it felt like to be completely consumed by someone else's presence. It's confusing, it's exhilarating, it's beautiful. But ultimately, I don't know. I don't know how to navigate this web of emotions that now entangles me, pulling me in every direction.

Her name alone elicits a twist in my stomach, a racing heart, and adrenaline rushes that I can't seem to control. Has love always been this potent? Or am I just infatuated by the latest hottest woman on the block? I never thought I would be so affected by someone, especially in a corporate environment like Maxwell & Co., where it's all about the bottom line and power plays. Yet, here I am, the CEO of the company, completely, or almost completely, distracted by a woman.

My father will not like this development, even though he always pushes for me to bring a woman home, to get married—but not to a worker of our company.

Isabella's presence in the room either makes me a little nervous or gives me a surge of confidence that I can't explain. It's like she holds this magnetic power over me, and my eyes find her even in the busiest conference room. I watch her as she works with such passion and talent, and it's mesmerizing. But it also makes me lose focus on my own work.

My father, the founder of Maxwell & Co., watches my infatuation with concern. The clash of power between us is evident, even if he doesn't openly oppose my relationship with Isabella. The chairman of the board, Robert Sinclair, is the real issue. He frowns upon office romance, and while he can't fire me as the CEO, he certainly doesn't like my relationship with an employee.

It's not that I'm willing to give up on love for my career, or vice versa. I don't want to choose between my heart and my work. But Robert's disapproval and the fear of jeopardizing the company's reputation are like weights pulling me in opposite directions.

However, he can't deny how essential Isabella has proven to be to the company's success. Isabella Rivera joined our company only a few months ago, and yet, we've made headlines on industry news. Still, although he may approve of her as a person, he frowns upon her connection with me.

I've always been a strong-willed person, never backing down from challenges, and I won't start now. But love is uncharted territory for me. I've had a fast-paced life with supermodels and RnB artists as my exes, but this relationship is different. It's genuine, and it's scary.

I'm learning to be romantic, to show vulnerability and care, things I never thought I'd embrace. Isabella makes me want to be a better man, not just for her, but for myself. However, with that desire comes the fear of losing control over my life, my decisions, and my career.

Love, work, and family intertwine in a complex dance that I struggle to follow. I know I can't let Robert's disapproval or the pressures of my position dictate my happiness. But I also can't ignore the potential consequences of our relationship.

Everyone who can remind me of it these days does so, frequently. Those that can't share hushed whispers and hurried gossip in the office. But Robert? Oh, good old Robert Sinclair, he, more than anyone, is capable of reprimanding me like my old man does.

And today, as I sit in my swivel chair, my back to the door, legs on my desk, a sudden knock interrupts my thoughts. Before I can respond, the door swings open.

Robert Sinclair.

He barges in like he owns the place. Well, I suppose he practically does, with his old-fashioned charm and age-defying looks. In his seventies, yet seemingly untouched by time, he walks in with the grace of a man half his age. It's been ages since I've seen him in my office, and I can't help but comment on it.

"You know, I can't remember the last time I saw you here in my office," I say, as I rise out of reverence for the chairman, trying to keep the unease at bay.

Robert chuckles and settles himself in front of my desk. "Well, back in the day when your old man was the CEO, we spent hours in this very office talking about baseball and fast cars. Those were the times, Sebastian."

Ah, the good old days—I've heard enough of those stories to fill a library. "Baseball's not my thing, I must admit, but fast cars? Now that's something I can get behind," I reply with a grin.

Robert glances out the window. "Mind if I smoke?" he asks nonchalantly.

I have a policy against smoking in my office, but before I can answer, he's already lighting a cigarette. I bite my tongue, feeling disrespected. *Keep your cool, Sebastian*, I remind myself.

The conversation drifts back to baseball.

"Ah, baseball—a game of strategy and teamwork," Robert muses, leaning back in his chair, a playful glint in his eyes. "You know, Sebastian, your father and I used to talk about it as if it held the key to life's greatest mysteries. Back then, we believed every pitch, every swing, and every catch had deeper meanings beyond the field."

I play along, feigning ignorance. "Oh, really? How so?"

Robert leans forward, his voice tinged with sarcasm. "You see, each player on the field has a role, a purpose. Just like in business, wouldn't you say? Your father was the pitcher, the one who set the pace, making the decisions that could change the course of the game. And he trusted his catcher—that'd be you—to have his back, to handle the curveballs life throws your way."

I nod, intrigued by the analogy. "I suppose you could see it that way."

He smirks, enjoying this game of words. "Of course, then there's the batter—the one who stands at the plate, facing whatever comes their way. They have to read the signs, anticipate the next move, just like the way you navigate through those boardroom meetings, huh? Always one step ahead."

Keeping my poker face pasted on, I reply, "I like the comparison, Robert. It's an interesting take on the game."

He leans back again, his tone becoming more serious. "You know, sometimes in baseball, a player can get caught stealing a base—reaching for something they desire, even if it's risky. And other times, they might have to sacrifice their own success for the team's greater good. Sacrifices, Sebastian, they're never easy."

I choose my words carefully. "Sacrifices are sometimes necessary, Robert. It's a part of life, both in business and personal matters."

He nods, as if he knows more than he's saying. "Indeed, my boy. And in this game of life, we all have our own roles to play, our destinies entwined like the stitching on a baseball. Sometimes, though, the seams can unravel, and we're left facing the unknown."

Growing more intrigued by Robert's cryptic words, I ask, "The unknown, huh?"

"You may think you've got it all figured out, Sebastian, but remember this—every pitch, every swing, it all leads to something bigger than the game itself. Life has a way of throwing curveballs when you least expect it," he says with a knowing smile. "You'll see what I mean someday."

I feel a mix of curiosity and caution, unsure of where this conversation is leading. "I'll keep that in mind, Robert."

He leans back, lightening the atmosphere. "Now, where were we? Ah, yes, the good old days of baseball and fast cars. Those were the times, my friend. But enough of that for now. We've got our own game to play, don't we?"

Patience is a virtue I've honed over the years, but it's waning as he continues to talk in riddles and parables. "Alright, Robert, what's the purpose of this trip down memory lane?" I finally interject.

Robert smiles gently, pulling out his iPhone from his breast pocket. He shows me blurry pictures of Isabella and me on a private beach in California. The headline screams rumors about the CEO of Maxwell & Co. dating his employee designer, Isabella Rivera. I scoff at the webpage as he tucks his phone away.

"Come on, Robert, my private life is hardly worthy of being front-page news," I retort.

He leans in, his voice lowering. "Sebastian, you're the CEO of one of the most successful fashion companies in the country. The media is painting you as a predator, taking advantage of a young woman working under you."

I can feel the anger rising within me, but I swallow it down. "With all due respect, Robert, you're overreacting. Isabella and I have a genuine connection, and I would never use my position to manipulate her."

"You don't get it, do you?" Robert's eyes bore into mine. "The media can be relentless. They're calling you a predator, who's leaving Isabella without a choice: date you or lose her job."

The room feels smaller, the air heavier. My composure slips, and I respond firmly, "That's not how it is, Robert." My voice is hoarse, cold, frozen to a crisp.

He sighs, disappointment evident in his expression. "I warned you this wouldn't end well, but you didn't listen."

As he stands to leave, I feel a mix of anger, frustration, and a nagging fear that there's more to this than meets the eye. But for now, all I can do is watch him go.

Later that day, I park my Rolls Royce outside my father's mansion, a bit tired after a long day at work. The butler, Andre, opens the giant, wooden door, and I give him a nod and a firm handshake before stepping inside.

As I enter the living room, there she is, my beautiful mother, almost sixty but looking like she's in her forties. She's engrossed in some show on the big TV, laughing heartily at goodness-knows-what. I can't help but smile at the sight; her laugh is infectious.

"Hey, Mom," I say, trying not to sound as tired as I feel.

She looks up, her eyes lighting up when she sees me. "Oh, Sebastian! You're home!"

"Yeah, just got in. Long day at the office." I plop down on the plush couch, sinking into its comfort. "What on earth are you watching, anyway?"

She chuckles, taking a moment to tear her eyes away from the screen. "A reality show. It's silly, but a good distraction."

I nod, leaning back. "Fair enough. Mind if I join you?"

"Of course not, darling." She pats the seat next to her, and I shuffle over.

"Where is he?" I ask.

"The courtyard," my mother answers with her eyes focused on the TV. "Robert is here, too. And they're both laughing like little boys."

"I bet he doesn't look as tired as I look. He works harder than the devil."

Catching my sarcasm, my mother laughs at my face. "Oh, please, Sebastian. What else does he do aside from lounging in his office and smoke like a chimney?"

"Well, you said it, not me." I relax onto the couch, my back propping against the pillows.

I spend the next ten minutes sunken onto the couch, occasionally talking and laughing with my mother before I jump to my feet to head to the courtyard to see my father.

These days, I dread going to see him. There's always something to lecture me about. He forgets that I'm a man, that I've been one longer than a decade.

I find him and Robert in the courtyard, heading towards the door.

"Sebastian, look who we have here!" my father exclaims, as if it's a big surprise to find me visiting my own parents. "Robert was just about to leave."

I nod at Robert, who wears his usual smirk and exudes an air of sarcasm. He gestures toward my father. "We are just having a little chat about how beautifully I've been running the company lately. You should've been here, honestly. Think of how lovely it would have been, all three of us, having tea, talking baseball, and fashion and politics. Do you think you young men nowadays dress better than men from thirty to forty years ago, Sebastian?"

He knows exactly how to push my buttons. I know he's hinting about his visit to my office earlier today. It's a well-practiced art of sarcasm and snide remarks, and he relishes it like a cat with a bowl of cream. But this time, I decide to play it cool. He's trying to gauge me like he always does. To see if I'm more of old school like my old man. "I think a lot of men dressed ugly forty years ago," I answer. Then, I pause a little. "I also think a lot of men dress ugly now."

My father smiles a little.

Robert chuckles, seemingly unfazed by my response. "Anyway, I should be on my way. Bye for now, John," he says turning to my father.

My father smiles and shakes Robert's hand. "Take care, Robert."

He taps my shoulder as he passes, and I fight the urge to swat his hand away. Taking a deep breath, I turn to my father, "He certainly has a way with words, doesn't he?" I say, only half-jokingly.

I walk over to the chair, and my father's intimidating gaze locks onto me. It feels heavy, as if he's trying to weigh my soul with just his eyes. I sit down, trying to project confidence, but the silence is suffocating. A whole minute ticks by, and I can't escape the tension building.

His gaze bores into me, unyielding and intimidating, a reflection of the man I've grown up fearing and admiring simultaneously. I take a deep breath, bracing myself for what I know is coming.

"What?" I ask, trying to muster my confidence against the weight of my father's stare.

"I've heard a lot of things," my father replies, his voice low and controlled, the words echoing with a mix of concern and disappointment.

"Of course," I retort, with a hint of resignation in my voice. I know what's coming. The same webpage of me and Isabella in California together, exposed to the prying eyes of the media.

I attempt to defend myself before he can get started with his lecture. "It's my private life, and besides, you've been asking me to find a wife. Now that I have a potential candidate, you shouldn't be against it."

My father's expression hardens. "Not at the expense of ruining your own reputation. I'm worried, and the media is relentless."

I roll my eyes, feeling exasperated. "Robert is filling your head with lies. You're listening to him more than me."

My father's tone grows stern. "You should listen to reason, not let emotions cloud your judgment. Find someone on your level, someone the media can't tear into. Or someone they don't even know."

"Oh, come on!" I scoff, frustration bubbling up inside me. "You, who never cared what anyone said, now cares about the media? Should they have a say in who I decide to give my love to?"

My father's eyes flash with intensity. "I didn't have anything to lose back then. But now, I have you, the company, and a reputation I've worked hard to build for years. Reconsider your choices, Sebastian. It's not too late to find someone else."

My patience wearing thin, I snap, "I've had a long day, and I'm leaving." I go over and tap my father's shoulder before adding, "Father, I'm a man now, not a boy. I'll do whatever I want."

Without waiting for a response, I turn and walk away.

— Chapter 18 —
Treacherous

Every year, the Council of Fashion Designers of America, or CFDA, awards fashion designers who made a notable achievement in the year. When the news of my nomination for the CFDA Emerging Designer of the Year came, my sister, Emily, almost lost her voice. That night, I didn't spend it in my apartment; I was at my parents', and my mother made sure to spend a lot of time on dinner.

"This is glorious, Isabella," he said.

My father didn't say much more, but at least he smiled a lot more than he does regularly.

Fast forward to the CFDA awards night. The venue is nothing short of breathtaking, a symphony of glamor and elegance. The chandeliers drip with crystal tears, casting a shimmering dance of light across the grand hall.

The clinking of champagne glasses, the hum of conversation, it all weaves together into this harmonious blend of excitement and tension.

Or maybe I'm the only one who's feeling the tension. Certainly, I can't be the only one. It's like stepping into a world where dreams are spun from silk and sequins. Well, this is a dream, too. It has always been my dream to be at this kind of event.

As I stand on the red carpet, the flashes of cameras almost blind me. The photographers shout my name, asking me to look here, there, everywhere.

"Hey, hey, hey, here."

"Miss Rivera."

Some just slap my first name around like we are friends.

"Isabella, look here. This side."

They add gestures, too. The camera flashes are enough to cause a seizure. I shift my weight from foot to foot, wondering how the photos are going to turn out.

I'm not very photogenic, I think. Even when everyone else says the opposite. But I've been around fashion models long enough for me to know how to make a good pose. So, I smile only a little, and when I stop smiling, I part my lips only a little, squint my eyes, too. I remember this trick from listening to the instructions models get. They say it makes your features even more pronounced. I don't doubt them.

And I'm feeling this mix of excitement and anxiety, like a roller coaster in my stomach. I wish Sebastian were here since his presence always grounds me. But he's on his way to Portugal for a business meeting. He left earlier tonight.

Just before the event started, Sebastian kissed me on the head and whispered, "Bring it home, Isabella." It was his way of saying that he believes in me. I watched him disappear into the sea of people at the airport, and the crowd's buzz of anticipation didn't make the goodbye any easier.

Tonight, I'm the only one from our office nominated for an award. Well, not entirely true. There's also Mr. Maxwell, Sebastian's father, as he's been nominated for the Lifetime Achievement award. Just knowing that we're both being recognized tonight adds a layer of pride to my fluttering nerves. But if you think about it, technically, he's not from our office because he's retired.

Sebastian speaks so fondly of him, of his achievements. He's gargantuan in the industry and almost everyone seems to know him. I'd be surprised if they don't, anyway.

The stage is like a work of art itself, adorned with cascading flowers and shimmering curtains. It's a beauty that somehow enhances my anxiety. The crowd's hushed whispers and occasional laughter heighten my self-consciousness, like I'm on display under a microscope.

When I walk past the host on the carpet, she calls me, grabs me by my wrist, and points her microphone towards me as I try to steady my racing heart. I can feel my nerves threatening to get the best of me. She smiles encouragingly, her voice smooth like honey as she asks, "Isabella, you're nominated for the Emerging Designer of the Year award. How does it feel to be here tonight?"

I take a deep breath, my eyes flickering around the dazzling scene before settling back on her. "Well, frankly, it's a lot of excitement for me," I reply with a nervous chuckle. "I mean, this award is such a big deal in American and International fashion, and being nominated...it's a bit surreal." My fingers brush against the fabric of my dress, a grounding touch amidst the chaos of the moment.

She nods, her eyes twinkling with curiosity. "And who's your biggest supporter? Any special shoutouts?"

I can't help but smile, a soft warmth spreading through me at the thought of Sebastian. "My family," I respond beaming with a smile. "Definitely my mother, my father, my sister, Emily," I wave at the camera swinging around my face. "They've been my rock, believing in me even when I doubted myself." I think about my love, Sebastian. I wonder how far he's gotten across the world. And it's him that I really want to add to the list. But I cannot, at least not right now, not when the world is watching like this.

"Anyone else, Isabella?" she asks, smiling. Why do I feel like she's waiting for me to mention Sebastian?

"Of course, my best friend, Charlotte," I reply, staring straight into her eyes.

Her grin widens, and she backs off, sensing the genuine affection in my voice or my eyes telling her to *fuck off* silently. "That's lovely. Now, Isabella, what's your signature style as a designer?"

My nerves start to ease a bit as I talk about something I'm truly passionate about. "I'd say my style is a blend of classic elegance with a touch of modern edge. I love playing with contrasts—mixing textures, patterns, and silhouettes in unexpected ways. It's about creating pieces that make a statement, but also feel timeless."

She leans in, genuinely intrigued. "Sounds like a winning formula. And finally, any pre-show rituals or superstitions?"

I chuckle, my tension melting away as I think about my quirky habits. "Well, I always wear this lucky charm bracelet my grandmother gave me when I started my journey in fashion. And I have this thing where I stand on one foot before stepping onto the runway. It's like my own little way of gathering courage."

She laughs softly, her energy infectious. "I love that. Isabella, thank you for sharing a bit of your world with us. Best of luck tonight!"

"Thank you," I reply, my gratitude sincere as I give her a small wave before moving along the carpet. As I walk away, I can't help but wonder if Sebastian would be proud of how I handled the spotlight. It's moments like these that remind me of how far I've come and how fortunate I am to have people who believe in me, even when I stumble through my words.

Amidst the sea of faces, I spot Sebastian's father. He's somewhere in the crowd, his salt-and-pepper hair catching the lights as he struts through the crowd. There's something intimidating about him, but also an air of calm that's strangely comforting. He's not as tall as Sebastian, yet he carries himself with a similar presence, a reflection of the man I love.

The evening unfolds with awards, performances, and speeches, each moment a blend of excitement and nervous energy. I can't help but scan the crowd, searching for familiar faces. And then, there's Mrs. Maxwell, Sebastian's mother, who catches my eye and smiles, making a little wave each time. Her warm gestures act like a lifeline in a sea of uncertainty.

As Mr. Maxwell passes me by, I muster up the courage to step forward. I offer a warm smile and extend my hand. :Mr. Maxwell, I'm Isabella. It's truly an honor to meet you.:

He pauses and squints his eyes, studying me for a moment before a small smile tugs at the corner of his lips. "Ah, you're the girl Sebastian speaks so fondly of," he remarks, his voice carrying a blend of curiosity and approval.

I chuckle softly, feeling a mix of embarrassment and pride. "Yes, that's me. It's been wonderful getting to know Sebastian and being a part of Maxwell & Co."

He leans in slightly, his interest piqued. "And what brings you to this event tonight?"

I take a deep breath, steadying my nerves as I answer, "I've been nominated for the Emerging Designer of the Year award. It's a bit nerve-wracking, but I'm excited."

Before Mr. Maxwell can respond, his attention shifts as his wife, Mrs. Maxwell, finds her way back to her husband from a group of older women she had been chatting with. She steals the spotlight effortlessly, and I find myself momentarily forgotten as she kisses her husband on the cheeks. I watch the interaction between the couple, their bond evident even from where I stand.

"Amelia," Mr. Maxwell starts, his hand on the small of her back. "This is Isabella," Mr. Maxwell introduces me.

Mrs. Maxwell's eyes light up as she looks at me. "Oh, the pretty woman Sebastian has been obsessed with lately," she exclaims. Her voice is warm and welcoming. She seems even more pleased to see me than her husband. She's warmer. More vibrant.

Blushing, I offer a shy smile. "It's a pleasure to meet you, Mrs. Maxwell."

She steps closer and pulls me into a gentle hug, her perfume enveloping me in a comforting embrace. "Congratulations on your nomination, dear. We're so happy for you."

"Thank you so much," I reply, genuinely touched by her kind words.

And then comes the moment I've been waiting for, and dreading. My category is called, and my heart tugs with fear as I walk to the podium. The applause reverberates in my ears, nearly drowning out the thoughts racing in my mind. I feel like I'm walking on shaky ground, but I'm determined not to stumble.

The spotlight feels blinding as I take hold of the microphone, my fingers trembling as I clutch it. My voice wavers as I begin to speak, my words stumbling over each other in a rush. "Um, wow, this is...I mean, thank you!" I manage to blurt out, feeling the weight of the moment settle in.

I glance down at the trophy in my hands, tracing my fingers over its intricate design. It's a symbol of all the hard work, late nights, and moments of doubt that I've poured into my craft. As I continue to speak, my gaze sweeps across the crowd, and I catch sight of familiar faces, their smiles and nods urging me on.

"First and foremost, I want to thank my incredible team," I say, my voice steadying as I find my rhythm. "You've stood by me through thick and thin, and this award is as much yours as it is mine." I feel a surge of gratitude for the talented individuals who've shared this journey with me.

Turning my attention to my family, I feel a lump forming in my throat. "To my parents and sister, you've been my pillars of support from day one. Your belief in me kept me going, even when I doubted myself." I see them beaming with pride, and it's a reminder that my achievements are intertwined with their love and encouragement.

"And to all the people who believed in my vision and pushed me to push myself," I continue, my voice gaining strength with each word, "this award is a testament to your unwavering faith in what I do." The crowd's cheers seem to swell, and their energy fuels my confidence. I want to mention Sebastian, I genuinely want to. But the time is not right.

"I know my hands are shaking," I admit with a nervous laugh, raising my trophy slightly, "but it's the best kind of shake there is." The audience responds with a chorus of laughter and applause, and it's a moment of connection that I'll cherish.

Stepping away from the microphone, I take a deep breath, feeling a wave of relief wash over me. The pressure that had built up throughout the evening has dissipated, replaced by a sense of accomplishment. I clutch the trophy to my chest, its weight a comforting reminder that I've taken a significant step forward in my journey.

As I leave the stage, I catch the eye of Mrs. Maxwell, and she gives me an encouraging nod and smile. It's a subtle gesture, but in that moment, I feel like she at least knows how messy my insides were from being in the spotlight.

As the night draws to a close, I find myself back in the crowd, surrounded by familiar and unfamiliar faces. The lights are dimmer now, the excitement still heavy in the air but softened by the passage of time. I take a deep breath, my heart still fluttering with a mix of emotions.

In the midst of it all, Mrs. Maxwell catches my eye one last time. She smiles and waves, like she's been doing all evening.

And there I sit, my mind still running with thoughts of Sebastian. I had imagined us walking down the red carpet. Hand in hand.. But these are treacherous times, and public shows of affection like that may have to wait.

— Chapter 19 —
Serenita

By the time my plane touched down in New York, all I wanted was to shower Isabella's face with playful kisses until she giggled like a child. I'd asked her to bring the award home, and she did. Now, it's up to me to find that perfect little restaurant to take her to, to celebrate in style. I've been to nearly every swanky joint in the city, especially the expensive ones. But now, the risky part is the recognition that comes with those posh places. As Isabella wisely puts it, "these are treacherous times."

So, I decide to stray from my usual path. One evening, coming back from work, I opt for a longer route to beat the traffic. I stumble upon this hidden gem of an Italian restaurant tucked away on Canal Street, Trattoria Serenità. The moment I see it, I'm captivated by the soft, warm glow seeping through its windows. I snap a quick picture of the entrance with the name in view, an idea forming in my mind.

Tonight, that's where I find myself, Trattoria Serenità, where I want to be tucked away with Isabella, away from the prying eyes of those who know us too well. I'm dressed comfortably in a linen shirt, a conscious choice to match the unassuming atmosphere of the place. Isabella, on the other hand, stuns in a two-piece ensemble of her own design. Her elegant walk, accentuated by her outfit that stops just above her tummy and flaunts her curves, draws every eye in the room as we step inside.

I let Isabella walk ahead. There's something about watching her move that's incredibly mesmerizing, the way she strides with a certain sensuality, each step adding to her allure.

Inside, the cozy restaurant is a mix of diners, both old and young, couples mostly, and a lone man engrossed in his meal. The ambiance is enhanced by the artwork adorning the walls—I find myself tempted to ask if any of it is for sale. Isabella's gaze lingers on the art as well, so I jest about stealing it for her. She laughs, and I quip that if I can't buy her the world, I'd gladly steal it instead. After another laugh from her, I'm content.

As we find a spot by the wall, the waiter arrives to take our orders. Isabella sits across from me, and the dim lighting accentuates her features—her cheeks, her hair, her face, all radiant in the glow.

"You know, winning the award was a dream come true," Isabella starts. "But I can't help but think how much more incredible it would have been if you were there to witness it, Sebastian."

I chuckle softly, a genuine smile forming on my lips. "I know, Isabella. I wish I could've been there, too." I take a sip of my drink, leaning back slightly in my chair. "So, since we're talking about incredible moments, what's your happiest day ever?"

Isabella's brow furrows as she ponders the question, her fingers tracing patterns on the edge of her napkin. "Hmm, that's a tough one. But if I had to pick, it would probably be the day I launched my first collection. Seeing my designs on the runway, knowing that my passion and hard work had come to life...that was something truly special."

"I can imagine that feeling," I reply, my gaze meeting hers. "For me, well, there have been a few moments that stand out. Graduation day was a big one, of course. But becoming a CEO, taking over the reins from my father—that was also a pivotal moment. However, if I'm being honest, I can't really pinpoint a single 'happiest' day. My life's been a series of exciting chapters."

Isabella's lips curve into a soft smile. "You're a man of many accomplishments, Sebastian. I think that's a sign of a content life."

I chuckle, a hint of playfulness in my voice. "Oh, you're giving me too much credit. Maybe I'm just a lucky guy to have you in my life. You've definitely added a lot of happiness."

Her laughter rings out, melodious and contagious. "Smooth as always, I see."

I lean in a little closer, a glint of mischief in my eyes. "Can't help it, Isabella. I've learned a few things over the years."

She raises an eyebrow, a playful challenge in her expression. "Oh really? Care to share some of those lessons?"

I lean back, feigning thoughtfulness. "Well, first lesson: always listen more than you speak. Second, a well-timed compliment goes a long way."

Isabella shakes her head, her laughter bubbling up again. "You're something else, Sebastian. But I have to admit, your smoothness does have its charm."

I grin and enjoy the banter between us. "Charm is my middle name, after all."

Then, after looking around the restaurant once more, I can see the worry about us being seen together take a hold of her once more. I gently place my champagne glass on the table, my fingers grazing hers as I seek to reassure her.

"You know," she begins, her voice soft yet laden with worry, "I've never really been in the spotlight like this before. It's overwhelming, to say the least."

I smile and my gaze meets hers. "I understand, Isabella. It comes with its own set of challenges."

She leans in slightly, her eyes searching mine. "How do you handle it? The public's attention, I mean."

My lips curl into a wry smile as I lean back in my chair. "Well, let's just say I've had my fair share of moments. Sometimes, I've just yelled 'fuck off' to the paparazzi, and on one occasion, I even tried to snatch their cameras."

Isabella bursts into laughter, the sound musical and infectious. "You? Snatching cameras?"

I chuckle and nod. "Yes, believe it or not. My father had to step in and remind me that cameras are expensive, and smashing them wasn't the wisest idea."

Her laughter continues to fill the air, a symphony that echoes in the cozy restaurant. "Oh, I can just imagine your father's expression."

I grin. "Yes, he was a mix of amusement and exasperation. But I'll admit, those moments brought a certain satisfaction."

Isabella's laughter eventually subsides, her eyes sparkling as she regards me. "You're quite the character, Sebastian."

Savoring the warmth of our conversation, I shrug nonchalantly. "Well, when life throws cameras and flashes at you, sometimes you've got to throw some words back."

Her fingers dance along the rim of her glass, a contemplative expression crossing her features. "It's just…I worry about the public's judgment, the constant scrutiny."

"Isabella, there's always a trade-off in life. But remember, you're the same amazing person you were before the spotlight found you. Don't let others' opinions define you."

She looks down at our entwined hands, a small smile gracing her lips. "You always know the right thing to say, don't you?"

I squeeze her hand gently, my gaze steady. "I'm here to support you, Isabella. No matter what."

Her eyes meet mine, and a mix of gratitude and affection shines in them. "Thank you, Sebastian. It means a lot."

"Anytime," I say softly, our connection deepening with each word. "We're in this together."

Isabella's fingers interlace more firmly with mine, a silent acknowledgment of the bond we share.

"You're right. We'll face whatever comes our way, together."

Just as we're deep in conversation, the waiter approaches with a confident smile, holding out a bottle of wine. I shoot a quick look at Isabella, and her nod accompanied by that playful smile tells me everything I need to know. I turn to the waiter. "Sure, go ahead."

He disappears briefly and returns with a couple of glasses, his expression a mix of excitement and anticipation. "Allow me to introduce this special wine to you," he says, his voice brimming with enthusiasm. "My boss noticed your presence and thought this would be the perfect selection for such a distinguished couple."

I chuckle, raising an eyebrow at Isabella. "Looks like we're making an impression, huh?"

Isabella's laughter tinkles like a melody as she leans in closer to me. "Seems like it. I wonder if they're trying to impress us."

Before the waiter can respond, a distinct voice cuts through the air, carrying a strong Italian accent. "Very much so.:

We both turn towards the source of the voice, and there he stands, a man with an air of authority, his eyes twinkling with amusement. I lean back slightly, my lips curving into a polite smile, and I can feel Isabella's subtle amusement beside me.

She can't resist, a playful glint in her eyes as she asks, "Is this your way of keeping your customers entertained?"

He chuckles, his accent lending a charming quality to his voice. "Ah, you caught me. But truly, I believe this wine is something you both will appreciate."

As he joins us at the table, I can't help but find his presence a tad intrusive, though Isabella's amused expression reassures me. He extends his hand towards Isabella, holding it just a touch too long as he introduces himself. "Pleasure to meet you, beautiful lady. I am Antonio, the proprietor of this humble establishment." I badly want to yank him off the table, but I restrain myself.

Isabella smiles politely, her tone laced with a hint of sarcasm as she replies, "Well, thank you, Antonio. Your establishment is anything but humble. It's quite charming."

I can sense the flirtatious undertone in his compliment, which both irritates and amuses me. I shift my gaze to him, extending a hand in greeting. "Sebastian. Nice to meet you, Antonio."

Antonio's attention shifts back to me, and he raises an eyebrow as he regards me. "Ah, you have the looks of a very important man."

I chuckle lightly, giving him a knowing look. "Just a man trying to enjoy a nice evening with his lady."

He pours the wine with practiced elegance, and I take a moment to appreciate his mastery. As he hands me the glass, I sniff it and take a small sip, letting the flavor settle on my palate. Isabella follows suit, her expression contemplative.

Antonio's eyes are fixed on us, trying to gauge my reaction, and when Isabella speaks, her voice is filled with genuine admiration. "This is one of the finest wines I've ever tasted, and I've tasted a lot of wine."

Antonio's smile widens, pride evident in his expression. "I'm delighted to hear that. Your approval means a great deal."

I can't help but join in with a nod of agreement. "She's right. It's excellent."

With a respectful bow, Antonio retreats, leaving us to enjoy the wine and each other's company. The warm, cozy atmosphere of the restaurant seems even more inviting now, and Isabella and I share a glance that's a mixture of amusement, appreciation, and a touch of mischief. As the conversation shifts back to us, we're reminded once again that it's these candid moments that make our connection all the more special.

I can't help but feel grateful for the serendipitous discovery of this charming restaurant. This night is about us, about Isabella's triumph and her concerns, about sharing stories and laughter in a place that feels as warm and inviting as the soft glow that first drew me in.

As the evening unfolds, we continue to exchange stories, memories, and dreams. Isabella opens up about her journey in the fashion world, how she pursued her passion despite challenges. She speaks of her family, her hopes for the future, and the excitement of receiving the CFDA fashion award. I'm enthralled by her words, the genuine enthusiasm in her eyes as she recounts her experiences.

"Remember that time you spilled coffee all over my design sketches?" she asks, a playful glint in her eyes.

I laugh in response. "Oh, how could I forget? You looked ready to murder me right then and there." The tension from those days has long dissipated, replaced by an easy camaraderie that's hard to miss.

Our reminiscing leads us to a series of inside jokes that we've built up over time. "And what about the 'mysterious disappearing pen' incident?" I tease, referring to a prank I'd pulled on her during a particularly stressful week. Isabella bursts into laughter, her infectious mirth echoing through the restaurant.

"You were impossible back then," she counters, her voice still tinged with humor. "I never would've thought we'd end up sitting here like this."

I lean in a bit closer, a suggestive smile tugging at my lips. "Well, you know what they say, there's a thin line between love and hate."

She playfully nudges my arm. "And which side of the line are we on now?"

I raise an eyebrow, meeting her gaze with a smoldering look. "I'll let you decide that."

Isabella's laughter subsides into a warm smile, and there's a moment of silence between us, charged with a different kind of tension. She takes a sip of her wine, her eyes never leaving mine. "Sebastian," she begins, her voice a touch lower, "did you ever...back then, did you ever think I was sexy?"

The question catches me off guard, and I chuckle nervously. "Well, I might have noticed it a time or two."

Her lips curl into a mischievous grin. "Oh, really? And here I was, thinking you were too busy being my enemy to notice anything else."

I lean in closer, my tone dropping to a huskier timbre. "Believe me, Isabella, it was hard not to notice."

A flush colors her cheeks, and she shifts in her seat, suddenly seeming more aware of the close proximity between us. "You're impossible." Her voice is barely a whisper.

"Only when it comes to you," I reply, my gaze locked on hers, the intensity of our connection palpable. The playful banter has given way to an undercurrent of desire that's been simmering beneath the surface.

As the night progresses, we delve into deeper discussions about the meaning of success, the pursuit of happiness, and the importance of staying true to oneself. Isabella's wisdom and insight leave me pondering my own values and priorities.

With the bottle of wine nearly empty, we raise our glasses for a final toast. The warmth of the restaurant, the clinking of glasses, and the murmurs of conversations around us all fade into the background as it becomes clear that this moment, this intimate conversation, is the highlight of the evening.

Trattoria Serenità.

I'll remember the name. The small, elegant restaurant tucked away on Canal Street. This place where I'll come over and over with Isabella to hear her laugh, watch her smile. Listen to the soft Italian music play in the background.

As we walk out of the restaurant, I catch sight of Antonio, the owner, standing by the entrance. He offers a warm smile, approaching to bid us farewell himself. "Thank you for gracing us with your presence tonight," he says, his Italian accent adding a touch of charm to his words. "I hope you both had a wonderful evening."

Isabella's gaze meets his, her eyes still glassy from the wine. "Antonio, the pleasure was all ours," she replies, her voice husky. "Your restaurant is truly enchanting."

Antonio's lips curl into a pleased smile, his eyes lingering on Isabella for a moment longer than necessary. "I'm delighted to hear that, bella signora," he says, placing a gentle kiss on the back of her hand. "Please do come back soon."

Stepping out of Trattoria Serenità, the lively streets embrace us with their vibrant energy. The hum of conversations, the distant sounds of car horns, and the rhythmic footfalls of pedestrians remind us that the city is very much awake, even as the night deepens.

Isabella's hazy eyes betray her state of slight inebriation, a result of the wine and the champagne we had earlier. Yet, her steps remain sure, and her laughter punctuates the air, a sound that's both intoxicating and heartwarming.

"Sebastian," she murmurs, her voice like a caress, her fingers brushing against mine as we walk side by side. "That was a wonderful evening, truly."

Captivated by her presence, even in the midst of the city's chaos, I smile. "I'm glad you enjoyed it, Isabella. You deserved every bit of it."

When we're almost to the car, camera flashes from lurking paparazzi immediately startle both of us. Curses escape my lips under my breath, my frustration welling up as they invade our privacy once again. Determination flares within me, and I make an attempt to catch one of the photographers, but he slips away in a flash. The swarm of paparazzi is too overwhelming to chase down individually, so with a resigned sigh, I give up.

Gently guiding Isabella by her arm, I steer her towards the awaiting car, the flashes of cameras continuing to assault our senses. The car doors close behind us, providing a brief respite from the chaotic scene. The car's engine purrs to life as we sit in silence, both of us processing the intrusion.

The drive home is mostly silent, save for Isabella's occasional comments. Her fingers trace patterns on the window, her gaze lost in the passing cityscape. Her sultry laughter from earlier has quieted, replaced by a more introspective mood. I steal occasional glances at her, marveling at the way her beauty glows even in the dimly lit interior of the car.

We arrive at her place, and I park the car by the curb. Isabella turns to me, her eyes locking onto mine with a mixture of emotions. The glassiness in her eyes has not faded, the wine still kicking hard, but her control remains unwavering. She leans in closer, her lips brushing mine in a soft, lingering kiss that conveys a depth of feeling that words could never capture.

When she pulls away, there's a moment of lingering intimacy, a silent understanding passing between us. With a whispered goodbye, Isabella opens the car door, stepping out onto the sidewalk. I watch her as she ascends the steps to her building, her figure bathed in the glow of the streetlights.

Only when she's safely inside and out of sight do I shift the car into gear and drive away. The passenger seat she occupied smells like her. As I navigate the streets, my mind replays the events of the evening—the laughter, the conversations, the stolen glances—until the city lights blur into memories. Sometimes, I laugh, sometimes, I smile as I replay Isabella's words in my head. Nothing beats a drive home after having a lovely night. I cannot wait to see her at the office tomorrow.

— Chapter 20 —
Follow Your Heart

Tuesdays are usually slow, causing them to be my least favorite day after Monday. Things are slower, or at least they feel like it. Jennifer complains more, and longer. The urgency of the beginning of the week, of Monday, is starting to wane, but it's still there.

This Tuesday, today, I've done a lot of things— sketched, draped fabrics, argued with a colleague— yet it's still morning. The sun streams through the large windows of our spacious studio, casting a warm light over the room. The air is filled with the scent of freshly brewed coffee and the soft hum of sewing machines.

As I stand in the center of the studio, surrounded by dress forms and mannequins adorned with my latest creations, I feel a sense of accomplishment mixed with anticipation. The fittings with models are about to begin, and I'm fully immersed in my creative process. The models stand around me, their postures elegant, embodying the spirit of my designs.

I adjust the hem of a deep blue gown on the tall, graceful model named Maya. The fabric cascades like water, and I can almost hear the rustling of waves as she moves. She turns, her eyes meeting mine, and a subtle nod tells me that the dress is just as she envisioned it. I smile, and my heart swells with pride.

Sebastian's entrance interrupts my moment of reverie. The room seems to shift as his commanding aura fills the space. I watch as he pats a few employees on the back, exchanging brief words with them. Then, his gaze finds mine. He winks, a playful glint in his eyes that never fails to make me blush. My fingers brush over the fabric, and I catch myself grinning as he disappears through the door.

Jennifer's voice breaks through my thoughts, her tone brisk and focused, "Isabella, we need to stay on track. Let's keep the fittings moving smoothly."

I nod, but my smile faded slightly. Jennifer's eyes scan the room, and I notice the models exchanging knowing glances. Their whispers flutter through the air like hushed secrets, and I can feel the weight of their speculation.

At that moment, our stylist, Alex, leans against a table, a knowing smile playing on his lips. He catches my eye and raises an eyebrow, as if acknowledging the obvious distraction Sebastian's presence has caused. Irritation simmers within me, directed both at Jennifer's reminder and the lingering attention from my colleagues and models.

Pushing aside my frustration, I focus on the task at hand. I give directions to the models, adjusting pins, and making notes on my sketchpad. The textures and colors of the fabrics come to life, and the room is filled with an atmosphere of creativity and anticipation.

As I continue with the fittings, I can't help but be reminded of the previous evening with Sebastian.

The memory floats in my mind like a delicate veil, tinged with laughter and the intimate conversations we shared. It's a private bubble of warmth that I carry with me, even as I work in this bustling studio.

A soft chime pierces through the atmosphere, and I instinctively reach for my iPhone. An unknown European number illuminates the screen, its country code elusive in my memory. With a curious mixture of trepidation and intrigue, I slide to answer the call.

"Hello," a woman's voice greets me, the words dripping with a strong French accent. Her tone carries a sense of mystery, leaving me momentarily frozen in place. Soon after, she adds, "I'm an Assistant of Adrian Hartley. He wants to speak with you. Bear with me for a moment, while I connect with him"

***

The call lasts for about an hour. It is inspiringly enjoyable to talk with him. The last and the only time I met Adrian Hartley, we didn't have enough time to talk and share ideas. A lot has changed since then. Adrian, the enigmatic fashion guru, has become more than just an idol. He is a mentor, a friend, a confidant. Our conversations in the spanning call have revealed a depth of connection that transcends the mere admiration of our creative works.

Tonight, I find myself seated at a dimly lit bar, the amber lights casting a warm ambiance. The chatter of the patrons and the tinkling of glasses create a soothing backdrop. I'm nursing a cocktail, fingers tracing the rim of the glass as I wait for Adrian. It's the first time meeting him in person since our last encounter.

As if summoned by my thoughts, I spot a figure entering the bar, blonde hair catching the light. Adrian's presence demands attention, even in a crowded space. He scans the room, and our eyes lock. A smile tugs at my lips as I stand, calling his name. His smile in response is genuine, his steps purposeful, as he navigates through the tables towards me.

After exchanging warm greetings and a hug that feels strangely familiar, Adrian settles into the seat across from me. He orders a whiskey, the clinking of ice punctuating the air. His intense gaze settles on me, and I feel a flutter of excitement mingled with a hint of nervousness.

"Isabella, those eyes of yours are truly captivating," he remarks, his voice carrying the weight of his sincerity.

I blush, grateful for the dim lighting that might mask the warmth creeping into my cheeks. "Thank you, Adrian."

Our conversation flows effortlessly, meandering through topics of fashion, his recent endeavors in New York, and his impending departure back to Paris. Adrian's humor is infectious, his laughter sending ripples of joy through the air. His eyes crinkle at the corners, a testament to the genuine delight he finds in sharing stories.

Amidst the casual banter, I gather the courage to broach the question that's been plaguing my mind. The ambience of the bar, cozy and intimate, seems fitting for such a conversation. As the hum of voices and clinking glasses envelops us, I draw a breath and ask, "Adrian, can I ask you something?" It's about the call I got earlier.

He sips his whiskey, a small smile playing on his lips. "Of course, Isabella. You know you can always ask me anything."

The question hangs in the air for a moment, my nerves tingling. "What would you do if you were offered an opportunity that could change your entire career trajectory? A chance to move to a foreign city, earn a much larger salary, and grow rapidly?" This one sounds like what Craig Stanton's promised to offer.

Adrian chuckles. "Well, Isabella, if I were to suddenly receive a salary a lot more than my current one, I'd probably find myself among the richest designers in the world."

I join his laughter, the tension in the air lightning. As his mirth subsides, he adopts a more thoughtful expression. "But seriously, my dear, it's not just about the money, is it?"

His words hang in the air, the question finding its mark. I nod slowly, my fingers tracing patterns on the table's surface. "No, it's not. It's about opportunity, growth, and...uncertainty."

Adrian leans back, and his gaze holds mine intently. He takes a sip of his drink before continuing, his voice tinged with a philosophical edge. "Sometimes, we're in such a hurry to reach the top floor that we forget the beauty of the journey. The lessons, the failures, the moments that shape us. I'm a man of method, Isabella. To me, everything is an experience."

His words resonate deeply within me, stirring a mix of emotions. The ambiance of the bar seems to cocoon us, isolating our conversation from the outside world. Adrian's gaze turns inward, as if he's contemplating his own journey.

"It shouldn't be a hard choice, really, if you truly want to grow fast," he says, his tone softer now.

I take a deep breath. His wisdom settles in my heart. "Thank you, Adrian."

He lifts his glass in a silent toast, a small smile curving his lips. "To growth and experiences."

As we clink our glasses, the conversation takes a turn. "Isabella, there's something else on your mind," he observes, studying me earnestly. His smile is knowing, like he's peering into the depths of my thoughts.

I meet his gaze, my lips curving into a coy smile. "You always were perceptive."

He leans forward slightly, and his expression is gentle. "This is about your boyfriend, isn't it?"

My surprise must show on my face, but there's no use denying it. "Yes," I admit, feeling a mixture of vulnerability and comfort.

Adrian's smile softens. His eyes reflects his understanding. "Love is the most beautiful thing ever."

I take a sip of my cocktail, my heart swelled by his simple affirmation.

"Follow your heart, Isabella," he says softly.

— Chapter 21 —
Keeping The Line

I read somewhere that love is selfish, and ever since then, the thoughts have mocked me. I have no shame in admitting that the reason I don't want Isabella to take the job offer she told me about and move to Paris is because I want her close to me.

What is love without the possessive raging desire to keep whom you love around you, or even follow them halfway across the world if it comes to that?

These days, my thoughts have become like tendrils reaching for her, even in the midst of board meetings and company strategies. I catch myself imagining her smile, her laughter, and how the light dances in her eyes when she's passionate about something. It's distracting, but in a way that fills my days with color and warmth.

It's Friday night, and I find myself standing outside Isabella's apartment, anticipation bubbling within me like a tightly sealed bottle of champagne. The city lights cast light on the streets, but all else pales in comparison to the sight that awaits me. Isabella steps out, and for a moment, time stills.

Her dress, a masterpiece she's designed herself, hugs her curves elegantly, like a canvas painted by a master artist. The fabric flows like a river of dreams, a cascade of midnight blues and stardust. She looks like a constellation brought to life, and I can't help but be in awe of her.

As she approaches, a delicate fragrance wafts through the air, a scent that's uniquely hers. It's a symphony of floral notes and hints of vanilla, a fragrance that lingers long after she's gone, just like the memory of her presence in my life.

"Hey, where are we headed?" she asks, curiosity dancing in her eyes. I flash her a playful grin, my heart racing with excitement.

"It's a surprise," I reply, taking her hand in mine and leading her toward a waiting car.

We arrive at Central Park, and the moon casts a silvery glow over the scene that's about to unfold. A small orchestra is gathered, their instruments poised, ready to bring my plan to life. Isabella's favorite song, "Midnight City" by M83, begins to play, and the night shimmers with enchantment.

The music resonates with an electrifying energy as I hold her close, swaying gently to the rhythm. It's as if the world around us has melted away, leaving only the two of us and the ethereal sounds that wrap us in their embrace. I start singing softly, my voice blending with the music from the orchestra. I see a spark in her eyes, a recognition of the significance of this moment.

The music carries us through a journey of emotions, each note a brushstroke painting a picture of our story. We share smiles, whispers, and stolen glances as the orchestra weaves its magic. And then, as "Midnight City" reaches its crescendo, I see her eyes glistening with unshed tears, a testament to the overwhelming joy that fills her heart.

She turns to me, her gaze searching for answers, for the meaning behind this orchestrated symphony of emotions. With a grin, I quip, "I bet there are orchestras in Paris, but none of them will play for you the way I'd make every orchestra play for you here in New York." My words are nearly swallowed by the music, but she laughs, a melodious sound that warms my very soul.

Her laughter slowly transitions into a smile of understanding, and in that moment, the distance between us, the uncertainty of the future, all of it seems to fade away. It's just her and me, immersed in the celestial sounds and the bond we share. As the final notes of the song linger in the air, I reach into my pocket, fingers brushing against the velvet of a bracelet box.

With tenderness, I open the box, revealing a bracelet adorned with delicate charms, each one a symbol of our journey together. She extends her wrist, and as I fasten the bracelet, our fingers touch, igniting a connection that transcends words. Then, beneath the canopy of stars and the lingering magic of the orchestra, our lips meet in a kiss that's as sweet and profound as the music that brought us here.

In that embrace, I feel a surge of emotions—love, desire, vulnerability—all intertwined like the harmonies of the orchestra. The world around us melts away once more, leaving only the echoes of the music and the resonance of our hearts. And as we break the kiss, her eyes shimmer with unshed tears, a testament to the depth of what we share.

Love may be selfish, but in this moment, it's also pure and undeniable. The music may fade, but the symphony of our love will continue to play, a melody that we compose together, even if life leads us to different corners of the world.

***

I still cannot decide which fact is greater: me wanting Isabella to stay because I am falling too hard for her, or the fact that she's currently our best designer. Here I sit, in the office conference room, facing Robert.

Across the table from me, Robert sits cross-legged, an unlit cigarette between his fingers. We've been going over minor issues in the business, navigating through challenges like skilled chess players on an intricate board. And now, as the smoke swirls around him like a shroud, I find myself broaching a topic that could further complicate our dynamics.

As we work through the final points of the conversation, a brief silence lingers in the air like suspended particles waiting for a gust of wind. It's as if the moment has been orchestrated for what I'm about to say next. I lean back, studying Robert's current expression: skepticism.

"You know, Robert, we're on the brink of losing Isabella to a fashion outfit in Paris," I say.

His eyebrows arch in mild interest, an unspoken question hanging in the air.

He takes a drag of his cigarette, exhaling a cloud of smoke as he leans back, the leather chair creaking under his weight. "And what's that got to do with us?"

I sigh, knowing that this path is fraught with the potential for discord. "She's getting offers because of her talent. Her award for emerging fashion designer at the CFDA is only the beginning."

Robert's lips curl into a slight smile, his eyes tracing patterns in the smoke. "So, she's good. It doesn't mean she's irreplaceable."

I take a deep breath, choosing my words carefully. "Isabella isn't just talented; her success isn't by chance or luck. It's calculated brilliance, and that's why people who understand her worth are eager to snatch her from us."

Robert's chuckle rumbles like distant thunder. He leans forward slightly, as if ready to share a secret. "Is that really the reason you want to keep her here, Sebastian?"

I meet his gaze, the intensity of our eye contact magnifying the weight of our conversation. "Of course. It's not just about personal feelings. Her designs are game-changers, Robert. She's hacked the industry, and it's reflected in our profits."

Robert's gaze doesn't waver, and I can almost see the gears turning in his mind. "I'm not doubting her talents, but I did some digging," he admits casually.

I raise an eyebrow "Digging?"

He leans in even closer, his voice dropping in volume as if sharing a confidential piece of information. "You've put more into marketing her collections than we've ever done for anyone else."

I lean back, processing his words. "Talent and marketing go hand in hand. They're two things that don't fail."

Robert's laughter rumbles in the room, a low, gravelly sound that reverberates off the walls. He leans back, his fingers drumming on the table. "Sebastian, you're quite the risk-taker, aren't you?"

I offer a wry smile in return. "In business and other aspects of life, I suppose."

He stands up, his movements slow and deliberate. He's heading toward the door, his hand on the knob, when he pauses and turns his head slightly, looking at me out of the corner of his eye. "If she wants to stay, she'll stay."

There's an unspoken understanding in his words, a hint of something beneath the surface. He adds with a nod of his head, "Don't blur the line that separates romance and work."

— Chapter 22 —
Solace

I hate interviews. The interviewer will tug and tug at you, asking generic or borderline intrusive questions. I hate doing them.

But Jennifer and Thomas, the head of marketing, insist that I take interviews more seriously now. After all, my recent successful collections and the prestigious award have thrust me into the spotlight. It's all part of the marketing and soft-selling approach to promote Maxwell & Co.'s brand and our newest collections.

So, here I am, in a studio that's illuminated by bright lights, surrounded by the faint buzz of cameras and crew members bustling about.

The studio is a blend of modern aesthetics and functionality. White-brown brick walls of the interior provide a traditional New York style backdrop for the set. The interviewer's desk is sleek and minimalist, contrasting with the plush chairs where guests are seated. The floor is polished wood, its reflection distorted slightly by the lights above.

As I take my seat across from the interviewer, his smug smile immediately grates on my nerves. The way he speaks on fashion with so much authority will make you think he's a man who walks his talk. I know him. I've seen his show. I see how harshly he criticizes styles and outfits.

But instead of walking his talk, he's a man who walks in an ill-fitting suit that bunches awkwardly around his chest and shoulders. The tension around the buttons of his jacket where it's closed is impossible to ignore, too. I wonder how no one backstage stopped him from going on live TV looking like this.

The host leans forward slightly, his eyes fixed on me with an almost calculated intensity. His voice drips with a self-assured charm that doesn't quite match his disheveled appearance. "Good evening, Isabella. It's a pleasure to have you here."

I offer a polite smile, masking my growing irritation at his demeanor. "Thank you for having me."

He flips open his notepad, a flourish that seems more performative than necessary. "Let's begin, shall we? Your work has been making waves in the industry. Tell me, what inspires you as a designer?"

I take a deep breath, focusing on the question and pushing aside the nagging annoyance. "I draw inspiration from a myriad of sources: nature, art, culture. It's about capturing the essence of those influences and translating them into my designs."

His brows arch in mock interest. "Fascinating. And what about your recent award? How has it impacted your journey?"

I sense a pattern in his questions, as if he's following a script designed to showcase my accomplishments. "Winning the award was an incredible honor. It's a validation of my creative vision and the hard work of my team."

He nods, as if he expected no less. "Indeed. Now, the fashion industry is known for its fast pace and relentless demand. How do you manage to keep up?"

I let out a soft chuckle, the tension in my shoulders easing slightly. "It's a whirlwind, but it's also where the excitement lies. Adapting to the ever-changing landscape requires a mix of passion, dedication, and the ability to stay ahead of trends."

He leans in closer, as though trying to unveil some hidden secret. "And you seem to be excelling at that. You've managed to navigate this demanding environment quite well."

I feel the veiled insinuation in his words, the implication that my success is somehow tied to something beyond my skills. My jaw tightens, but I maintain a calm exterior. "I appreciate your kind words. It's a team effort, really."

A small smile plays on his lips, and I sense a shift in his approach. "Isabella, sometimes success in this industry comes from unexpected sources. Especially when there's someone unlikely helping you get ahead as fast as you can."

His words hit me like a slap, the audacity of his suggestion threatening to break my composure.

My heart skips a beat, and an inferno of irritation ignites within me. Is he really going to go there? I plaster a pretentious smile over my face, masking the annoyance that's bubbling just beneath the surface.

I force a tight-lipped smile, my fingers gripping the armrest of the chair. "I'm not sure what you're referring to." I raise an eyebrow, feigning curiosity. "What do you mean?"

He maintains his smug grin, seemingly undeterred by my cool response. "There have been rumors, you know. Rumors of a certain romantic relationship with your boss that might have contributed to your rise in popularity in the industry."

My fingers clench slightly at my sides. How dare he insinuate that my success is solely tied to my relationship with Sebastian? My smile remains steady, betraying nothing more than a polite curiosity. "I'm not sure what you're referring to."

He chuckles softly, his eyes glinting with mischief. "Oh, I think you do, Isabella."

My heartbeat quickens, but I refuse to let his tactics unsettle me. "I don't believe that discussing my personal life is relevant to this interview."

He raises an eyebrow in mock surprise. "Of course, of course. We're here to talk about your career and your achievements."

His attempt at playing coy infuriates me, but I maintain my composure. "Exactly."

The interview continues, the host posing questions and steering the conversation toward various aspects of my work. I answer dutifully, my responses well-practiced. But my mind is preoccupied, grappling with his thinly veiled attempt to undermine my accomplishments.

As the interviewer drones on, I find myself zoning out, my focus slipping. The questions blend together into a monotonous hum, as if I'm hearing them from a distance. The memory of his comment lingers like a dull ache. The audacity of his insinuation, the way he attempted to belittle my efforts by attributing my success to my relationship, gnaws at me.

By the time the interview concludes, I'm emotionally drained. I offer a gracious smile to the host, my eyes betraying nothing of my true feelings. He offers a final nod, a smirk playing on his lips as if he's won some sort of petty victory.

As the studio lights dim and the crew begins to pack up, I'm left with a mixture of anger and frustration. Jennifer's and Thomas's voices echo in my mind, reminding me of the importance of interviews in shaping my public image. But this encounter has shown me the darker side of media exposure, the way it can be manipulated to undermine my achievements.

***

The last time I was at the Grand Bazaar flea market was when I started at Maxwell & Co. and I hated Sebastian with every fiber of my being. Or I thought I hated him.

I haven't been here in a while; I've been almost too busy for it. But today is different—it's Sunday, and I've decided to make it a ritual to visit the Grand Bazaar whenever I can on Sundays. Now, I'm here with Sebastian, arm in arm, amidst the bustling crowd.

Sebastian looks around, his eyes scanning the eclectic stalls and vibrant displays. "How come I didn't know there's a place like this in the city?" he asks, with genuine curiosity in his voice.

I chuckle, nudging him playfully. "Believe it or not, not even you know everywhere in New York. There's still a lot I can show you."

He grins, his hand finding mine, fingers entwining. "I like the sound of that. How about I show you this?" He leans in and presses a soft, warm kiss on my lips. It's a brief, affectionate connection that sends a comforting tingle through me.

"How did the interview go, Isabella?"

I release a sigh, a mixture of frustration and resignation. "You know how much I hate interviews. They're like a necessary evil in this industry."

He nods sympathetically, his fingers gently squeezing mine. "I understand, but you always handle them so well."

I give him a wry smile, appreciating his attempt to comfort me. "I do my best. Did you watch it?"

Sebastian shakes his head. "I didn't. I didn't know what time it aired yesterday."

I shrug nonchalantly. "Well, you didn't miss much. The interviewer was annoying."

Sebastian chuckles, and I elaborate, "First of all, he dressed ugly."

Sebastian bursts into laughter, his amusement infectious.

I continue, my tone more serious, "And secondly, he implied on live television that my success has been because of our relationship."

Sebastian's laughter fades, replaced by a flicker of irritation. "That's just ridiculous. He's a very stupid fellow for that. I'd have yanked him off his chair."

Now it's my turn to laugh while my fingers playfully graze his arm. "With those strong muscles of yours?" I tease, measuring his bicep with my hand.

Sebastian grins mischievously. "Exactly."

He announces his intention to get us milkshakes from a corner stand he spotted, leaving me waiting alone amidst the bustling market. The moment he leaves, a familiar voice breaks through the chatter.

"Bella?"

I turn, my heart suddenly racing, to find Tyler standing there. Tyler, my ex-boyfriend from my university years, the one who disappeared when he went to Brazil. His appearance is like a shock to my system, and I find myself unable to believe my eyes.

A smile graces Tyler's lips, and he approaches me, his arm extended as if to prove his presence is real. "It's me."

Before I can say a word, he pulls me into a warm embrace. The shock of seeing him mingles with the familiarity of his touch. "I thought I'd never see you again," I admit softly as he releases me.

Tyler's gaze travels over me appreciatively. "You look incredible, Bella. It's been too long."

A flutter of emotions swirls within me, a mixture of surprise, nostalgia, and perhaps a hint of unresolved feelings. He mentions seeing me on TV, acknowledging the changes in my life since he left.

I laugh, slightly flustered. "Yeah, I've been keeping busy."

Tyler grins, an enigmatic twinkle in his eyes. "I can see that. So, what have you been up to?"

I'm about to answer when he leans in and kisses my hand. My breath catches, and I'm momentarily transported to the past, a time when he used to be a significant part of my life. He assures me that we can catch up another time, that he has a lot to share, but now isn't the right moment.

With that, he disappears into the crowd, leaving me standing there, stunned. It's only when Sebastian returns with two milkshakes that I'm brought back to the present. He notices my surprise and asks who I was just speaking to.

"Just an old friend," I reply, my tone casual as I take one of the milkshakes from him.

***

I hate Mondays. A lot more than I hate Tuesdays. Everyone and everything move so fast. As if everyone is in a hurry to alter the course of their lives in one day.

Today has been a whirlwind of work, meetings, and deadlines. By the time I leave the office, the sun has already set, and the city's skyline is painted with a cascade of lights. I'm exhausted, mentally and physically drained. Yet, there's a glimmer of anticipation in my heart—Sebastian, my solace, is waiting for me.

I spot him leaning casually against his car, his tall, confident figure standing out even amidst the bustling city streets. His eyes light up as he sees me approaching, and a warm smile graces his lips. It's a small gesture, but it's enough to make the weariness fade away, even if just for a moment.

"Rough day?" he asks, his voice a soothing balm to my senses.

I nod, leaning into him as he wraps an arm around my waist. "You have no idea."

He chuckles softly, pressing a gentle kiss to my temple. "Well, I've got something that might help."

He leads me to a nearby bar, a quaint place tucked away from the hustle and bustle of the city. The ambiance is cozy, and the low hum of conversations fills the air. We find a secluded corner, a dimly lit table where we can unwind.

As we sip our drinks and exchange stories of our days, I feel a sense of relief wash over me. His presence has a way of grounding me, of reminding me that there's more to life than the stresses of work. But just as I start to relax into the moment, his phone rings, and his expression shifts.

Sebastian glances at the screen, his brows furrowing.

"I'm so sorry, Bella," he says, his voice tinged with regret. "I have to take this. It's something urgent at the office."

I offer a reassuring smile, though disappointment nips at the edges of my mood. "Go ahead, I understand."

He leans in and kisses me, his lips soft against mine. "I'll make it up to you, I promise."

Sebastian hurries off, leaving me at the bar. I finish my drink and step outside, the cool night air hitting me like a welcomed gust. I signal for a taxi, and it drops me off in front of my apartment building. I'm almost ready to retreat into the comfort of my home when a familiar voice cuts through the night, jolting me from my thoughts.

"Bella?"

I turn around, and my heart skips a beat as I spot Tyler, standing there across the street. He's wearing a simple t-shirt and jeans, a ball cap shading his features. The beard and the tattoo on his neck are new additions I hadn't noticed at the flea market, transforming him into someone even more striking than before.

"Tyler," I greet with a genuine smile, feeling a rush of happiness at the sight of him after all these years.

He gestures to the coffee shop across the road, explaining how he was waiting for me. I'm intrigued and amused. "How did you know where I live?"

He grins, his eyes holding a hint of mischief. "It's not that hard to find."

Crossing the distance between us, he envelops me in a warm hug. It's a familiar embrace, and I'm caught off guard by how much I've missed it.

Pulling back, I hold his face in my hands, studying the changes in him. "Where have you been all this time?"

He shrugs nonchalantly, his smile laced with a hint of sadness. "Around the world, mostly."

He's a different Tyler from the one I knew in school, yet he's still the same at the core. He asks to come in, and without hesitation, I agree. He takes my bag, joking about its weight after my long day at work.

As we head to the elevator, we encounter a couple of repairers working on it.

"I'm too tired for stairs," I mutter, feeling the exhaustion settling in my bones.

Without a word, Tyler sweeps me off my feet, and I'm caught between laughter and surprise. As he carries me up the stairs, memories of our carefree days flood back.

"I missed this," he admits, his tone tinged with nostalgia.

I chuckle, a mixture of emotions swirling within me. "Carrying me up the stairs?"

He grins, his gaze locked on mine. "No, just... us."

We reach my apartment, and he sets me down gently. As I open the door, he steps inside, his eyes exploring every corner in wonder.

"You've got a nice place," he remarks, his fingers brushing against various objects with a childlike curiosity.

He settles onto my couch, his words laced with humor. "Feels like I'm visiting someone's house for the first time."

I laugh, feeling a sense of comfort in his presence. "Well, make yourself at home."

Before I head to my room to change, I sneak a moment to smile to myself at the unexpected reunion. When I return, Tyler is engrossed in watching something on his phone, the sound of music filling the room.

"What's that?" I ask as I pour us both some whiskey and settle onto another couch.

He lifts his eyebrow playfully. "Just some of our band's performances."

I raise my eyebrows in surprise. "You're in a band?"

Tyler takes a sip of whiskey before answering, revealing a glint of amusement in his eyes. "Yeah, I formed a band after school."

I chuckle, genuinely surprised. "I didn't know you were into music."

He laughs, shaking his head. "I'm not the singer, don't worry. I'm the drummer."

Memories of his drumming skills back in school flash through my mind. "I do remember you being pretty good at that."

He grins, taking another sip of his drink. "Well, we all found our paths."

He leans back, and his gaze focuses on me. "You know what brought me back to New York?"

I shake my head, genuinely curious. "No, what?"

A smile tugs at his lips, his voice soft. "You."

I'm taken aback by his admission, and a blush creeps onto my cheeks. "Oh."

Tyler's eyes hold mine, an intensity in his gaze. I can sense his unspoken thoughts, his lingering feelings from the past. And then, with a deliberate slowness, he leans closer, his intent clear.

Just as our lips are about to meet, an internal alarm goes off within me. I pull away abruptly, standing up. "I'm sorry, Tyler. I can't."

He smiles gently, his understanding evident. "Your heart belongs to another man."

"Sebastian," I confirm, feeling a mix of emotions: guilt, relief, and a hint of sadness.

Tyler's smile doesn't falter. "I can see why."

He claims he needs to leave, and I watch as he walks out of my apartment. Standing by the window, I see him step onto the street. I notice his car not too far away. A Ford Mustang. And then, as if on cue, Sebastian's Rolls Royce pulls up to the curb.

— Chapter 23 —

Insecurities

There's hardly a time where I hang out with Isabella that she doesn't leave something behind. Tonight, it's her purse. I would have waited until tomorrow, but I won't be at work for the rest of the week. So, here I am, parked in front of Isabella's apartment building, my Rolls Royce gleaming under the streetlights. As I stop the car, my gaze catches a man descending the short flight of stairs. But this isn't just any man.

It's the same guy I saw at the Grand Bazaar, kissing Isabella's hand before disappearing into the crowd. The same man I asked Isabella about, and she assured me he was just an old friend. I remember feeling a pang of jealousy as I watched him from a distance, the familiarity and affection between them leaving an impression that lingered in my mind.

My chest tightens as I watch him, my eyes narrowing instinctively. He glances in my direction, pausing in his steps as our eyes meet. I stand there, silently sizing him up, trying to gauge his intentions. He stares back at me as I get out of the car, his expression almost as if he's on the brink of saying something, as if he recognizes me. Of course, he knows me. Everyone knows me.

"You must be Sebastian," he finally says, extending his hand for a handshake.

I hesitate for a moment, then take his hand. "I'm not sure we've met," I reply, my grip firm as I maintain a steady gaze.

"Almost," he says, a mysterious smile playing on his lips. "We almost met. But we are meeting now. I know you well. Who wouldn't?"

Managing a slight smile, I respond, "Well, a lot of people don't know me. In fact, there are more people who don't than those who do." I can feel the tension in the air, the unspoken curiosity and underlying scrutiny.

He introduces himself as Tyler Cooper, his name carrying an air of mystery that makes me uneasy. I gesture towards the Ford Mustang parked nearby and ask if it's his car.

"Yes," he confirms, his eyes lingering on the vehicle. "A gorgeous beast."

I chuckle and actually find myself agreeing with him. "What year?"

"1969," he replies with a proud grin.

"My father has a 1967," I remark. "He claims it's the greatest car ever made."

Tyler nods, a hint of intrigue in his eyes. "Traditional man, I see."

I nod in agreement. "Very much so."

He turns his attention to my Rolls Royce, gesturing towards it. "Obviously."

A subtle grin forms on my lips. "I guess you came to visit Isabella?"

Tyler shrugs nonchalantly. "Just catching up with an old friend."

I offer a curt nod, my gut twisting with skepticism. "Right."

He lets out a casual laugh. "You don't have to worry. Just old pals."

I don't fully believe him, but I don't press the matter further.

"I better get going now, Mr. Sebastian Maxwell," he says.

I nod in response, watching as he disappears into his Ford Mustang. I keep my eyes on him until he's out of sight.

With a heavy sigh, I finally make my way out of the car and into Isabella's apartment building.

***

The climb up the stairs is the longest I've ever climbed. Not because Isabella's apartment is on the 8th floor, but because I still can't make anything out of meeting Tyler. I wonder what Isabella has to say. My heart pounds as I reach her door, my knuckles hovering over the surface for a moment before I finally knock. The seconds stretch into eternity, my chest tightens with every passing moment.

I raise my hand to knock again, my chest tightening as I hold her forgotten purse in my hand. The door opens, and Isabella stands there, looking somewhat...at home. As she should be. Her ruffled hair and attire, simple t-shirt and sweatpants, contrast with my grim mood. I don't know where to start, how to unravel the knot that's formed in my stomach.

"Can I come in?" I ask, my voice sounding gruffer than intended.

"Of course," she replies, stepping back to make way. I walk in and sink into her couch, feeling the weight of the day pressing down on me. There are two glasses on the center table—one with a tiny bit of whiskey left, the other empty. Isabella's eyes catch mine, and she hurriedly collects the glasses and takes them to the kitchen.

She returns, her demeanor slightly uneasy, a mirror to my own feelings. "I see you had a visitor," I say, my tone neutral.

She shrugs, snuggling into me on the couch. "Just an old friend," she answers, her voice casual.

I raise an eyebrow, my gaze fixed on her. "The man I saw at the flea market?" I inquire, already knowing the answer.

She nods. "Yes, Tyler."

"Just an old friend," I repeat, my words laced with skepticism. Her reaction only fuels the suspicion that's been simmering within me.

I pull away slightly, my eyes locked onto hers. "I don't believe it," I say, my tone firm.

Her posture stiffens, and her voice grows defensive. "There's nothing to talk about."

I stare at her, my eyes searching her face for answers. She avoids my gaze, then finally admits that Tyler is her ex-boyfriend. The words hit me like a blow to the chest. My jaw clenches as I turn my gaze away, processing the information. A mix of emotions floods me: jealousy, anger, hurt.

I nod, unable to form a coherent response. Isabella pulls away from me, her voice wavering as she insists it's not what I'm thinking. She tries to explain, but my mind is a whirlwind of emotions, thoughts spinning out of control. I can't think straight, can't make sense of what I'm feeling.

The air is thick with tension, every word exchanged a heated accusation. "You've been keeping this from me," I snap, my voice laced with anger. "An ex-boyfriend, Isabella? How am I supposed to believe there's nothing more to it?"

Isabella's eyes blaze with frustration, her voice rising to meet mine. "You're overreacting, Sebastian! Tyler is just an old friend. There's no reason for you to be this jealous."

My jaw clenches as I struggle to control my emotions. "Jealous? Is that what you think this is? You had a whole history with him that you didn't even bother to mention. How do you expect me to trust you now?"

She throws her hands up in exasperation. "Trust me? You don't trust me because of my past with Tyler? That's ridiculous!"

"Ridiculous? I saw you together at the Bazaar, the way he kissed your hand. And now he's just showing up at your apartment? How am I supposed to believe this is all innocent?"

Isabella's eyes narrow, her frustration giving way to hurt. "You know what, Sebastian? You're being unfair. You're letting your insecurities get the best of you."

"Insecurities?" My voice rises, matching the intensity of the argument. "I trusted you, Isabella. I thought we were building something real. But now, with all this secrecy, I don't know what to believe anymore."

She takes a step closer, her voice quivering. "You're not the only one who's been hurt before, Sebastian. You're not the only one with a past."

My frustration collides with a wave of guilt, her vulnerability taking me aback. "Isabella, this isn't about our pasts. It's about honesty and openness in our relationship. I thought we had that."

Her shoulders slump, and her voice softens. "I never meant for it to come to this. I didn't tell you about Tyler because I was afraid it would change things between us."

I let out a heavy sigh, the anger slowly dissipating into a mix of sadness and regret. "Isabella, it's not about your past. It's about us, about building a future together. Keeping things hidden only makes it harder."

The silence is deafening. Isabella stands there while her eyes well up with either anger or sadness, I'm not sure which. She turns around and bites her lower lip in frustration. There's nothing left to say for either of us.

And then, unable to bear the intensity any longer, I storm out of her apartment, my footsteps echoing in the hallway.

The drive home is quiet, the car filled with the haunting melody of slow jazz, sad music that matches the turmoil inside me. My grip tightens on the steering wheel, my mind replaying the argument, the feeling of betrayal, the sharp pang of jealousy. I struggle to make sense of it all, to find a way to calm the storm that's raging within me.

As the city lights blur by, I'm left with the weight of uncertainty and a sense of disconnection. The world outside may be bustling, alive with its own rhythm, but inside the confines of my car, there's a silence that starkly contrasts the chaos in my heart.

***

I didn't envision that I would be at the office today, or even for the rest of the week. But here I am all the same. A part of me thinks if I knew I'd be at the office today, it would have been better if I just gave back Isabella's purse today. Then I wouldn't have gone over to her apartment to get my heart broken

I can't even get it out of my mind. My chest tightens and my fist balls up without my consent just remembering our fight. I couldn't even sleep last night. I got into the shower, thinking hard of the sound of her voice when she kept saying "just a friend."

Another part of me wonders if I'm not just overreacting, if it is really nothing to be vexed about. Another part of me insists it's good that I went there last night and I saw what I saw. The voices in my head aren't just like thoughts. They feel like different people with different personalities, tone and perspectives arguing in my head, having tough conversations that I cannot shake away.

So, today I'm late to the office. At least three hours late. I spent more time in the shower than I normally do. Perhaps this was what Robert and the rest of the board meant when they say office romance is a distraction. Because I've been distracted enough. I reluctantly climb into my car, my mind reeling through what Tyler Cooper and I said about cars.

I walk by Isabella's office, stopping by her window for a little while as our eyes meet. I can't tell if what I see flicker in her eyes is remorse or conviction. Without saying a word to her, I leave as she looks like she wants to say something but her throat won't let her.

I replay every worst possible scenario in my head. *Why didn't she tell me? What else did they do inside there?* All she needed to do was apologize and explain how things really went. I asked so many questions and when I didn't get adequate responses, I made up answers in my head.

I spend the rest of my day fighting those thoughts, pushing them out of my head almost as quickly as they are suggested.

I pick up my phone from the top of my desk, swipe it open, and go straight to our DMs.

Hey, what you doing after work?

I pause a little to collect my thoughts.

We need to talk.

I delete the message before I hit send, and then, I drop my phone back on my desk. I heave a deep sigh and stare out of the window. That sounds desperate. Just the thoughts of those words make my chest tighten some more. I can walk over to her office to speak to her.

No.

If she really cares, she should come here instead. She's not the only one who's had an ex.

It's a few minutes past the closing, and Isabella still isn't here. I'm standing by my window watching the city below when my phone buzzes in my breast pocket. I pull it out, hoping it's Isabella's text.

I kiss my teeth, seeing it's just another email.

But before I can put it back in my pocket to continue staring at the street below, my phone chimes again. This time, it's Isabella's notification. It has become my favorite notification ever. It's a picture with the caption: "I'm sorry. It isn't what you are thinking."

My heart races with anticipation as I open the picture. A smile creases my face as I stare down at my phone. It's a mirror selfie of her in a red nightdress. Silky and shiny with a lace pattern barely covering her breasts as I can see, albeit faintly, her brown areola and stiff nipples.

I start to breathe through my mouth. I can feel the tension coursing from my brain through my body until it settles somewhere in the bulge underneath my fly. As I look away from the phone, my thoughts are all over the place.

Is she trying to seduce me? Is she trying to seduce her way out of our problems? She's definitely succeeding.

Before I can catch my breath, another few two texts drop in quick succession. I find myself a little too eager to tap on the pictures. The same style. Looks like she took them in the morning. Her hair looks ruffled, her eyes still heavy from sleep. The last one, she turned so her back faced the mirror.

She's built like a fitness model. Not tall enough to be a runway model but with curves more visible than most. With thicker thighs, too. I salivate at the thought of her right there in my office. I chuckle to myself as I close my phone and slip it back in my breast pocket.

A knock on the door interrupts my thoughts. Before I can answer, the door clicks open. I turn back to see Isabella standing right there by the door.

— Chapter 24 —
The Thrill

I can't gauge what mood Sebastian might be in. So, my knocking fist hovers around the door for a little while longer before I attempt to press the bell. But I don't. I remember Sebastian telling me once that he hates the bells.

I take a deep breath and finally find the courage to knock. Three sharp knocks on the heavy, wooden door. I wonder if he hears me at all.

I think I hear him say "come in" or something that sounds like it. I twist the handle until the door clicks open. I find him standing by the large window of his office. He turns almost as soon as I open the door.

He's wearing a striped suit with a plain, royal blue tie. There's something sinful that a well-fitted stripe suit does to me. Plus, the man wearing it doesn't hurt. I struggle to find balance with a lump in my throat as I try to speak. He turns fully towards me as I wonder if he has opened the photos I sent.

The room is silent. As if we are both waiting for the other to break the silence.

"I thought you left already," I say, my voice gruffer than I intended.

Sebastian is unmoving. I'm still trying to gauge his thoughts. He's wordlessly staring straight into my eyes, and frankly, it's making me tense and nervous.

And when I get tense and nervous, I get horny.

A little tingling sensation starts down there, in between my legs. I breathe out slowly, trying to hide my discomfort. He's not making it any better by staring me down like that, too.

"No," he says calmly. His voice is deep enough to send volts of electricity down my spine. "I've had things to take care of." His tone is cold.

"Oh," I reply with a nod. "I didn't even know you'd be coming to work today."

"I didn't know that, either."

I take one or two steps closer to him. My hands nervously entangle as I inch closer. "I know what it looks like, Sebastian, but trust me, it's not what you think at all."

Sebastian walks closer to me, closing the gap between us until he's staring down at me. "What do you think it looks like, Isabella?"

"I'm sorry, he's nothing to me anym…"

Before I can finish my sentence, Sebastian closes the tiny gap between us with a kiss. His lips press almost violently against mine as if he yearns to eat the rest of my words straight out of my mouth.

I'm stunned for a few seconds, my eyes wide open. I soon shut my eyes and ease into him as he continues to mouth me like a hungry man mouths a steak. I cannot hold back the moans escaping my mouth, finding their way into his. His hands and his mouth don't hold back as he firmly gropes my heart.

My mind buzzes with the what ifs: *what if someone walks in on us, especially Robert?* I wouldn't know how to react.

He pulls away from my lips to rasp, "I've missed you, my love."

I lick my lips while my eyes are locked lustfully on his as our heads are joined at the forehead, breathing each other's air. "I've missed you, too." My voice is soft, and my breath is so warm on his face that I feel it on mine, too. "Did you see my pictures?"

"They got me a little too excited," he admits with a small, mischievous smile creasing the corners of his lips.

I let out a small laugh as I rub my hands over his face and then his hair. And in a split second, he lifts me off my feet like I weigh nothing at all and drops me on his desk. I watch him sweep some paperwork off the top in frantic excitement.

I've never had the urge to please any man as much as I want to satisfy him. I want to take the rigid part of him in my mouth and watch him squirm on his feet to whatever I do with my tongue. But before I can collect my thoughts enough, Sebastian grabs the back of my neck, his hand firm and gentle on my skin as he lunges gracefully forward. His mouth digs into mine, and his tongue desperately tries to find mine.

By the time he finds it, starts to suckle on it, his hands continue to do the dirty job of undressing me. I push him back a little.

"What if someone walks in on us?" My voice is raspy; too much intensity in such a short time will leave a woman gasping for oxygen.

"That's the thrill," he says with a smile stretching on his lips. His breath on my neck makes me want to throw all caution to the wind and just tear his shirt and suit off him. But the seams of his suit look too strong for my fragile hands.

"You look too enticing in those photos," he says as he starts to kiss me on my neck. "I just couldn't resist anymore."

It was a long time coming, us clashing together at the office. I shut my eyes as I desperately move in sync with the movement of his hands, my hips thrusting forward against him. What he's doing is my absolute weakness. The way he sucks on the skin on my neck. Biting it softly, leaving trails of hickeys along my flesh.

Before he can continue any further, I unfasten the buttons of his suit and help him slip out of it. Then, carefully, with methodical ease, I loosen his tie and fling it somewhere on the floor. Frankly, I don't care where anything is anymore.

He's a lot more in a hurry than I am. So, I watch him burst his shirt open, and in a split second, he's tearing it off himself before tossing it on the couch behind us. He tries to unzip my dress from my back, but I stop him before he can.

"What?" he mutters.

"I'm in control today," I whisper in his ear before I slip gracefully off the tabletop. His eyes are as dirty and lustful as I want them to be. I watch him swallow hard as I carefully descend on my knees. He's without words as my hand grazes his bulging fly. I can feel the stiffness of his arousal growing inch by inch, protesting against the zipper holding it hostage.

I pull down the zipper until I'm eye level with his white briefs. I'm breathing through my mouth now. He throws his head back, grunting loud enough I feel the vibrations. He makes throaty sounds I cannot spell out.

Without hesitation, I pull the briefs down, and his cock flies in my face, a little moist on the tip before I even grab the stiff, meaty and veiny flesh. A gasp escapes me as I struggle hard to control myself. I look at him with a smile on my face.

I absolutely love what I'm seeing.

The cap is reddish, as if it's been begging to be let out for so long that it threatened to burst through.

"Fuck!" I whisper as I grab his cock and lick the moistness off its cap. But it doesn't stop seeping out, almost as if teasing me.

"Do that again," Sebastian whispers as he grabs my hair. His grip around my hair tightens as I lick the moisture off his head again. He lets out a loud moan. So deep that I worry that someone might hear him and be tempted to look in.

Watching him from where I kneel is probably the most beautiful view I've seen in a while. I keep my eyes on him as I push his length halfway in my mouth until I can feel it warmth, pulsing, and moisture in my mouth. I start to bob my head as my eyes remain on him, trying to gauge his reaction.

"Where did you learn how to do that?" His voice is raspy. It's rhetorical as he throws his head back, frantically glancing around the room. I can feel the pleasure bubble somewhere inside him. I bob my head while working my tongue around the tip, flicking and slapping it on the insides of my cheeks.

"I don't cum from getting head," he says. He's staring down at me, biting his lower lip in a lustful, sinful gaze. "But you are getting me close. Keep going." He pushes my head back to work.

I stroke my tongue over him, then I bite him until I know he can feel the sensation. When he cannot take it anymore, he pulls away, his hips looking like they will cave in, and his legs give up on him.

He throws me over his desk and unzips my dress before pressing his weight on me. My dress drops to the floor until I'm wearing nothing but my thong and my strapless bra. For the first time ever, I feel his arousal press against my bare ass.

"Now it's my turn," he says before dropping lower. I can feel his face where his cock should be.

"Fuckkk!" I cannot contain my surprise as his lips and nose graze my slit. I feel too moist. Almost a mess. He shakes his face in between my legs, mumbling inaudible noises through the act.

I cannot keep my voice down.

"Don't…stop…please….fuck…yesss…more."

There's something about make up sex that hits harder than anything else. Maybe it's the anger and resentment that has built up now pouring out in torrents. Sebastian doesn't stop. He ignores my loud moans and the inaudible words I jumble around. He starts to make conscious efforts to suck me from the back. His tongue reaches my slit, flicking and circling around my clit. I hold one hand out behind me as I try to push his head off me.

I want it. I want him.

But the pleasure is getting too intense for me.

My breath seizes as I'm bent over the desk. He spends the next few minutes on his knees, spreading my ass cheeks with his hands while his whole face is buried in between my ass. His tongue goes deeper, almost to the point that I feel it touching my soul as he continues the rhythm that gets me wriggling. He continues to assert pressure. A familiar feeling continues to build up like the rhythm of a heart beating slowly at first.

Then it doubles, tightens, harder and harder. Every build up makes it harder for me to breathe.

Sebastian isn't helping either. He's not stopping. He's making grunting noises. Talking in between. Saying words that I can't make out without taking his face away.

I can't think of anything else as the pressure continues to build up. I reach a mind-blowing release of endorphins. I'm clenching hard as I desperately try to push Sebastian off me. I'm screaming loud now with no fucks left to give. My body wriggles against the desk. My vagina clenches hard.

So, I give in, and I hit the ceiling of all kinds of pleasurable feelings. This is definitely it. The feelings implode through my body, and I feel it course through me from my clit to my thighs. Fingertips. Head. My head starts to do me in, and I feel lightheaded, even sleepy.

Sebastian takes the cue and towers over me. I can feel his eyes burning through my back as he watches me all spent and exhausted, lying on the mess that is his desk.

"You taste good," he says right before he spanks me on the butt.

"Ouch!" I cannot hold back the sensation his spanking sends through me.

"You said you were sorry," he says gently. "Well, I want you to show me how sorry you really are."

I'm still bent over. My eyes shut. Still vulnerable. The next spank takes me by surprise, and my eyes melt into a screwed-up expression. He spanks me again. And again. And again. Harder and harder until I find myself moaning and thirsting over him again. The warmth in between my legs bothers me so much that I can almost feel myself dripping down my thighs.

Sebastian spanks me again before holding me down to his desk, the weight of his strong forearms bearing down on my back. He reaches out and unhooks my bra. He pulls me off the desk to remove the bra before discarding it into a corner.

It's already getting dark outside, but I don't give two fucks about anything else more than how badly I want Sebastian inside me. He pushes me over the tabletop again. His arm goes back to holding me down right before he pushes his length inside my warmth.

"Fuckkkk!" He lets out a loud gasp.

I turn my head in a desperate attempt to catch the expression on his face on his first entry. He's biting his lips as he starts to thrust slowly. His other hand grabs my waist, and then my hips, and then my ass.

He starts slowly, saying things I can barely make out. His throaty moans and grunts start to propel something inside me as I feel myself leaking again. The sound of our bodies colliding fills the air.

Then he pauses, and begins grinding his waist on me. As slowly as he can. It's a lot better than anything I've ever had.

"Don't stop…harder….please…"

Sebastian pulls me up by my hair, grabs my neck to feel the pulse under my jaw. He presses the two sides of my neck until I'm lightheaded whilst he's still inside me. He pulls out of me, then flips me over.

Pleasure-induced tears fill my eyes. The office is fully dark now, the only lights being the those from the other buildings.

He kisses me on the lips and lets his tongue linger a little long before carrying me on his chest, his cock bobbing under my ass as he heads to the sofa by the wall.

"I love kissing you," he says right before placing me gently on the sofa.

"And I enjoy fucking you," I reply.

A small smile crawls up his face before he leans over me to kiss me again. His lips are warm and wet against mine. I get so lost in his kiss that I lose track of time. I get so lost in everything that I forget about how we shouldn't be doing this. Anyone can walk in on us.

I don't even remember locking the door when I walked in. What if the janitors come around?

Sebastian isn't giving room for long thoughts. Instead, he cuts them into short, urgent ones. He's all over me. His breath is intense against my ear and neck. It does something crazy to me.

His fingers find my slit, and he slides his middle finger inside me, the moistness of my warmth swearing his fingers and hand as he increases the tempo of his thrusting.

"Oh my God! Fuck it. Yes, Daddy. Don't stop, please."

Almost as if he's a master craftsman, he takes his time to study my body. He pulls away from me and grabs my neck, pressing against my pulse gently while his other finger works through my warmth. His strong forearm shakes my core until I feel myself approaching the edge again. He slows down.

Pauses.

Starts again.

And as he starts to make a circling motion inside me, his ha…

A knock interrupts the moment.

Sebastian stops. Stares straight into my bewildered eyes. Without words, I jump onto my feet and start to find my clothes in the dark. I rush to his desk and turn the lamp on. The beam from the lamp makes a soft halo on the desk while lending some of its light around the room. Not too far. Not too bright. Just enough for me to scamper to find my clothes.

Sebastian is sitting on the couch. Unmoved as he watches me desperately hurry for my things. He's smiling when I turn to him. I beckon to him with my head to get dressed.

The knock comes again.

"Hold on!" Sebastian says. His voice is loud, deep, and gruff. Loud enough to get through the heavy door.

The silence on the other end of the door is alarming.

I feel a little bit…I can't find the right words for how I'm feeling. Perhaps embarrassed. I watch Sebastian slip into his pants and put shirt back on. The table is still a mess. The room smells like sex.

Thankfully, there's no surveillance camera. But if the walls could speak, they'd definitely have a lot of stories to tell everyone who walks into the office.

Sebastian walks over to me, kisses me on the head, then on the lips. "I love you," he says.

"Your desk is a mess," I say with a smile.

"Wilson will take care of it," he replies.

When we open the door, we find Wilson walking down the hallway. I'm a little too embarrassed to face him because I feel like he knows what happened in that room. Even if he doesn't have the audacity to mention it to our faces, I'm sure he'll say something to someone else, who will in turn say it to another person. It's how hearsay becomes rumors, and rumors get passed around until the truths in them become so stretched out that they become fables.

I smile as I walk down the hallway. Sebastian joins me in the elevator and holds me in an embrace. There's a glint of satisfaction in his eyes every time he looks over at me.

The drive home is mostly quiet. My dress rides up my thighs, leaving them bare and vulnerable to Sebastian's grip, leaving me battling a tingling sensation. The memories are new, but I keep getting flashbacks of his lips against mine. His face in between my legs. The way his fingers work with so much mastery, how his hands and fingers seemed so refined by years of experience. Even better than the magic of a master guitarist like Jimi Hendrix.

"There's a lot more I wanna show you," Sebastian says after a while of silence between us. His hand is still on my thigh. I turn slowly from the road to smile at him.

"I want to see," I reply. "I want to see all of it. I'm not leaving, Sebastian," I add.

"What?" He glances at me.

"I'm not leaving the company. I'm not going to Paris. I'm not leaving you."

— Chapter 25 —
A Warm Reception

One thing Isabella and I have in common is our aversion to Mondays. I hate it almost as much as her. She once told me over a glass of red wine that she hates Mondays more than anyone alive. Of course, I laughed, the wine making her words sound more dramatic than they probably were. She was tipsy, already in her fifth glass or so. With a playful grin, she even confessed that if I were only her boss and not her boyfriend, she wouldn't have shared this secret with me. It was a privilege I was apparently privy to, she said.

I chuckled and muttered "privy," then paused, turned to her, and quipped, "Is that why they call it 'privilege?'"

Her laughter filled the room, loud, carefree, and endearing. I couldn't help but laugh along, her happiness infectious. But today, another Monday morning, laughter is far from my mind. There's nothing to laugh about.

Before Isabella came into our fold, we had Aiden Martinez, the best designer we've ever had. Aiden has been a pivotal part of our team for years. His creative genius and innovative ideas have given our company a unique edge. Yet this morning, Jennifer, my head of design comes to inform me that Aiden is leaving. Leaving for Paris. It appears that the same

French company that pursued Isabella has now set their sights on Aiden.

I let out a sigh as Jennifer delivers the news, my heart feeling a little heavier. Aiden's departure is a blow to our team, and to me personally. He's not just a talented designer; he's become a friend, someone whose presence has enriched our work environment. Jennifer, noticing my solemn expression, offers a sympathetic smile. "I know how much Aiden means to you, Sebastian."

I nod, running a hand through my hair in frustration. "I can't believe he's leaving. We can't afford to lose someone of his caliber."

Jennifer's gaze meets mine, her concern evident. "Should I summon a meeting? Discuss this with the team?"

I nod again, appreciating her proactive approach. "Yes, let's gather everyone. Heads of departments, Mr. Johnson, and the HR as well."

An urgent meeting is called, everyone assembling in the conference room. I anchor the discussion, addressing the elephant in the room. "As most of you have heard by now, Aiden Martinez, our esteemed designer, has decided to leave us." The room fills with a mix of disbelief and sadness, confirming the impact Aiden has had on our company.

Various concerns are raised—how to fill the void left by Aiden, the potential impact on ongoing projects, and the need to retain other talented designers. Jennifer expresses the sentiment shared by many: "Aiden was more than just a designer. He was an inspiration to all of us."

After the meeting concludes and everyone starts to leave, Abigail, the fifty-six-year-old HR admin who I admire immensely, approaches me in the hallway leading to my office. There's a sense of respect and wisdom that emanates from her presence. "Sebastian," she begins, her tone gentle yet firm, "I have a suggestion."

I nod, intrigued by her insight. "Go on."

She takes a deep breath, her gaze steady as she speaks. "Considering Aiden's departure and the potential of others following suit, I believe it's time to consider increasing the salaries of our design team."

I lean against the wall, my thoughts racing as I consider her proposition. "I'm all for compensating our employees fairly," I reply, "but we did just recently increase their remuneration."

Mrs. Thompson nods, acknowledging the fact. "Yes, but inflation is kicking our ass, Sebastian. We need to keep up with the changing times, provide a little incentive that keeps our designers from seeking opportunities elsewhere."

I sigh, rubbing the back of my neck as I process her words. "I understand, but we can't just outlay our budget for salaries to keep everyone from leaving. What if it sets a precedent? What if other departments start demanding the same?"

Her smile is knowing, a touch of wisdom in her eyes. "Perspective, Sebastian. Not everyone is Isabella.

Not everyone has personal ties to this company like she does, like you do, like I do, or even Robert. Investors might come and go, but people like us, we stay."

***

The only thing I love about Monday is that it ends. And just like we do at the end of workday, Isabella and I leave work together. It's a small pleasure that adds a touch of joy to the otherwise dreaded day. Even when we don't come in together in the morning, we always manage to leave side by side.

As I walk over to Isabella's office, I see her busy packing her bag. I lean against the doorframe, twirling my car key in my hand. "Ready to go?" I ask, a hint of a smile on my lips.

Isabella turns around, and her face lights up when she sees me. She walks over to me, her steps graceful as always, and I feel my heart skip a beat. She kisses me for a few seconds, a sweet warmth passing between us. "Hey," she says with a soft smile, "I'm not going home directly tonight. Having dinner at my parents' place."

"I'll drive you there and head back home," I reply, the thought of her spending time with her family warming my heart.

She looks straight into my eyes, her gaze holding a mischievous glint. "Just drive me there?" she asks, her tone playfully teasing.

I raise an eyebrow, a bit puzzled by her question. "I guess?"

Isabella chuckles, nudging me out of the way as she walks past me. I follow behind, still slightly confused. We make our way to the elevator, and as the doors close, she looks at me with a smile. "You'll have to come in and join us for dinner," she says.

My confusion replaced by surprise, I laugh. "What if I don't want to meet your parents just yet?"

Isabella holds my arm in hers. "Don't worry, they don't bite."

By the time we arrive at her parents' home, I'm feeling a mix of excitement and nervousness. Meeting her parents feels like a significant step, one that's both thrilling and intimidating. Isabella opens the door, and I step inside, greeted by the warmth of a cozy living room.

Her father, Mr. Rivera, stands by, his demeanor reserved. He extends his hand, and I shake it, introducing myself. Isabella's mother is a burst of energy, her smile infectious, as she approaches me and pulls at my cheeks in a playful manner.

Mr. Rivera's attention turns to my attire. "Nice suit," he comments, and his tone is slightly gruff, yet approving. "Made it at your company?"

I nod, glad that I'm wearing something I've designed. "Yes, we did."

Isabella stands nearby, a smile playing on her lips as she watches the interaction between her father and me. I feel a bit shy, glancing at her from time to time. I want her to come save me.

The conversation turns to Isabella's younger sister, Emily, who isn't present. Her parents explain that Emily has a party to attend tonight, and Isabella shakes her head with a fond smile, indicating that her sister's social life is always bustling.

Dinner is served, and the table is filled with a variety of Italian dishes. There's lasagna, creamy risotto, and tiramisu for dessert. I dig into the food, enjoying the rich flavors and the comfortable atmosphere around the table. I make sure to compliment Isabella's mother on her cooking, and she beams with pride.

Mr. Rivera leans forward, his eyes lighting up with a fervent gleam as he recounts his life experiences. "You know," he begins, "I was part of the team that designed and built the Barclay Tower. It was a monumental project, pushing the boundaries of engineering and design."

I lean in, intrigued by his storytelling. "The Barclay Tower? That's an iconic building," I comment, impressed by the significance of his contribution.

Isabella nods in agreement, her admiration for her father evident. "I've heard you talk about it before, Dad, but it never gets old."

Mr. Rivera smiles. There's a mixture of humility and pride in his expression. "Every building has its own story, its own challenges. But when you see it rise from the blueprint to reality, it's a feeling that's hard to describe."

I find myself nodding in understanding. His passion for his work resonates with me. "Absolutely, the process of turning an idea into a tangible structure must be incredibly rewarding."

Isabella's mother chimes in, "He'd spend nights poring over blueprints, sketching and recalculating. We used to joke that he was more married to his buildings than to me!"

Laughter ripples through the room, and Mr. Rivera joins in with a chuckle. "Well, it's true that engineering and architecture have always been my second and third loves," he admits, his gaze warm as he looks at Isabella's mother.

Isabella leans towards me, her voice a soft whisper. "My dad's stories are endless. He could talk about architecture for hours."

I smile, appreciating the insight into her father's passion. "I can see that. His enthusiasm is contagious."

By the time dessert is served, the conversation naturally drifts towards other topics, and the room is filled with the warm buzz of camaraderie. As the evening winds down, I find myself feeling grateful for the opportunity to witness the genuine love and connection that define Isabella's family.

As we prepare to leave, Mr. Rivera stands and extends his hand towards me, a gesture that speaks of respect and acceptance. "Thank you for joining us tonight," he says, his voice genuine. "It's good to know Isabella has found someone who appreciates her as much as we do."

I shake his hand, touched by his words. "Thank you for having me. It's been an honor."

Isabella's mother offers a warm smile as she approaches, her eyes twinkling with affection. "You're welcome here anytime, dear. Family gatherings are always more joyful with new faces."

I glance at Isabella, gratitude and contentment filling my heart. Her parents' warm reception and the sense of belonging I've experienced tonight reaffirm the connection we share.

. Isabella and I step outside, and she walks with me towards my car. "They like you," she says with a smile.

I chuckle, feeling a mix of relief and satisfaction at her confirmation. "Why do you say that?"

Her eyes sparkle with affection. "Because they don't talk much to anyone they don't like."

— Chapter 26 —
Just Like Always

I sit on a park bench in Central Park with my best friend, Charlotte. Our eyes wander across the different couples passing by—some old, some young. We often point at someone doing something silly and laugh together.

"This is my favorite thing to do," I say, nudging Charlotte as we watch a couple trying to fly a kite with no wind. "Just sitting outside somewhere and watching people scurry around. Everyone with their story, casually blending into the background like side characters when they are actually main characters in their own lives."

Charlotte nods, sharing my sentiment. "Yeah, it's like we're all part of a big story, with little subplots going on simultaneously."

"Oh, by the way," Charlotte says as her mood turned serious. "Emily stopped by the hospital a few days ago to say hi. She mentioned something that happened with you guys."

Sighing, I brace myself for the conversation. "Emily and her stories again. What now?"

"She told me you turned down a huge career opportunity with Craig Stanton's company in Paris because of... Sebastian?"

"Because of him?" I reply, my defensiveness rising. I wonder what she will say if she ever learns that I turned down another big opportunity in Paris for Sebastian.

"Yeah, and I think your relationship with him might be clouding your judgment," Charlotte explains. "People in love can be delusional sometimes."

"I'm not delusional," I assert firmly. "I know Sebastian loves me as much as I love him."

Charlotte probes further, "So it's all about him then?"

I turn away, reluctant to admit the truth. Silence hangs in the air before Charlotte continues, " Sebastian wouldn't refuse a big career opportunity because of you. A man like him would always put his career first."

"Did you put your career first?" I counter, catching her off guard.

Charlotte stumbles to find an answer, but I don't stop there. "Is that why you left your fiancé? To put your career first?"

Before she can reply, I ask her another question, "Have you ever been in love? True love?"

Charlotte's eyes widen, realizing where I'm going with my counter interrogation.

"He has a funny reputation," she finally says. "The media calls him a predator."

I turn to her, my mind swirling with conflicting emotions. "A predator?" I repeat, my voice trembling with disbelief. "That isn't true." I let out a small, annoyed laugh. "You know how the media twists things for sensationalism."

Charlotte sighs, her eyes filled with concern. "I'm just saying, maybe you should be cautious. You've been head over heels for Sebastian, and that's amazing, but it's okay to step back and consider things objectively."

"I know he has a past, Charlotte, but come on, Sebastian isn't a predator. Who's the prey here?" I laugh again. "Me?" It's ridiculous, but even I can hear the defensiveness and vulnerability in my voice. "I believe in him, and I believe in us."

Charlotte reaches out and gently squeezes my hand. "I'm not trying to attack your relationship. I just don't want to see you get hurt."

My gaze hardens, and the small smile dissolves on my face. "I appreciate that, really. But let's change the topic. We should hang out this weekend, yunno?"

"Isabella," Charlotte says, and her voice is as soft as the evening breeze. "I'm worried about you."

My brow furrows, my thoughts churning. "You don't have to be," I say. "I'm happy at Maxwell & Co., and Sebastian supports me in everything I do. It's not a sacrifice if I'm genuinely content with my choices."

"You know how much I support you, too. It's just…" she trails off as if her words went off the tracks, as if resigning herself to my unwillingness to listen to her.

I'm taken aback. "Do you believe those lies?"

Charlotte goes silent, her hesitation speaking volumes.

Knowing the truth, I stand up, grab my bag, and leave without saying a word.

On my way back home, I sit in the back of the taxi, my mind a whirlwind of emotions. Charlotte's words linger in my thoughts, and I can't shake off a strange feeling. I don't know what name to call it, what adjective to use. But I saw the look on her face, and I know for sure what I saw in her eyes.

How could she believe those lies about Sebastian being a predator? She doesn't know him like I do.

My stomach twists into knots as I replay our conversation in the park. Charlotte's concern for me is genuine, I know that. But her doubts about Sebastian and our relationship hurt more than I'd like to admit. It's been a rollercoaster, balancing love, work, family, and friendship, but I never imagined it would become this complex.

Sebastian has given me so much in such a short time. He's the reason I'm making a name for myself in the fashion industry. And now, the offer from Craig Stanton's is a tempting chance to soar to the top. But it feels like a betrayal to even consider leaving Maxwell & Co., where I can still be around Sebastian every day.

The whispers and gossip at the office only add to the pressure. I can feel the board breathing down Sebastian's neck because of our relationship. And after the headlines about our weekend getaway surfaces on the internet, I can't help but wonder if it's all worth it.

But then, there's the trust and support Sebastian has shown me. He's fought for me, for us, against all odds. Leaving now would be like letting him down, like abandoning the love we've built together. I can't bear the thought of hurting him, of breaking his heart.

Yet, there's also a part of me that wonders if I'm losing myself in this relationship. Have I become too entangled in love to see things objectively? My heart races, and I feel the adrenaline rushing through my veins. The conflict within me is tearing me apart.

I look out of the taxi window, the city blurring into a haze. New York, the city of dreams, has become both a sanctuary and a battlefield for me. It's where I found love and success, but it's also where I face the toughest decisions of my life.

I take a deep breath, trying to steady my thoughts. I need to find clarity in this chaos, to remember who I am outside of this relationship. I need to talk to Sebastian, to know if he's truly the man I believe him to be.

The taxi arrives at my apartment building, and I pay the driver absentmindedly. As I step out onto the bustling streets of New York, I feel a mixture of determination and vulnerability. Love, work, family, and friendship—these are the threads that weave the tapestry of my life, and I need to find a way to balance them all.

I take the elevator up to my floor, lost in my thoughts. The key turns in the lock, and I step into my apartment, feeling the weight of the day on my shoulders. The soft lights and familiar surroundings offer comfort, but my mind is still restless.

As I sit on the couch, I realize that I need to have an honest conversation with Sebastian. I need to address my doubts and fears, and I need him to understand how much this decision is tearing me apart.

Love can be messy and complicated, and I have to embrace that reality. It's not all rainbows and butterflies; it's a journey of self-discovery, compromise, and vulnerability.

But as I pick up my phone to make the call, I hear a knock on my door.

I swing open the door, and there stands Charlotte, looking as concerned as she was at the park. My first instinct is to slam the door on her face, but she's too quick for me. She barges in, holding a tabloid that screams scandal in bold, garish letters. I can practically feel my stomach churn at the sight of it

"I'll leave this here," she says, tossing the tabloid onto the kitchen cabinet. "Make your choice, Isabella."

And with that, she turns on her heels and leaves, leaving me dumbfounded and shaking with a mix of anger and confusion. What the hell was that about? I pick up the tabloid, eyeing it warily as if it was a venomous snake about to bite me.

The headline details a love triangle involving Sebastian and two supermodels from his past. My heart sinks as I start skimming through the pages. The story suggests that he is involved in a messy romantic affair with both models simultaneously, leading to heartbreak and betrayal. My mind races with conflicting thoughts.

Surely, they are all lies, right? But what if there's a grain of truth in this whole mess? Doubts about Sebastian's character begin to creep in, and I feel the weight of uncertainty bear down on my chest.

I dial his number, hoping to get some answers. The phone rings, and I can't help but think about how he was with me just last night, whispering sweet nothings in my ear, and now this?! Is any of it real?

As the call goes unanswered, my mind starts playing tricks on me. What if he is avoiding me because there is some truth to the tabloid's claims? My stomach knots with worry and anger. I can't believe he would betray me like this. We have something special, or so I thought.

The words on the tabloid keep taunting me, and I can't shake off the feeling of being played like a fool. I trusted him, given him my heart, and now, I feel like I'm just a pawn in his game of deceit.

I pace around the room, my emotions all over the place. Should I believe the tabloid, or should I have faith in our love? How could he do this to me? Why can't things just be simple and straightforward?

I pick up the tabloid again, rereading the headlines that are now burned into my mind. The public questions Sebastian's ability to be faithful and committed to me, raising doubts about his character.

My heart sinks even further. Is our love just a façade? Are his sweet words just empty promises?

But then, I remember all the times we've laughed together, the late-night conversations we've had, the stolen kisses, and the way he looks at me like I was the only woman in the world. Surely, that can't be fake, right?

I shake my head, trying to clear my thoughts. I can't let a stupid tabloid ruin what we have. I need to talk to him, to hear his side of the story. I call again, hoping he'll pick up this time.

As the phone rings, I can't help but wonder if my world is about to come crashing down. But when he finally answers, I hear his voice, and for a moment, all my doubts fade away. His voice is warm and familiar, just like always.

"Isabella? Is everything alright?"

— Chapter 27 —
A Dangerous Game

"Isabella? Is everything alright?" My voice quivers with concern as I pick up the phone. She's called multiple times, and I know something's wrong.

Somehow, I can't help but think that someone has told her about Victoria's visit to my apartment last night.

***

"The good old days," Victoria reminisced before she put her wine glass to her face.

"The old days, but not the good old days," I replied.

"That's a shame because your life now is so boring, moving so slowly, tending to your father's fires while letting the fire in your heart die out," Victoria prodded.

"I've grown up now," I said calmly as I leaned back into my chair.

"Have you outgrown me now?" Victoria was relentless.

I laughed. "No, Victoria," I replied. "It's just that you represent a life I'd rather leave buried in the past."

"That life?" Victoria teased, "does it bore you now?"

I leaned back and sipped my whiskey, watching her every move. Then, I glanced over the city's skyline from my balcony. I turned back to her. "Look, Victoria," I said, "I'm not that man anymore. I'm madly in love with Isabella. I'm happy with her. What exactly do you want visiting me?"

"I want you back, Sebastian," she said as her eyes sparkled with mischief. She stood up, holding her wine glass, and her backless dress revealed a spine tattoo that oozed sensuality. I was momentarily lost in lust as she sauntered towards the balcony railing.

"What could you possibly be doing with that bore of a designer you're passing time with?" Victoria snarked.

My expression grew serious. I turned to her as I said, gently but firmly, "Isabella is not a bore, and I'm head over heels in love with her."

"Are you, though?" Victoria asked, her tone sly and sarcastic.

I was momentarily conflicted, as if her words had somehow sowed seeds of doubt in my mind. But I shook it off. "I think you need to leave, Victoria."

"Maybe you're right," Victoria said. She walked up to me, kissed my cheek, and then, unexpectedly, dropped her wine glass, letting it shatter on the floor.

"I wonder what Isabella would think of you when she sees those pictures of us in Vegas and Miami, putting coke in your nose. Those sex-tapes. Those pictures. The threesomes. I wonder how she'd look at you after that," Victoria remarks.

***

Isabella's voice comes through the phone, and I can tell from the tone that something is off.

"Hey, Sebastian, there's something I need to talk to you about," she says.

My mind races with possibilities, but I try to remain calm. "Sure, what's up?"

"I'm staring at a tabloid right now, and they have a cover story about you," she says, and her voice is still tinged with concern.

My heart sinks as my mind starts spinning. A story about me? What could they possibly be saying?

"What story?" I ask, trying to sound nonchalant.

"It's about alleged affairs, Sebastian. They're insinuating that there's something you're not telling me." Her voice gets firmer the more she speaks.

I feel a mix of anger and frustration bubbling up inside me. How could they make such baseless accusations?

"Isabella, you know I would never lie to you," I say, although my voice is tinged with defensiveness.

"I want to believe you, Sebastian, but this is all over the news. People are talking about it."

I take a deep breath, trying to find the right words. "Anything they say is in my past, Isabella. Long before I met you. You know I've changed, right?"

There's a pause on the other end, and I can feel the tension building between us.

"I thought I knew you, Sebastian," she says, her voice breaking. "But now I don't know what to believe."

I can feel my own frustration rising. How could she doubt me like this?

"Isabella, please," I plead, my voice filled with emotion. "I would never do anything to hurt you. You have to believe me."

"I don't know what to believe anymore," she says, her voice distant.

My heart races as I hear Isabella's frustrated voice on the other end of the line. "Isabella, frankly, it's all in the past! I've changed, and I swear I'd never do anything to hurt you."

I can almost feel her hesitation, her doubt seeping through the phone. "But how can I be sure, Sebastian? These accusations, these stories, they're all over the news. People are talking about it."

Trying to stay calm, I take a deep breath. "I know it's overwhelming, but you gotta trust me, Isabella. I love you, and I've been honest about everything."

Her voice wavers as she admits, "I wanna believe you, but it's hard. I thought I knew you, but now I don't know what to believe."

I desperately search for the right words. "Isabella, please listen to me. Those moments from my past are long gone. I've worked my ass off to be a better person, for you and for us."

She needs time to think, and I can't blame her. "I need some time to process, Sebastian. This is a lot to take in."

"I get it," I say, my voice tinged with concern that she'll still give up on us. "But don't let this tear us apart. We've been through so much together."

"True," she says, still unsure. "But I can't help but feel hurt and confused right now."

"Isabella, let's talk this through. I don't wanna lose you over something that's not even true."

She sounds torn, and I wish I could hold her hand right now. "I don't wanna lose you either, but I can't ignore what's out there. I need to be sure."

I rack my brain for the perfect response. "Is there anything I can say or do to prove that I'm not that person anymore? That I'm committed to you and only you?"

Her hesitation is evident, and it gnaws at me. "I don't know, Sebastian. It's not just about what you say; it's about how I feel."

I take a deep breath and look straight into her eyes. "I know I was foolish in the past. I don't have a good reputation in that sense. And I'm truly sorry for any pain I've caused you because of the past trace. But please trust me that I'm not the person that I used to be. You're everything to me."

There's a pause on the line as Isabella sorts out her thoughts. The disbelief is loud in her silence.

"Why won't you believe me?" I say, my voice cracking.

"I want to believe you, Sebastian, but this is all so overwhelming," she admits, her voice softening slightly.

I take a deep breath, trying to steady myself. "Isabella, we've been through so much together. Don't let some stupid tabloid stories come between us."

There's a heavy silence on the line, and I can tell that Isabella is struggling with her emotions. The tension between us is palpable, and I wish I could reach through the phone and hold her, reassure her that everything will be okay.

"I need some time to think," she finally says, her voice distant.

"Isabella, please," I say, and my voice is desperate.

But before I can say anything else, I hear a click on the line. She's ended the call.

I sit at my desk, the weight of a boulder in my stomach, my mind racing.

The trust she once had in me was shattered by that damn tabloid. How do I mend this mess? How do I convince her it's all a load of rubbish? Isabella means everything to me, and the thought of losing her sends shivers down my spine.

And then, there's Victoria, lingering like a shadow in the background. I can't shake the feeling that she's somehow behind this media circus, trying to reclaim me. I need to find a way to get rid of her once and for all. But how can I prove it?

Adrenaline courses through my veins, urging me to fight back against the media and protect my relationship with Isabella. I'm torn between wanting to win her back and the need to put Victoria in her place.

Maybe I should talk to Isabella, bare my soul, and spill out my feelings. But what if she doesn't believe me? What if she's already made up her mind?

It's a Friday afternoon, and I'm trapped at my desk, my anxiety growing with each tick of the clock. I can't afford to waste time; this situation demands action.

I need to be smart about this, to keep my emotions in check. Gathering evidence to find out who's behind this malicious rumor seems like a logical step. But where do I start?

Love and hate are two sides of the same coin, and I'm caught in the middle. I'm torn between fighting for my relationship and fighting against those who want to tear it apart. It's a dangerous game, one I must win—for my heart, my ego, and, most importantly, for Isabella.

— Chapter 28 —
A Commitment

I sit at my desk in my office, my eyes fixed on the computer screen, but my mind is consumed by thoughts of him—Sebastian. Our once flourishing relationship is now treading on treacherous grounds. The silence between us is deafening, the tension palpable.

I pretend to be engrossed in my work, but I can't help stealing glances out of the corner of my eye whenever Sebastian passes by my office. He does the same, our eyes locking together for brief moments before quickly looking away. The connection that was once so strong is now frayed, hanging by a thread.

My heart aches with anger and hurt. The feeling of betrayal and humiliation washes over me whenever I think about those scandalous words. I wonder if my colleagues have seen the tabloid, too, given the way they exchange glances or grow awkward whenever I'm around or when Sebastian and I are in the same space.

I want to confront him, demand answers, but the words stick in my throat, stifled by the fear of what I might discover. Instead, I choose silence, using it as a shield to protect my already fragile heart. But with every passing moment, the tension between us grows, mirroring the storm that rages outside the office windows.

As I pretend to sift through some documents, my heart leaps when I hear the soft knock on my partially open door. I know it's him before he even steps inside. Sebastian's tall figure fills the doorway, his dark hair slightly disheveled, a hint of guilt in his eyes.

"Isabella," he begins, his voice gentle but unsure. "Can we talk?"

I avert my gaze, my hands gripping the edge of the desk. "I'm busy right now, Sebastian."

"Please, just a few minutes," he persists and takes a hesitant step closer.

I take a deep breath, mustering the strength to look at him. "Fine, but make it quick."

He enters the room, closing the door behind him. The air thickens with unspoken words and unresolved emotions. He leans against the wall, as if unsure of where to start.

"I know you think what the tabloid said is true," he finally says, his voice tinged with regret.

I clench my jaw, trying to maintain my composure. "And what am I supposed to think, Sebastian? The rumors, the stories..."

He interrupts, his eyes pleading for understanding. "It's not true, Isabella. I promise you. Those stories are fabrications, lies meant to tarnish my reputation."

My voice tinged with bitterness, I retort, "Why should I believe you?"

Sebastian steps closer, his eyes locked on mine. "Because you know me, Isabella. You know the truth in your heart."

Tears well up in my eyes, and I blink them back, refusing to show any vulnerability. "I thought I did."

Sebastian reaches out, as if to touch me, but he hesitates, his hand suspended in the air between us. "Please, let me explain. Let me prove to you that I'm not the person they're painting me to be."

I feel torn, my heart warring between love and doubt. I want to believe him, to trust that our love is strong enough to weather this storm, but the uncertainty gnaws at me.

"Give me some time," I finally whisper. "I need space to process all of this."

Sebastian nods, his expression pained. "I understand. Take all the time you need."

He turns to leave, and my heart aches at the growing distance between us. As he reaches the door, he pauses, looking back at me with a mixture of longing and hope.

"I love you, Isabella," he says softly. "And I will do whatever it takes to earn back your trust."

I nod, my throat tight with emotion. "I love you, too, but I need to figure things out."

With that, Sebastian leaves me alone with my turbulent thoughts and emotions. The silence lingers, but now, it feels heavier than ever. As the storm outside begins to subside, I know that the storm within my heart is far from over. The road to healing our fractured relationship will be long and uncertain, but I'm determined to find the truth and, above all, to rediscover the love that once bound us together.

Later that day, at the cafeteria, I'm lost in my thoughts, staring blankly at nothing in particular, when a voice interrupts my internalized debate.

"Hey, Isabella! Mind if we join you?" Mark, one of my closest friends at work, asks with a warm smile, gesturing to a few other coworkers behind him.

I manage a weak smile in return and gesture for them to sit down. Soon, my table is filled with laughter and chatter, but despite my colleagues' best efforts, I can't fully engage. I appreciate their kindness, but there's a heaviness in my heart that I can't shake off.

Maria, another colleague, tries to lift the mood with a joke. "So, did you guys hear about the new intern who spilled coffee all over Mr. Henderson's files this morning?"

I chuckle, trying to play along, but my mind keeps drifting back to my own troubles. I can't escape the tabloid rumors about Sebastian's affairs, and the uncertainty gnaws at me.

The conversation meanders through office gossip, weekend plans, and new fashion trends, but I find myself zoning out more frequently. I wonder if my colleagues know about the rumors but choose to remain silent out of respect for me. Maybe they think talking about it would only make me feel worse.

"Hey, Isabella, are you okay?" Mark asks, his concern evident.

I snap back to the present and force a smile. "Yeah, just a bit distracted, that's all."

"We're here for you, you know? If you ever want to talk about anything," Maria adds, her voice gentle.

I nod, touched by their support. I know they mean well, but the weight of the rumors about Sebastian lingers in my mind, clouding my thoughts.

As the lunch hour goes on, I find myself growing more restless. The cafeteria, usually filled with laughter and camaraderie, now feels suffocating. I excuse myself from the table, claiming I have an urgent email to respond to, and retreat to a quiet corner of the office.

I pull out my phone and stare at a photo of Sebastian and me taken during our weekend getaway in California. Doubts and questions plague me, and I can't bear the idea of losing him. But the uncertainty of his loyalty keeps haunting me.

Later that day, I find myself in the elevator with Sebastian, our eyes meeting briefly before he looks away. We exchange polite but distant greetings, and my heart sinks further.

The days pass, and I continue to navigate the office with a heavy heart. My colleagues try to be there for me, but some things are just too difficult to discuss. I appreciate their efforts, but I can't bring myself to burden them with my personal turmoil.

As I return to my desk after another long day, I can't help but feel the weight of the uncertainty bearing down on me. The cafeteria, once a place of camaraderie, now feels like a reminder of everything I'm trying to escape. The rumors and the distant behavior from Sebastian have made my days feel longer, and the future more uncertain than ever.

I know that, eventually, I will have to confront the truth and have an honest conversation with Sebastian, but for now, I need time to gather my thoughts and find the strength to face whatever lies ahead.

***

My fingers dance across the keyboard, fully immersed in my work on the latest fashion collection. The soft hum of the computer and the occasional scribble of a pencil are the only sounds in my serene office.

Suddenly, the door creaks open, and my heart skips a beat. It's Jennifer, the head of design, a formidable woman known for her high standards and meticulous eye for detail. She rarely graces my office with her presence unless she has something to critique or complain about. Her visits often leave me feeling uneasy, making me doubt my abilities and push myself even harder to achieve perfection in my work.

But as Jennifer enters the room, something feels different. Her normally stern expression is replaced by a warm smile, and her eyes hold a glimmer of appreciation.

"Isabella," Jennifer begins, her voice surprisingly gentle. "May I have a moment?"

"Of course," I reply, trying to maintain my composure despite the anxiety bubbling inside me.

Jennifer takes a seat across from my desk and leans forward. "I wanted to talk to you about something important."

My chest tightens, expecting the usual critique that leaves me feeling inadequate. However, Jennifer's words take a different turn.

"I need to apologize," Jennifer admits, her smile faltering just slightly. "In the past, I may have doubted your abilities and overlooked your talent and successes. I realize now that I haven't given you the recognition you deserve."

My eyes widen in astonishment. This is not the conversation I expected. Jennifer, the woman who rarely shows vulnerability, is acknowledging her own shortcomings and apologizing for them.

"You are a brilliant designer, Isabella," Jennifer continues, her tone sincere. "Your creativity and passion shine through in every piece you create. I should have acknowledged that earlier, and I regret not doing so."

My heart swells with mixed emotions. On one hand, I'm grateful for Jennifer's unexpected praise and apology. On the other hand, the weight of her previous doubts still lingers, making me wonder if I truly deserve this newfound recognition.

"I appreciate your words, Jennifer," I reply. My voice is soft but genuine. "It means a lot to me to hear this from you."

Jennifer nods, seemingly relieved to have finally expressed her feelings. "You've proven yourself time and again, and I want to assure you that your work is valued here."

As I absorb Jennifer's words, a sense of validation washes over me. This simple interaction, though unexpected, lifts a burden from my shoulders. I may still be grappling with my troubles outside of work, my turbulent relationship with Sebastian weighing heavily on my heart, but for this moment, I feel a little at peace.

"Thank you, Jennifer," I say, my voice steadier now. "Your acknowledgment means more to me than you know."

Jennifer rises from her seat, her smile returning. "You're welcome, Isabella. Keep up the great work, and don't hesitate to reach out if you need anything."

With that, Jennifer leaves the office, gifting me with a newfound sense of confidence and pride in my work. It's a small step, but a significant one in mending the relationship between the head of design and me.

As I return to my work, my mind shifts away from the troubles that have been consuming me. The weight on my chest eases, if only for a moment, as I continue to pour my passion into my designs. Jennifer's apology has opened a door to a new understanding, one that makes me believe in my talent and abilities once again.

I know that my relationship with Sebastian still needs attention and resolution, but for now, I find solace in the fact that someone at work, especially someone as influential as Jennifer, appreciates my artistry. With a renewed sense of purpose, I delve back into my designs, determined to make my mark in the fashion world, both in my career and in my personal life.

***

As the soft glow of the evening light streams through the windows, I'm lost in my thoughts, trying to find clarity in the middle of all the madness. It's been about two weeks since I last spoke to Sebastian.

Suddenly, a knock at the door snaps me back to the present. I approach cautiously, peeking through the peephole to see who it is. My breath catches as I see Sebastian, standing there looking strikingly handsome, brushing his hair back with his hand, holding a single flower.

He knocks again, and I hesitate before finally opening the door. I stand in the doorway, keeping a slight distance between us. Sebastian's eyes soften as he sees me, and he holds out the flower to me.

"Can I come in?" he asks gently. His voice makes my heart melt, but I am still upset. I cannot show him any softness yet.

Reluctantly, I step aside and allow him to enter. He walks in, and the scent of the flower fills the room. Sebastian looks at me, searching for any sign of forgiveness. I can't bring myself to meet his gaze fully, so I focus on the flower in my hands.

"I know it won't fix everything, but I hope it shows you how much I care about you."

He takes a deep breath and takes a step closer, reaching out to touch my cheek. "Isabella, I need you to know that I'm truly sorry. I should have been honest with you from the beginning about my past. But I was afraid of losing you, and I thought keeping it a secret would protect us."

I turn away, trying to hold back tears. "You should have trusted me enough to tell me. Keeping secrets only breeds more mistrust."

Sebastian gently turns me to face him again. "I know, and I've learned my lesson. I promise I will be completely honest with you from now on. You are the most important person in my life, and I can't bear the thought of losing you."

I want to believe him, but the wounds are still fresh, and I can't shake the feeling that I'm not enough for him. He's successful, charming, and attractive—a magnet for attention. The media story about his affairs with other women has fueled my insecurity, making me doubt our relationship.

He takes both my hands in his, looking into my eyes with sincerity. "Isabella, those flings were a reckless part of my past, but they mean nothing to me now. None of those women matter. You matter, and only you. I love you, with all my heart, and I want to spend the rest of my life with you."

Tears spill down my cheeks as I try to hold back my emotions. But my walls are crumbling, and his words are breaking through the barriers I've built. I turn briskly away from him towards the window, staring straight ahead into the street below.

By the time I turn back to say something, I find him on one knee, pulling out a small box with a beautiful diamond ring inside. "Isabella, will you marry me? I want to prove to you that you're the only one I want, that you're the one I choose every day."

The words run back down my throat, and my eyes well up some more.

I'm speechless, my heart torn between my lingering doubts and the love I still feel for him. But as I look into his eyes, I see the vulnerability and sincerity in them. This moment is different; he's not just apologizing, he's making a commitment, a promise for the future.

"Yes," I blurt out, my voice choking with emotion. "Yes, Sebastian, I will marry you."

Sebastian's face lights up, and he slips the ring onto my finger. I throw my arms around him, finally allowing myself to fully feel his embrace. The walls around my heart begin to crumble, and I let go of the pain that has been consuming me.

"I love you, Isabella," Sebastian whispers, holding me close. "I will spend the rest of my life making it up to you and showing you how much you mean to me."

— Chapter 29 —
Meant To Be

I think planning a wedding is difficult, but attending one where you are the groom is even more tasking than I thought. I stand there with my heart in my mouth, the priest one step above me, my eyes steadfast on the door. Isabella will enter anytime from now.

It's the beginning of winter, and everyone is dressed almost to their teeth. Weather aside, the pews hold some of the most dignified fashion icons in the world, from New York to Europe. Everyone has come to show off, to show out. I'm not complaining, though. It's a fitting atmosphere for a fitting wedding, for a fitting couple.

The majestic cathedral church in downtown New York City stands tall and proud, its grand facade an imposing sight against the backdrop of the chilly winter sky. The opulent decorations adorning the interior, including white orchids and roses in crystal vases, create an atmosphere of pure elegance and luxury, befitting the fashion world elites gathered here to witness the union of Isabella and me.

As I stand at the altar, my heart races with a mix of excitement and nerves, waiting for the moment that will change my life forever. The soft music begins to play, signaling the arrival of my beloved Isabella. My breath catches in my throat as she steps into the cathedral, looking like a vision of beauty in her exquisite designer gown. Her father, Mr. Rivera, walks her down the aisle, pride and bittersweet emotion visible in his eyes.

As the seconds tick by, my old friends clap me on the back, offering a reassuring smile. "Sebastian is getting married! You've got this, man." they shout, reflecting the same disbelief we all share about how our lives have changed since Isabella's talent graced our company.

Suddenly, a soft melody begins to play, and the atmosphere grows more ethereal, signaling Isabella's imminent arrival. All heads turn toward the grand entrance, where her silhouette slowly emerges. My breath catches as I lay eyes on her, and the world seems to stand still, leaving only her in focus.

Isabella glides down the aisle like a goddess, her gown a masterpiece of her own design, accentuating her every curve with grace and elegance. The guests gasp in awe, and I feel pride swell within me, knowing that she isn't just joining my life; she is merging our artistic souls into a single force to be reckoned with.

The closer Isabella comes, the more my nerves transform into an overwhelming sense of certainty. It is as if the universe has conspired to bring us together, two creative souls destined to create not only fashion but a love story that will outshine every collection we'll ever showcase.

As she reaches my side, our eyes lock, and I can see the love and determination in her gaze. There is no doubt in her heart, just as there is none in mine. The priest begins the ceremony, his voice resonating like a harmony amidst the silence, binding our destinies together.

"Dearly beloved, we are gathered here today to witness the power of love and the union of two souls," he begins, capturing the attention of the guests.

Isabella looks into my eyes, her heart brimming with emotion, as she begins her vows. "Sebastian, from the moment we met, I knew there was something special between us. You are my rock, my confidant, and my biggest supporter. I promise to stand by your side through thick and thin, to cherish and honor you, and to love you unconditionally for all the days of my life."

Tears glisten in my eyes as I hold her hands, feeling the weight and sincerity of her words. "Isabella, you are my everything," I say, my voice filled with love. "You make my world brighter and complete. I promise to be there for you in every moment, to hold you close during the storms of life, and to be your biggest cheerleader in all your dreams and aspirations."

As we exchange vows, the cathedral becomes a cocoon of love, with the warm support of our cherished guests enveloping us. The air is thick with emotion, and we can feel the love and happiness surrounding us.

"I, Sebastian, take you, Isabella, to be my lawfully wedded wife, to have and to hold, from this day forward, for better, for worse, for richer, for poorer, in sickness and in health, until death do us part."

"I, Isabella, take you, Sebastian, to be my lawfully wedded husband, to have and to hold, from this day forward, for better, for worse, for richer, for poorer, in sickness and in health, until death do us part."

Before I can hear the words, "You may kiss the bride," I lean in, and sink my lips down onto hers, and everything else fades in the background. Even the sounds of hands clapping in applause.

Later, we perform the unity candle ritual, and as the candle's flames merge into one, I fight back tears threatening to roll down my cheeks.

***

The Rolls Royce eases into the driveway of the majestic mansion, tucked away between trees in Staten Island. I feel a surge of pride and disbelief as I look at the grand building before me. Just a couple of weeks ago, my relationship with Isabella was hanging on a thread, and now, here we are, married and about to start a new life together in this beautiful house.

"Where are we, Sebastian?" Isabella asks, peering out of the tinted window as the car comes to a stop.

I smile at her with a glimmer of excitement in my eyes. "This is going to be our new home," I say, feeling a mix of nervousness and anticipation. I purchased the place a week ago, wanting something that reminded me of my father's estate, a place where we could build a life together.

As I help Isabella out of the car, delicate snowflakes begin to fall from the sky. She gasps with excitement, and in that moment, I can't resist the urge to sweep her off her feet. I scoop her up into my arms, relishing the warmth of her body against mine, and carry her towards the front door.

Isabella laughs playfully as she wraps her arms around my neck. "Oh, Sebastian! You romantic fool!" she teases, her eyes sparkling with love and happiness.

I grin, feeling a rush of affection for my new wife. "I can't help it," I confess, my voice filled with tenderness. "You make me want to do all these crazy, romantic things."

As we step inside the house, Isabella's excitement only grows. She rushes from room to room, exploring our new home with childlike wonder. "This place is incredible!" she exclaims, running her fingers along the elegant furniture and admiring the artwork on the walls.

I watch her, unable to tear my eyes away. She's like a whirlwind of joy and beauty, and I find myself irresistibly drawn to her. I loved her from the moment we met, but seeing her now, so full of life and happiness, makes my heart swell with love.

"You're incredible," I whisper, unable to hold back my feelings any longer.

Isabella turns to me, her eyes softening with emotion. "And you're my everything," she replies and takes a step closer to me.

I wrap my arms around her, pulling her close. The snow outside falls gently, creating a cozy and intimate atmosphere inside the house. "I can't believe we're married," I admit, my voice tinged with awe.

She smiles as her fingers gently caress my cheek. "I can't believe it, either, but I'm so glad we are."

I lean in, my lips meeting hers in a tender kiss. It's a kiss filled with love, promise, and the hope of a beautiful future together. We stand there, holding each other, as if we're the only two people in the world.

At this moment, I know that this is where I'm meant to be. With Isabella by my side, in our new home, I feel complete. The past no longer matters; all that matters is the love we share and the life we're going to build together.

As we pull away from the kiss, Isabella looks up at me with eyes that hold a lifetime of love. "I love you, Sebastian," she says, her voice barely above a whisper.

"And I love you, Isabella," I reply. Such a perfect day.

— Chapter 30 —
Now And Forever

Sebastian wasn't lying when he said he knew how to dance. But what I'm currently not sure of is how he's going to teach me how to dance like he promised. So, I watch him lock the door as soon as he enters the room.

He's wearing a large T-shirt that's doing so little to hide his broad shoulders. Anyone can see, even while he's clothed, that whoever carved him was as patient as a monk. Maybe even more patient. He's certainly the most beautiful man I've ever laid my eyes on. Especially the way the lights are touching his face right now.

The room feels warmer now, and the soft glow of the lamp adds to the romantic atmosphere. I'm not sure what he has in mind, but I'm eager to find out.

Sebastian walks towards the vintage record player in the corner of the room, a mischievous grin playing on his lips. He takes out an old vinyl record and places it gently on the turntable. The familiar tune of "Hotel California" starts to fill the air, and my heart skips a beat. It's one of our favorite songs, and it was on repeat when we visited California together.

He extends his hand towards me, and I can't resist taking it. As I stand in front of him, he places his other hand on my waist, pulling me closer. We sway gently to the music, our bodies moving in perfect harmony. It's like we've danced to this song a thousand times before, and yet, it feels fresh and new, just like our love.

"You remember the first time we danced to this song?" Sebastian asks, his voice soft and nostalgic.

"Of course," I answer. "How could I possibly forget?"

"Good," he says, "because I'm going to do things to you tonight that you'll never forget, either," he whispers, almost as if there's someone else in the room who can hear him if he speaks up.

But I like it, the hot breath on my neck, which sends shivers down my spine for so many reasons.

Sebastian's eyes soften, and he pulls me even closer, our bodies pressed together.

We start to dance, lost in each other's embrace, the world outside the room fading away. With every step, every sway, I feel the love and connection between us grow stronger. It's as if time stands still, and in this moment, there's only us and the music that binds us together.

As the song nears its end, Sebastian dips me slightly, and I laugh in delight. It's a move he's always loved to do, and it never fails to make me feel like we're in our own little fairytale.

When the song finally ends, we remain in each other's arms, catching our breaths. The silence between us speaks volumes, and I know that despite the challenges and changes we've faced, our love is still as strong as ever.

"You promised to teach me how to dance," I remind him playfully.

Sebastian chuckles, the sound like music to my ears. "Well, I think you've got the hang of it already," he says, his eyes twinkling with love and admiration.

"But I want you to teach me some more," I say, not ready to let go of the moment just yet.

He raises an eyebrow, a teasing glint in his eyes. "Are you sure? I might be a tough dance instructor," he teases.

I grin, feeling bold and adventurous. "I'm up for the challenge," I reply.

Sebastian pulls me closer until I can feel my stiffening breasts pressing against his muscular chest. My night dress does so little to hide the feeling of my nipples on his chest. As we continue to dance, his voice fades into the background, and all I can hear is the music wafting around the room. I pretend to dance along with him when all I just want to do is rip his T-shirt off his shoulders and have him sit on the edge of the bed as I worship the entirety of his body.

I wonder if he wants the same, too. If he's thinking of me the way I am thinking of him. If he's looking at me with lustful eyes, thinking about the easiest way to rid me of whatever I'm wearing now. If he wants me just as much as I want him and he's only pretending to dance to while away time.

By the time the music stops, there's nothing left for Sebastian and I to do. So, we just stand there, his hands around my waist, our eyes locking together.

I can feel myself tingling in between my inner thighs. There's something eye contact does to me. And Sebastian knows this, so he doesn't hold back. Instead, he stares harder, letting the silence beat me into wanting him more with each passing second.

There are a lot of things Sebastian is good at. He knows how to hold a room by the scruff of the neck. The way he handles himself, the way he moves in rooms full of sharks and crocodiles. The way he dresses. A lot of things.

But I wonder if anyone has ever told him how good he is in the art of kissing and sex.

Perhaps he knows this, perhaps he doesn't. And if he does, maybe it's the reason he's so confident as a man. As confident as any man can be. Perhaps it's knowing how much ability he has to bend any woman to his will. To make them feel things they didn't know they could feel. Reach points and parts of their bodies they didn't know could be reached.

Is it atrocious to think of your husband's past sex-capades with other women on your wedding night? Wondering has never killed any woman.

I want him to touch me, in the most inappropriate way possible. I want him to toss me around like a rag doll and rail me like it's his last night with me. His eyes are still burning through me, and his gaze drops as he stares down at my breasts.

Without hesitation, I reach out and cup his face in my hands and stretch to meet his lips. As our lips meet, he sweeps me closer until he's almost squeezing me in his embrace. Our eyes are closed, and our lips are like gateways through which we can simply walk in to search each other's soul.

I started it. But Sebastian doesn't stop as I start to moan in his mouth. Then, frantically, he pulls away and pulls his T-shirt over his head with so much vigor. I watch him fling it somewhere on the floor as I retreat onto the bed behind us.

Sebastian moves over me slowly to me, like a hunting tiger. Sebastian reaches for my dress and yanks it until my left breast becomes visible. Before I have any more time to react, he stares wordlessly into my eyes and grabs me. I smile a little as he keeps eye contact while twirling his tongue around my areola, teasing me. He always starts with my left breast. Then, slowly, he starts to ease into me, his body swelling and diving like waves of the oceans.

"I want nothing more than this." His voice is raspy, almost out of breath. "Right now, and right here. And forever."

— Chapter 31 —
The Unspoken Understanding

The Rolls Royce pulls up to the towering glass building that houses my Maxwell & Co. Isabella takes a deep breath, and I can see that she's nervous. Hell, I'm nervous, too. I mean, what do you expect after spending a glorious week in paradise with the woman you love, only to be thrown back into the chaos of the corporate world?

The entrance is adorned with massive floral arrangements, courtesy of our overenthusiastic PR team. They must've thought it'd be a great idea to celebrate our return like some celebrity couple. I can't blame them; Isabella does have that star quality. As we step out of the car, the staff stands in a neat line, clapping and cheering like we just won the fashion Olympics.

"Bit over the top, don't you think?" I whisper to Isabella, trying to hide my amusement.

She giggles softly, her hand squeezing mine. "Just a tad, but it's sweet. They missed you, you know."

I smile, feeling a warmth in my chest. "They missed you too, Bella," I say, using the nickname that always makes her blush.

We walk hand in hand, and as we approach the entrance, I feel a mix of pride and anxiety. I know I should be elated, given the success of the company and the amazing honeymoon, but there's this nagging feeling at the back of my mind. The weight of responsibilities bears down on my shoulders like never before.

Frankly, I'm used to being in control. As the CEO, I'm supposed to have all the answers, make all the tough calls. But right now, all I want to do is hold Isabella's hand and escape to a beach somewhere.

The staff is cheering, and I spot familiar faces, some of them giving me thumbs-ups and others sending playful winks. I can't help but chuckle. "You're quite the sensation, you know," I tell Isabella.

She rolls her eyes playfully. "Oh, please. They're just excited to have their favorite boss back."

"They're excited about us," I correct her, a teasing glint in my eye.

Isabella blushes, and I know she loves the attention as much as she pretends not to. We finally make it through the staff line and step into the bustling lobby. The energy is contagious, but there's a part of me that longs for the quiet serenity of the home we left behind.

"I hope you know what you're getting into," I say to Isabella as we head towards my office. "Things might start to get crazier."

"I've dealt with divas and drama queens on the runway. I think I can handle a few suits," she quips, a hint of sass in her voice.

I laugh. "You have no idea, but you know I'm not just talking about suits. I'm talking about the people in them."

Once inside my office, I sink into the leather chair behind the desk, and Isabella perches on the edge. I can see the excitement in her eyes as she takes in the grandeur of space.

"You know, I never imagined I'd be here, in this position," I confess, my tone turning more contemplative. "But I'm grateful for everything. For you, for the company's success. It's just that sometimes, it feels like I'm living two different lives."

Isabella leans closer, her hand finding mine. "You don't have to be two different people. You can be Sebastian, the CEO, and Sebastian, the man who loves his wife and enjoys lazy days on the beach."

"I know." I sigh, feeling a weight-lifting off my shoulders just by her touch. "I guess I'm still figuring it all out."

"That's okay," she says, her voice reassuring. "We'll figure it out together."

And in that moment, I realize how lucky I am to have her by my side. She's not just my wife; she's my anchor, my confidante, and my inspiration. As I look into her eyes, I know that no matter how crazy the corporate world gets, as long as I have her, everything will be alright.

So, maybe I don't hate this Monday after all. It's the day I return to work, yes, but also the day I return with the love of my life, and that's something worth celebrating. With a smile on my face and a newfound sense of determination, I know that together, Isabella and I can conquer anything that comes our way. Even the craziest of Mondays.

***

Almost as if she's been waiting for our honeymoon to be over, the head of design, Jennifer, tells me that Isabella wants all of us to see her new designs.

Her new designs?

We've been together for a week, so how am I the last to hear she's got new designs?

So, I just sit there, in the room, watching everyone scurry around the table. Her presence commands attention, and as I watch her, I can't help but get lost in the sway of her every movement. There's something mesmerizing about the way she presents her vision for the upcoming collection.

She's wearing a gown that perfectly complements her artistic spirit—a flowing, colorful masterpiece that accentuates her every curve. It's impossible not to be attracted to her, to the way she effortlessly blends elegance and creativity. I try to shake off my thoughts, knowing this is not the time or place for such distractions. Dirty thoughts, indeed.

"Thank you all for being here," she begins, her voice carrying a mix of confidence and humility. "I've been working on something I truly believe will take us to new heights, challenge us to explore uncharted territories in the world of design."

Her words hang in the air, and I watch as the team leans forward, eager to hear what she has in store for us. Isabella gestures to the projector screen, and with a click, the room is bathed in the soft glow of her presentation.

"We've had incredible success with our current collection, and I couldn't be prouder of what we've achieved together," Isabella continues, her gaze sweeping across the faces of our colleagues. "But as artists and creators, we must not be content to rest on our laurels. We have the talent, the passion, and the courage to push boundaries and redefine what's possible in the fashion world."

She starts unveiling her designs, and a gasp ripples through the room. They are bold, daring, and undeniably unique. The colors, the textures, the silhouettes—everything is a departure from the familiar aesthetics we've grown accustomed to. It's as if she's tapped into a well of inspiration that knows no bounds.

"These pieces are an exploration of contrasts," she explains, her hands moving gracefully to emphasize her point. "They blend the traditional with the avantgarde, the past with the future. It's about celebrating individuality and empowering the wearer to embrace their true selves fearlessly."

The team is visibly impressed, their eyes glued to the screen, soaking in the vivid details of Isabella's designs. But as the initial excitement settles, I notice the flicker of uncertainty in their expressions. They exchange glances, unspoken questions passing between them. Is it too soon to venture into a whole new territory? Will our customers embrace such a radical departure?

I can understand their apprehension, for I, too, feel a twinge of doubt. But as I steal a glance at Isabella, I'm reminded of her unwavering belief in her creative instincts. She's never been one to shy away from taking risks, and those risks have paid off time and again.

"You might wonder if it's too soon," Isabella says, her voice a calming presence amidst the sea of thoughts swirling in the room. "But that's the beauty of creativity—it's boundless. Our current collection has been a resounding success, and I'm immensely proud of what we've accomplished. But if we stay within the safe confines of what we know, we'll never discover what we're truly capable of."

As her words wash over us, I feel a mix of pride and concern. I'm proud of the fearless woman before me, the one who isn't afraid to challenge the status quo, but I worry about the risks involved. However, in her eyes, I see passion burning bright, and I know I can't stand in the way of her creative journey.

So, I decide to trust her, to trust the spark of her genius. After all, she's not just my wife; she's an artist, a visionary. And though it's a delicate balance, I choose to embrace her vision wholeheartedly.

As the presentation continues, my thoughts drift to our journey together. I recall the first time I saw Isabella's sketches, her artistry leaping off the pages and into my heart. She bewitched me then, just as she does now, and I realize that my romantic obsession with her is not just based on her physical allure but also on her boundless creativity and unwavering spirit.

In a world full of conformity, Isabella is a beacon of individuality. And that's why I'm drawn to her like a moth to a flame, unable to resist the magnetic pull of her brilliance.

As her presentation comes to an end, the room erupts into applause. I clap, too. Maybe even louder than everyone else. But I still do not agree with her.

. Isabella's vision is inspiring, but a part of me worries that we should milk the current collection for a while, bask in its glory. I glance at her, hoping she would notice my unease, but she's entirely immersed in her presentation.

"Sebastian, what do you think?" Robert finally asks, breaking the silence. I know the intentions behind the question. The old man likes to put me in tight corners. I know he feels the same way I feel about this new approach.

I'm torn between supporting my wife's creativity and expressing my reservations. I clear my throat, trying to find the right words.

"It's a fantastic concept, Isabella, there's no doubt about that," I begin, choosing my words carefully. "But maybe we could give the current collection a bit more time in the spotlight. People have fallen in love with it, and we should savor that success."

Isabella turns to me, her eyes searching for understanding. She knows me too well not to notice my hesitancy. "I get what you're saying, Sebastian," she replies, her voice steady, "but we can't let fear of change hold us back. We need to take risks, push boundaries. That's what got us here in the first place."

***

The dim light from the bedside lamp bathes the room as Isabella steps out of the bathroom, her hair cascading down her shoulders in waves. She's wearing cozy pajamas that somehow manage to make her look even more beautiful. I can't help but smile as she climbs into bed next to me, her eyes sparkling with mischief.

"Hey there, handsome," she says, leaning in for a kiss.

I gladly meet her lips with mine, savoring the taste of her sweetness. "You look gorgeous," I murmur against her lips.

She chuckles, running her fingers through my hair playfully. "You always say that," she teases.

"Well, it's true," I reply, pulling her close as we settle into a comfortable embrace. "You know, I think you should wear pajamas all day, every day.""

She laughs, a melodic sound that warms my heart. "And who's going to take me seriously if I do that?"

"Who needs to be taken seriously?" I chuckle. "Where are the pajama police in this room?"

"Are you saying I look better in pajamas?" Isabella asks, her eyebrows locking as she squints, almost as if she's waiting to assess my answer.

I laugh. "You look great in anything you wear, my love," I say. I lean in to plant a kiss on her lips. "It's just that you look much more vulnerable sauntering around like that."

"You like vulnerable?"

"I like carefree."

Our bodies press closer, and I feel the heat rising in my cheeks. There's something electrifying about this moment, a solid energy that draws us together.

Amidst the laughter and teasing, I can't help but wonder why I was the last to know about Isabella's new ideas for the collection. "Why keep it a secret from me?" I ask, my tone curious.

Isabella looks at me, her expression contemplative. "I like surprises," she replies with a mischievous glint in her eyes. "Besides, it's unprofessional to discuss work at home."

I chuckle, shaking my head. "Says the one who was designing during our honeymoon," I tease, recalling the times she couldn't resist sketching new ideas even then.

She playfully nudges my shoulder. "Workaholic, remember?"

"But you're my workaholic," I say, my voice tinged with affection.

As the playful banter subsides, the air between us becomes charged with an unspoken tension. I can tell there's more to her decision than just wanting to surprise me. There's a depth to her emotions that she hasn't fully expressed.

"Why didn't you tell me earlier?" I ask again.

Isabella takes a moment to compose her thoughts, her fingers tracing patterns on my chest. "I wanted to make sure the ideas were fully formed before sharing them," she begins. "And honestly, I was afraid of facing objections. I knew you'd be cautious about jumping into something new."

I nod, understanding her perspective. "You're right. I do like to take things slow, especially when it comes to big decisions. But it's not that I objected to your ideas; I just thought we should give the current collection more time to shine."

Isabella's eyes soften, and she leans in to place a tender kiss on my cheek. "I know you always have our best interests at heart, Sebastian. I appreciate that about you."

As we lie there, wrapped in each other's embrace, I can't help but feel a deep sense of connection. It's not just physical attraction; it's a soul-deep bond that makes us melt into each other's bodies and hearts. Our desires simmer beneath the surface, the unspoken tension palpable.

I look into her eyes, and for a moment, everything else fades away. There's an intensity in her gaze that makes my heart race. It's as if she's baring her soul to me, and I can feel the raw emotions coursing through her.

"Where do you see yourself in the next five years?" I ask, genuinely curious about her dreams.

Isabella's expression becomes contemplative, and she takes a moment to gather her thoughts. "I want to be big in the industry," she begins, her voice filled with determination. "I want to create designs that are not just beautiful, but meaningful. I dream of having my own fashion line, one that's known worldwide for its innovation and authenticity. I want to make a mark, leave a legacy."

Her words send a shiver down my spine. There's a fire in her, a passion that ignites something primal within me. I can't help but be drawn to her ambition, to the woman who dreams so big and works so hard to make those dreams a reality.

As we lie there, our bodies pressed together, the sexual tension between us is palpable. It's a dance of desire and restraint, a magnetic pull that leaves us both yearning for more. The room feels charged with electric energy, and I can sense that Isabella feels it, too.

Her fingers trace lazy patterns on my chest, and I catch my breath as she leans in, her lips hovering just inches from mine. Our eyes lock, and in that moment, there's nothing else in the world but the two of us, caught in the intoxicating dance of desire.

But as the moment lingers, we both pull back, our lips barely grazing. We exchange a knowing smile, the unspoken understanding lingering in the air.

— Chapter 32 —
Navigating

It's been two years since Sebastian and I tied the knot. Jennifer retired, and I was promoted to head of design at Maxwell & Co. But convincing my colleagues that my marriage to their boss isn't the sole reason for the position is a bit of a struggle. Sure, maybe it contributes a little, but Jennifer herself recommended me for the role, claiming I had some fiery potential to take the company to higher places. Or so Sebastian said.

But was he just lying to make me feel better?

Who knows. In two years, a lot has happened—problems, solutions, you name it. Yet, I can't shake this feeling of stagnation at Maxwell & Co., though I keep it all to myself. Everyone I meet praises me, telling me how proud they are. But deep down, I yearn to break free from my comfort zone, to explore new avenues, and embrace creative freedom. Starting a fashion line has always been my dream.

However, where do I even begin? I can't collaborate with Maxwell & Co. and risk them taking a cut of my profits while using their marketing budget for my independent designs. That's just not going to work.

Speaking of things happening in two years, Craig Stanton's expansion hit a roadblock due to some internal conflict among the boards. Many pulled out, leaving Daniel Stanton stranded. I noticed they were going to lease the building they bought for the New York expansion just two weeks ago.

So, impulsively, I pick up Daniel's card and call.

"Hello, Isabella," he greets. "Long time no see."

As I hesitate a little over the phone, Daniel's distinct British accent crackles through the static. It's odd, yet comforting, to hear that familiar voice after so long.

"How have you been, Isabella?" he inquires politely.

"I've been doing well, Daniel," I reply, trying to match his composed tone.

"I apologize for not attending your wedding, Isabella. It was all over the news. But I was in Milan at the time," he says, and his tone is sincere.

A soft laugh escapes my lips. "Time flies, doesn't it? Well, we're talking now, and that's what matters."

We continue chatting about the problems he's been facing with Craig Stanton's expansion. He sighs heavily, revealing the weight of the challenges he's dealing with. "I'll be returning to London soon, and we'll have to put the expansion on hold for now," he admits.

Sympathy swells within me, and I can't help but feel for him. "Daniel, I might have an idea," I say cautiously. "I've drawn up a plan for a potential collaboration with Craig Stanton's. Maybe we can work together and find a solution."

He sounds intrigued. "Oh, really""

"Of course," I say confidently. "I've also been harboring some designs I want to bring to life. You know, creative and artistic freedom."

"Why aren't you doing that at Maxwell & Co. now that you're the head of design?" he inquires, genuine curiosity evident in his voice.

I pause, considering how to phrase my response. "While I'm grateful for the position, I can't ignore the desire for something more. I want to step outside my comfort zone and pursue my vision without any constraints."

He seems to understand, and after a moment of silence, he suggests, "This isn't something we should discuss over the phone. Let's meet for lunch tomorrow. I'll clear my schedule."

I agree wholeheartedly. "That sounds like a plan," I say with a newfound sense of excitement. "We can talk in detail about everything then."

As we're about to say our goodbyes, the phone line starts to go static. "See you tomorrow, Daniel," I say, hoping he hears me.

"I'm looking forward to it, Isabella," he replies, his voice slightly distorted by the interference. "Until then."

***

We're sitting at the dinner table, Sebastian and I, relishing the delicious lasagna he cooked. Oh, my husband, the culinary genius! As we dig in, I can't help but chuckle at the hilarious incident that happened at the office today.

"Do you remember that intern, Tommy?" I ask, trying to stifle my laughter.

Sebastian's eyes light up with amusement. "Ah, the one with the crazy hair and mismatched socks?"

"Yeah, that's the one!" I reply, unable to keep a straight face. "He accidentally spilled coffee on Mr. Jenkins' new suit, and the look on his face was priceless!"

We both burst into laughter, and I reach over to touch Sebastian's hands, feeling the warmth of his touch, and for a moment, everything feels perfect. But then, I remember what I wanted to talk about, and my laughter fades.

"Actually, there's something serious I need to discuss," I say.

Sebastian notices the change and immediately drops his napkin, folding it neatly on the table. The smile on his face dissolves, and I can see the concern in his eyes.

"What is it, Isabella?" he asks gently, giving me his full attention.

I take a deep breath and muster the courage to say it out loud. "I've decided to leave Maxwell & Co. after we launch the new collection next week."

"What? Why?" he asks, his voice tinged with disbelief.

I nod, affirming my decision. "I've been thinking about it for a while now. Don't get me wrong; I'm happy and grateful to be working here, but I want to start my own fashion line."

He furrows his brows, searching for an explanation. "But aren't you happy here at Maxwell & Co.?"

Trying to ease the blow, I reach for his hands again. "I am, honestly. But I want creative freedom, and I want to build something of my own, with my name on it. I don't see that happening here, no matter how supportive you and the company are."

Sebastian looks visibly heartbroken, and it breaks my heart to see him like this. He gets up from the table abruptly, leaving his food unfinished, and starts pacing.

"Why?" he asks again, this time with a mix of frustration and sadness. "Why do you want to leave? Can't we figure something out together?"

I swallow hard and try to hold back tears. "I need to do this for myself, Sebastian. I want to build my own brand, my own legacy. I don't want to be known as 'Isabella from Maxwell & Co.' I want my designs to carry my name."

He stops pacing and looks at me, his eyes searching for something. "Is it because you think I'll hold you back?"

I shake my head. "No, it's not that at all. It's just...I need to know that I can do this on my own, without anyone's help. I need to prove it to myself."

Sebastian lets out a sigh and leaves. No words. Just silence.

Cold, haunting silence.

***

It's been several weeks since I told my husband about my decision to leave Maxwell & Co. And during this period, I can count on my hands how many times he's spoken to me about something. Never anything intimate, serious, or with any depth. Just shallow "good mornings" here and there. Or perhaps to ask me where I kept this or where I kept that. Every attempt to pull him out of his hole has been futile. Charlotte suggests that I give him some space and let him feel his feelings, and eventually he'll come around.

I know it's only been weeks, but for someone you love? It feels like it's been an eternity.

As we walk into the fashion exhibition, I can feel the tension in the air, as palpable as the designer clothes on display. Frankly, I can't shake off the feeling of being an intruder in my own world. It's not just the fashion on the racks that feels foreign; it's the very presence of my husband, Sebastian, and the man I share everything with. At the moment, we share nothing but awkward glances and polite nods.

The exhibition is in full swing, and I hug the back of my chair, desperate for something to hold on to. Sebastian is nearby, his body language stiff and guarded. A pang of sadness courses through me as I recall all the joyous exhibitions that we attended together.

"Professional disagreement," he says, lifting a shoulder carelessly, like it's no big deal. But to me, it's everything. I want his support, his understanding, but instead, I get a wall of ice between us.

I notice what he's wearing. A pale green shirt I've never seen before. I've spent today trying to decide if it's a harbinger of doom, or if I love it. Perhaps it's just my emotions playing tricks on me, searching for meaning in the smallest details.

"What's with the green shirt?" I ask, my voice sounding a bit too sharp even to my own ears.

"Green seemed appropriate," he replies, and I can't tell if he's being sarcastic or sincere. It's so hard to read him now, and that thought stings.

We're both summoned backstage for some last-minute preparations. As I walk toward the bathroom, the need to be alone overwhelms me. I slip in, closing the door behind me, finding solace in the temporary solitude.

Minutes pass, and I feel a bit of respite, a moment to collect my thoughts. But then, the door suddenly opens, and there he stands, Sebastian. And without a word, he steps in and closes the door behind him.

I'm taken aback, unsure of how to react. Sebastian and I have always had a close friendship, but this is different. He looks at me with a mix of concern and understanding, and before I can say anything, he kisses me.

It's unexpected, but strangely comforting. There's warmth in his touch that I've been missing, a connection that's been lost between us. For a moment, I feel conflicted, but also alive in a way I haven't felt in a long time.

As he pulls away, I can see the sincerity in his eyes. "You deserve to be with me, here at Maxwell

& Co.," he says, his voice soft and reassuring. It's the first time since that he has tried to talk me out of leaving.

My heart aches with a longing for the life and closeness we once had. But starting my own fashion line is something I want for myself, and I can't deny that.

I take a deep breath and step away from Sebastian, mustering the strength to face whatever comes next. The truth is, I don't know how things will unfold with Sebastian, but I know I can't let fear dictate my path.

The exhibition goes on, and I'm tucked away in a corner, stealing glances at Sebastian, my designs on display for the world to see. There's a mix of anxiety and pride inside me, knowing that this moment marks the beginning of a new chapter in my life.

As I glance at Sebastian, I see a flicker of something in his eyes—perhaps regret, or maybe just a touch of admiration. I can't help but wonder if he's finally realizing that I'm not giving up on my dreams, and maybe, just maybe, he'll come to understand and support me.

***

I stare at the blank resignation letter on my desk, my fingers hovering over the keys. It's early afternoon, but the light outside seems dull and lifeless, much like the weight in my chest. Leaving Maxwell & Co.

feels like I'm about to step into the unknown. And it scares me, frankly, more than I care to admit.

Should I stay, stick to the familiar, the comfortable, and the secure path that I've carved here? Or should I take the plunge, risk everything to pursue my own vision, collaborating with Craig Stanton's?

My head and heart are tangled in a fierce tug-of-war, and I can't seem to find clarity in the midst of this.

I've had countless discussions with myself, battling love and hate, trying to weigh the pros and cons of both choices. It's like being torn between two extremes, my stomach twisting with every thought of leaving. But strangely, there's also a strange kind of exhilaration that comes with the idea of venturing into uncharted territory.

Sebastian remains silent about my decision. The kisses we had at my last exhibition are a stark contrast to the lack of communication we have now. I wonder if he hates me a little for leaving, just like I feel a pang of hatred for myself for being unable to stay content with what I have. It's as if love and hate are mirror versions of the same game, and we're both trying to win. Yet, the battle rages on, and it's consuming me entirely.

My hands tremble as I finally type my resignation letter. But with every letter I type, the adrenaline spikes, and it feels like my body is barely under control. It's like plunging into the depths of love and hate simultaneously, and it both excites and terrifies me.

As I press the send button, I can't help but wonder how the fashion world will react to my departure. Fashion journalists and tabloids, always hungry for a story, will speculate wildly about my reasons for leaving Maxwell & Co. The media frenzy will be relentless, and I can already imagine the sensational headlines they'll cook up. I'm not just leaving a job; I'm stepping out of a life I've known for years, and everyone will want to know why.

The pressure of public scrutiny weighs heavily on me, and I feel like I'm being judged even before I've taken a single step towards my new venture.

But then I ask myself, do I care about what others think? Do I let their opinions dictate my life choices?

The answer is, frankly, no. I've always danced to the beat of my own drum, and I won't let the noise of the world drown out my intuition.

As I embark on setting up my own fashion studio, the challenges are many. Securing funding seems like an uphill battle, but I remind myself that even Rome wasn't built in a day. I'm determined to find a way, to make my vision a reality, and that will require resilience and unwavering commitment.

Building a team who shares my passion is another hurdle I face, but I believe in surrounding myself with like-minded individuals who can elevate my ideas. It's not just about business; it's about creating a family who believes in my dream as much as I do.

But it's not all smooth sailing. Doubts and vulnerabilities creep in at times, and I find myself questioning my abilities and decisions. What if I fail? What if it's all just a pipe dream? These doubts can be suffocating, but in those moments, I'm reminded of the support I receive from unexpected sources.

A friend from my early design school days, Helen, reaches out, encouraging me to keep going. She's someone who's witnessed my journey from the very beginning, and her words lift my spirits. I realize that while love and hate may be all-consuming, support and understanding can be equally powerful forces.

So, here I am, navigating the rollercoaster of emotions, striving to turn my dreams into reality. It's not an easy road, and I stumble and fall along the way. But with each setback, I remind myself of the passion that fuels me, the vision that drives me forward.

I may not have all the answers, but I'm willing to find them as I go. It's about more than just starting a fashion line; it's about finding myself and embracing the uncertainty of life. It's about taking a leap of faith, not just in my career, but in myself.

Tomorrow, I'm heading to London to meet with Daniel Stanton. All the times that I have been to London, it's been with Sebastian, running professional errands. And now, this is going to be different, strange maybe. But new.

— Chapter 33 —
The Emptiness

The car is quiet, the only sound being the soft hum of the engine and the snowflakes hitting my windshield. I steal a glance at Isabella sitting beside me.

Her eyes are fixed on the passing scenery. She doesn't seem very interested in what's out there. There's just nothing else to look at. Nothing else.

She tries to say something, mutter comments to herself, hoping I'll respond. But my eyes are focused on the road, the snow packed on the sides making it a treacherous drive.

I only speak when necessary, keeping the silence between us intact.

The drive to the airport is longer than it should be. No traffic on the road, just the one in my mind, and the silence between us is making the roads stretch on and on like a forever journey.

So, by the time we reach the New York airport, I notice how busy it is, even in the middle of winter.

Where's everyone traveling to in this cold?

It's about a week until Christmas, so people are probably traveling home. Or away. Probably a long way from here, maybe California or New Mexico, where it's hot. Maybe Australia, where it's summer at this time.

But Isabella is heading to London.

She told me about how she's partnering with Craig Stanton's and she's heading to London to speak to the board. I'm upset. But I don't blame her. Robert and the rest of the board wouldn't have allowed it, anyway. Even my father, too. Like my friend told me, Isabella's like a bird, and I should let her fly.

My breath comes out in white puffs, and I warm my hands with my breath as I help Isabella with her small handbag. Even though I'm angry with her for leaving the company, I can't deny that I still love her, maybe even more than the day before or even a year ago.

Isabella moves closer to me, and I get a better look at her eyes, those mesmerizing Tuscan sunset eyes that I fell in love with. It's the first time I've seen them up close since I kissed her at the exhibition.

"I've missed you, my love," she says softly, her breath freezing. She's searching my eyes as if there's love lost in there somewhere.

But the love in my eyes isn't lost.

"I've been right here, Isabella," I reply.

She laughs. A short, small laugh. I watch her cover her mouth as she cracks up.

I've missed her little laughs, but I wonder why she's laughing now. A small smile creases half of my face.

"Isabella?" she says amidst her laughter.

"Last time I checked, that's your name," I say smiling. I know what's coming next.

"Isabella?" she asks again. "I call you 'my love' and this is what I get in return?"

I don't say a word. Instead, I pull her closer until I can feel her breasts press on me through my suit. She's still smiling.

"Do you not miss me, too, my love?" Isabella asks as she searches my eyes for answers.

"I've missed you so much, Bella. So much that it hurts."

"All you just needed to do was talk, Sebastian."

"I was upset about your decision to leave," I start. "But I understand. Not like Robert and the rest will let you have your way, anyway."

She's smiling. Looking up to me with so much love. So much admiration. So much love.

"But I love you," I continue. "I love you more than anyone. More than anything in the whole world."

She leans back, visibly holding back the tears welling up in her eyes. "I love you so much, my love. I love you so much, Sebastian."

The airport speakers announcing her flight interrupt our moment. "Go ahead, then." I nudge her. But before she can leave, I pull her close and sink my lips onto hers.

When I pull away, she reluctantly takes her bag, and I kiss her on the head before she starts to walk away from me.

As she struts into the crowd, a mix of soulful, sad, and happy tunes play in my head. I watch her disappear from view, and she looks back at me more than twice before she's out of sight.

I glance at my watch; I'm running late for work, but I can't leave until I know her plane has taken off.

The wait feels long and heavy, but finally, the flight status updates, indicating that her plane has flown. It's time for her new journey, and I can't help but feel a mix of pride and sadness.

Driving back home before I get to work, I replay the events in my mind. The quiet car ride, Isabella's attempts to talk, our exchange of feelings at the airport. It all feels like a whirlwind, and I can't shake the emotions that surge through me.

Back at home, the emptiness of the house reminds me that she's not here anymore. I sit down, taking a moment to collect my thoughts and emotions. There's a part of me that wishes she hadn't left, that we could have worked things out at the company somehow. But I also know that she's following her dreams, and I can't stand in her way.

The emptiness follows me everywhere.

***

The morning at the office feels eerily empty without Isabella. I stand by my window, gazing out at the snow falling gently onto the ground below.

Winter has always been my favorite season; I could stand here all day, mesmerized by the dancing snowflakes. But today, even the beauty of winter can't shake the sadness that weighs on my heart.

This is officially my worst winter ever.

A knock interrupts the serenity. It could be any of the employees. I wonder what this person has come to say now.

"Come in," I say without turning to see who it is.

"Whatever it is you are watching outside and down there must be more interesting than a movie." It's Robert. You can't mistake his deep, hoarse voice, or his sarcasm.

"Robert," I say after I turn to watch him as he makes his way towards my desk.

"Morning, Sebastian," he says as he takes a seat at my desk. I wonder what he's here for this time.

"Good morning, Robert," I say. My mug of coffee is still in my hand. It's keeping my breath and hands warm.

I watch Robert open a pack of cigarettes, cross his legs, and light one up. I scoff, not impressed by his habit. He's always trying to show me that he's the only one who doesn't give a flying fuck about me.

"So, why don't you join me by the window to watch the snow fall, I bet it's better than any movie you've seen this year," I say, my eyes still on the street below. Watching people scurry around, the sides of the road packed with snow. From here, you can't see their faces. Just figures and different winter jackets.

"I don't see movies anymore," Robert answers. Smoke swirling around him. "Okay, maybe not as much as I used to. Like twice a year."

I scoff.

"I've never been a fan of winter either," he continues as he smokes his cigarette. The end gleams into a bright red every time he draws his breath.

I move away from the window and walk to my desk, as I sink into my swivel chair. I drop the mug on the desk, staring straight at Robert.

"Coffee won't keep you warm enough, Sebastian," he says with a wry smile on his face. "Here." He throws the cigarette pack on the table before me. "That's a fitting, warm companion for men whose wives are far away."

I laugh. A short, brief laugh that stops right before my lungs can echo it. Then, I stomach my sadness again. I shouldn't be laughing. I'm missing my wife.

"Autumn is my favorite season, anyway," Robert says. "I thought you'd ask."

"Autumn, really?" I raise an eyebrow, amused. "I've always loved the quiet beauty of winter. It's like the world is covered in a soft, white blanket, and everything feels calm and peaceful."

He chuckles, taking a drag from his cigarette. "Well, I guess we all have our own poisons, don't we?"

"So, tell me," I say as I take a sip from my coffee. "You must have a reason for your visit this morning."

Robert likes his riddles, but I'm in no mood for games.

Robert nods knowingly, his expression softening. "She was an essential part of this place, Sebastian." He's talking about Isabella. "The success we're experiencing now, she played a significant role in making it happen."

A pang of sadness tugs at my heart as her absence becomes even more evident. "I know," I reply quietly. "It's just strange to think that she won't be walking through these doors every day, full of energy and ideas."

"Change can be tough, but it can also bring new opportunities," Robert says, tapping the ashes of his cigarette into an ashtray. "Speaking of which, there's something we should discuss."

I look at him curiously. Robert is known for his cunning ways, but I trust him enough to hear him out.

"The head of design position is vacant now, and it needs someone who can fill Isabella's shoes," he says with a hint of seriousness. "Many of our designers are talented, but they lack the experience to lead at the highest level."

I take a moment to consider his words. Being head of design was never part of my plan, but I can't ignore the opportunity to ensure Isabella's legacy lives on in the company.

"I'll take on that role for now," I say finally, my decision firming up. "Until we find the right person who can truly carry on her vision."

Robert raises an eyebrow, seeming surprised by my choice. "You, the head of design? I've never known you to be a designer, Sebastian."

"There's a lot a man can learn from watching his wife do it every day," I reply with a touch of pride in my voice. "I may not have formal training, but I know what makes great design, and I've seen firsthand the passion and dedication she poured into her work."

Robert smiles, his eyes reflecting a mixture of respect and admiration. "Well, I can't argue with that. I suppose it's worth a shot. Just remember, you'll have a lot on your plate as the CEO and head of design at the same time."

I nod, understanding the challenges ahead. "I'll manage," I say with determination. "And I'll do it for Isabella."

As I watch the snowfall outside, a mix of emotions floods me. I wonder what I'm now supposed to do. Where to start from. It's like a huge chunk of the company has gone with the plane that took off that day.

I've asked Isabella what she's going to call her line. She paused for a little while and said she doesn't know yet. It was one of those days that I wasn't speaking to her much.

I should have spoken more to her before she traveled. Now I'm just going to wander around the house, force feeding myself coffee and pretending I'm not missing her.

Perhaps I should visit my parents; my mother is always happy to see me. My father? He always has something to say about whatever. Something to complain about. I'm not always happy to see him. But today, I think I should visit them.

— Chapter 34 —
Bella Sogno

Winter in London has its own unique charm, but it still takes me by surprise every time I visit the city. As I step out of the taxi, I wrap my coat tighter around me since the air is so crisp. As the taxi wheels away, the city's aesthetics shoot past in a slightly blurring motion.

And my God, it's a fashionista's paradise.

The sights and sounds of London never fail to inspire me, and I find myself mentally sketching new designs as I make my way towards the colossal building of Craig Stanton's.

The building's facade is impressive, with the words "Craig Stanton's" emblazoned on its glass exterior. My eyes scan the surroundings, taking in the little details that make London unique. The red double-decker buses passing by, the sounds of people chatting with their distinct accents, and the smell of tea, coffee, beer, and cigarettes from nearby cafes, pubs, and roadsides all contribute to my sensory overload.

Just as I'm about to enter the building, I can't help but think about how different it is from the bustling New York fashion scene I'm accustomed to. The London fashion world has its own charm, and I feel a little internal turmoil, excited about the potential collaboration but also unsure about what the future holds.

As I step into the foyer, Daniel Stanton himself stands there to welcome me. His British accent adds a touch of refinement to his words as he warmly calls out my name. "Isabella, my dear! It's wonderful to see you again," he says, leaning in to peck my cheeks and give me a warm hug.

"Daniel, it's always a pleasure," I reply, smiling. "Thank you for inviting me."

As we walk towards the elevator, Daniel continues to talk. Oh, how he loves to talk. "You know, Isabella, it's no secret how much I've always admired your designs. You bring something fresh and bold to fashion. It's no surprise that you're a big name in the industry." I watch him press a key in the elevator as it shuts and starts to hum gently.

I chuckle. "Thank you, Daniel. I believe that fashion should be an expression of oneself, and I'm glad my work resonates with so many."

Daniel smiles back. "Most world-class designers I know wouldn't dare dress as you do. They worship minimalism, but I find it rather refreshing to see someone who embraces extravagance in style."

I raise my eyebrow playfully. "And what about you? What do you worship?"

Daniel laughs heartily. "Ah, I'm barely a designer, but yeah, I'm quite the opposite. I like to dress nicely. I like to dress a lot. I'm fucking extravagant."

"But being minimalist does not mean they dress badly," I say.

"Of course," Daniel says with a smile. "But a lot of them don't dress well, either. I'd rather over-dress than under-dress."

The elevator opens on the top floor, and we walk into the sleek and modern boardroom. The members of the board greet us warmly, some expressing their admiration for my work.

"Thank you all for the warm welcome," I say. The room falls silent, and all eyes are on me as I begin my presentation.

I stand confidently at the front of the boardroom, my sketches and ideas displayed on a large screen behind me. My voice is clear and passionate as I begin my presentation.

"Ladies and gentlemen, thank you for having me here today. As you know, fashion is not just about clothing; it's about storytelling, it's about emotions, and it's about creating a connection with the audience. With my experience as a fashion designer and having worked at a big fashion brand in New York, I've learned that the key to success lies in pushing boundaries and staying true to your vision."

"I've seen the potential in Craig Stanton's brand, and I believe our collaboration can elevate both our brands to new heights. Your brand already has a solid foundation, a loyal customer base, and a reputation for quality. My creativity and unique design perspective can infuse new life into your collections and open doors to new markets."

I click to the next slide, showing some of my avantgarde designs. "Take a look at these designs. They challenge conventional norms and redefine fashion's boundaries. By incorporating elements like these into your collections, we can capture the attention of a broader and more diverse audience, driving more sales and increasing brand recognition."

I pause, gauging the reactions of the board members. Seeing nods of approval, I continue, "Now, I understand the challenges you faced in the past with expanding to New York. The market there is fiercely competitive, but my name and reputation in the fashion world can help create a buzz that will cut through the noise. As a former head of design at Maxwell & Co., I have extensive connections and know the industry inside out."

"I propose we develop a limited-edition collection that marries my artistic flair with the essence of Craig Stanton's brand. This collection will be an amalgamation of bold and visionary designs, drawing from the legacy of your brand and the innovation of my work. It will be a conversation starter, a must-have for fashion enthusiasts, and it will put Craig Stanton's brand back on the map in New York and beyond."

My passion fills the room, and I can sense the excitement building among the board members. "In addition to the collaboration, I also recommend embracing digital marketing and social media strategies to create a stronger online presence. The fashion industry is rapidly evolving, and we must adapt to new consumer habits. Let's leverage my social media following and influence to amplify our message and reach a wider audience."

I go on to discuss other marketing strategies, retail partnerships, and potential collaborations with influencers and celebrities, all aimed at building hype and excitement around the brand. I highlight the importance of sustainability and ethical practices, aligning with the values of modern consumers.

"As partners, we will inspire each other to take risks and innovate, merging traditional craftsmanship with contemporary artistry. Our combined strengths will forge a path towards a new era of fashion."

As I conclude my presentation, the boardroom erupts in applause. Daniel Stanton smiles, his confidence in my plan evident. "Isabella, your vision and creativity are truly remarkable. We believe in your ideas and see the tremendous potential in this collaboration. Let's move forward together and bring Craig Stanton's brand to new heights!"

The member who had previously expressed admiration for my work speaks up, "Isabella, we are thrilled by your ideas and would be honored to collaborate with you. Your creativity and boldness are precisely what our brand needs to revitalize our expansion plans."

I can't contain my enthusiasm. "Thank you all for this opportunity. Together, we can create something truly extraordinary and bring a fresh wave of excitement to the fashion world."

The room erupts in applause.

And when it dies down, Daniel's voice cuts through the room, "Do you have a name for your line yet?"

***

Sebastian always loves watching the snow fall. It's one of his favorite things to do during winter in New York. He sits by the window, just like I'm doing now in my hotel room in London, and marvels at the delicate dance of snowflakes as they descend from the sky. The snow in London isn't as freezing as New York's winter, but it's still chilly enough to evoke the season's charm.

As I sit by the window, with my notepad open on my lap, I can't help but think of my husband back in New York. Sebastian has a unique sense of humor and often teases those who seek refuge in warmer places during winter, calling them "cowards" with a playful laugh. I miss his warmth, both figuratively and literally.

Feeling the pang of loneliness, I pick up my phone impulsively, intending to FaceTime Sebastian. However, as the phone rings, I remember the time difference and that it's early morning back in New York. He might still be asleep or deeply immersed in slumber. I hesitate for a moment before deciding not to disturb him and end the call as it's ringing.

I set my phone down and gaze out at the London streets where the snowflakes lazily drift down, lost in my thoughts of my beloved husband. Then, to my surprise, my phone begins buzzing again. Glancing at the screen, I see that it's Sebastian FaceTiming me.

A smile spreads across my face as I quickly pick up the call. "Good morning, sleepyhead," I greet him, hearing the hoarseness in his voice, a sign that he has, indeed, just woken up.

Sebastian chuckles softly, rubbing his eyes. "You caught me. I couldn't resist calling you as soon as I woke up."

I laugh affectionately. "I knew it! You're a terrible liar, my love."

"I suppose I am," he admits with a grin. "But I've missed you so much, Bella. I couldn't wait to hear your voice."

My heart warms at his words. "I've missed you too, Sebastian. It's just not the same being here without you."

He looks earnestly at me through the screen. "You look beautiful, as always. London seems to suit you."

I blush, feeling a surge of happiness at his compliment. "Thank you. I'll tell you all about it when I return home."

Sebastian's eyes sparkle with excitement. "I can't wait to hear all about it. By the way, have you thought about what you'll call your fashion line?"

"Yes, I have," I reply. "'Bella Sogno.'"

***

As the plane touches down in New York, I eagerly look out of the window, my heart racing with anticipation. I'm finally back home after spending weeks in London, the longest I've been away from Sebastian. I'm scanning the crowd at the airport, trying to spot him among the sea of people. My eyes dart over the heads of the passengers, stretching to find my six-foot-three man, at least a head taller than anyone around him. And then, there he is. Sebastian has already seen me before I even catch sight of him.

He stands out effortlessly, wearing a gray suit that reminds me of the first time we met at Maxwell & Co., when he was still my boss. Back then, I thought I hated him, or at least I convinced myself I did. But now, as I see him irresistibly hot in that gray suit and his black leather gloves holding a bouquet of flowers, I can't help but marvel at how time has transformed my feelings for him.

In the middle of the bustling airport crowd, Sebastian walks over to me, a confident smile on his face. Maybe it's because I haven't seen him in person for over a week, or maybe it's the beard he's growing out, adding to the rugged charm, but he looks so much hotter than the last time I saw him. Without saying a word, he grabs me into his arms and kisses me passionately, making me momentarily lose myself in the intensity of the moment. The rest of the airport fades away around the two of us, and it's as if we're the only ones in the world.

"I missed you," I whisper when we finally break the kiss.

"Of course, you should have," Sebastian replies with a playful smirk. "There's no man as hot as I am in London, I'm sure of it," he jokes.

"You're insufferable," I say, though there's a hint of amusement in my voice.

Sebastian chuckles and pulls me closer, wrapping his arms around me protectively. "Come on, let's get out of here," he suggests, nodding towards the airport exit.

As we walk hand in hand towards the exit, my mind starts to drift, and my internal emotions surge. I can't help but imagine the building that Craig Stanton's wanted to lease out for my fashion line. I see it as a canvas for my creativity, a reflection of my character as fierce, daring, and intensely detailed. I envision the space filled with unique designs and eye-catching displays, a place where fashion enthusiasts from all over the world would come to experience my vision.

I want the walls to exude boldness, with striking patterns and colors that draw people in. The floors would be adorned with intricate and luxurious carpets, a testament to the attention to detail I pour into my designs. Large mirrors would line the walls, reflecting not only the clothing but also the confidence and empowerment they bring to those who wear them.

My thoughts continue to wander as we step outside into the bustling city of New York. The possibilities seem endless, and I can feel the fire of inspiration burning within me. With Sebastian by my side, supporting and encouraging me, there's no doubt that my fashion line, Bella Sogno, will become a force to be reckoned with.

— Chapter 35 —
The Age Old Rivalry

It's been one year since Isabella left Maxwell & Co. to pursue her dreams, and the company has weathered both highs and lows. As I sit in my office, staring out at the bustling streets of New York City, I can't help but reflect on how much has changed since she departed.

Firstly, I look different now. My once neatly trimmed beard has grown fuller, and Isabella never fails to tease me about it whenever we meet. She finds it amusing how I've embraced this rugged look, but it's a small change compared to the upheaval that has occurred in the company since she left.

In the beginning, things were promising. Isabella's designs had brought about a new era of prosperity for Maxwell & Co., and we experienced unprecedented profits, even surpassing the records set by my father, the company's founder. Her talent shone like a beacon, drawing attention to us both. But all that glory seemed fleeting when she decided to leave.

At first, I was supportive, even though a part of me felt a pang of sadness. I wanted to see her succeed, but I also couldn't deny the impact of her departure on the company. We struggled to find someone who could fill her shoes with a similar flair and creative genius. Three designers were hired, but they couldn't recreate the magic that Isabella effortlessly wove into her designs. In the end, we had to let go of two of them, as their work didn't meet our expectations.

The last remaining designer is a young man from Chicago, full of enthusiasm and fresh ideas, but he is no Isabella Rivera. His designs are good, but they lack that certain spark that made Isabella's creations so exceptional. It's been a challenge for me to accept that no one can replicate her style, and we've been running on the designs she created before she left, with only minor tweaks from the new designer.

Meanwhile, Isabella's journey has been one of growth and success. Her fashion line took off like a rocket, leaving me both proud and melancholic. I attended her fashion exhibition last week, and I couldn't help but feel a mixture of emotions as I watched her confidently present her latest collection. She has become an internationally acclaimed designer, and just two weeks ago, she won a prestigious award. I was there, clapping the loudest, my heart swelling with pride.

Life has been kinder to both of us in the past year. Isabella and I have grown closer, and we now visit our parents more often, cherishing the precious moments we have with them. However, as Isabella's stardom rises, my role as the CEO of Maxwell & Co. has become more challenging than ever.

The pressure weighs heavily on my shoulders. Overseeing the department of design is no small task, especially when our shining star is no longer among us. Every decision I make now carries the weight of keeping the company afloat and maintaining its legacy. I feel as though I'm navigating treacherous waters, trying to steer the ship in the right direction, but the waves are rough and relentless.

The bitter-sweet reality is that we owe much of our success to Isabella's designs, and while she is flourishing, Maxwell & Co. is struggling to regain its former glory. It's a paradox that haunts my every step, and it's something I've learned to carry with a heavy heart.

I find myself yearning for the past, for the time when Isabella was by my side at Maxwell & Co., igniting the fashion world with her brilliance. But I know I must also embrace the future, adapt to the changes, and find a way to move forward without her. It's not easy, but I won't let Maxwell & Co. falter.

Perhaps it's time to take a leap of faith, to explore new avenues and push the boundaries of our creativity. The fashion industry is ever-evolving, and maybe we need to redefine what Maxwell & Co. represents in this fast-paced world.

***

My father calls Augustus the greatest menswear tailor in America. Augustus is our seventy-year-old tailor, he has been for at least three decades now, and in that time span, he's been the one making my father's suits.

Tonight, the suit I have on is one of Augustus' finest masterpieces. It's a tradition to have him suit me up for important occasions; like the CFDA ceremony I'm attending with my wife, Isabella.

The suit is American, sleek, black, and perfectly fitted, tailored to accentuate every angle and contour of my frame. As I adjust my tie in front of the mirror, I feel a twinge of nervousness.

It's not the award itself that has me on edge, nor the grandeur of the ceremony that awaits us.

No.

It's the competition with Isabella that's causing this unease to coil within me. We've both been nominated for Brand of the Year. In a surreal twist of fate, we find ourselves pitted against each other in a race where only one can claim victory. Or neither of us.

The problem is, my father raised me to be a little too competitive, in that my sentimental attachment doesn't wane my determination to win any race I enter. Even if it's against my wife.

As I stand in the dressing room, adjusting the cufflinks on my shirt, my thoughts swirl like the echoes of a distant storm. Isabella is in her own dressing room, I imagine, preparing for the evening's events.

A sense of melancholy tugs at my heart, not only because she left Maxwell & Co., a company that holds my name, but also because in losing her, we lost a creative force that breathed life into our designs. In just two years, she had become a design luminary, her creations sweeping through the industry like wildfire.

The sound of heels tapping on the floor outside the dressing room heralds Isabella's arrival. I turn and catch my breath as she enters, the embodiment of elegance and strength. The gown she wears hugs her figure in all the right places, its design a testament to her impeccable taste. A sense of pride swells within me, witnessing the transformation of the woman I fell in love with into a powerhouse of her own making.

She smiles, and my heart skips a beat. The once-shared dreams of collaboration have given way to separate paths, but the connection between us remains unbreakable. Tonight, however, that connection is tinged with an unspoken rivalry, a competition that threatens to cast a shadow over the evening's festivities.

The time comes to leave for the awards ceremony. We step out of our mansion, the grandeur of our surroundings juxtaposed against the weight of anticipation that hangs in the air. The Rolls Royce awaits, the driver poised and ready. I take my place at the back. She bursts through the front door, a whirlwind of energy and purpose, and I can't help but smile at her.

This isn't the Hollywood-style power that I once fantasized about. It's a power that emanates from within, a strength born of determination and a relentless pursuit of one's vision. Isabella slides into the car, her eyes meeting mine, and for a moment, all the competition and rivalry fade into the background. We share a silent understanding, a knowing that despite the odds, despite the competition, we are in this journey together.

The drive to the CFDA is mostly quiet. Her hand is quietly placed on my thigh. Occasionally, she turns to me and slips a kiss on my lips.

By the time we reach the venue, the buzz in the air is palpable. Flashing lights, the hum of excited conversations, and the occasional burst of laughter create a vibrant atmosphere. As we step out of the car, Isabella is immediately enveloped in a whirlwind of attention. It's not surprising; her presence is magnetic, drawing in the gazes of onlookers and photographers alike. I smile, both proud and in awe of the woman beside me.

The dress she's wearing shimmers like liquid silver under the bright lights. Its sleek lines hug her form gracefully, flowing like molten metal as she moves. The cameras flash relentlessly, capturing every facet of her elegance.

"Perfect! Hold that pose!"

"...thank you...smile, Sebastian..."

"Yes, that's it!"

Camera shutters click.

"...Isabella and Sebastian, a power couple..."

"Sebastian, can we get a shot of just you?"

"Sure," I say. "Right here."

Camera shutters click again and again.

I stand by her side, my arm naturally finding its place around her waist as we pose for the rest of the photographers. I can't help but wonder how the pictures will turn out—capturing a moment of anticipation and celebration, a snapshot of our intertwined fates.

As Isabella moves further down the red carpet, engaging in conversations and effortlessly navigating the sea of industry peers and journalists, I follow her with my gaze. Her words are a blend of creativity and innovation, a testament to the designer she's become.

The crowd is loud. Everyone is speaking all at once. You have to tilt your head and listen closely or else you'll miss out on some of the words. As if the buzz is eating part of their sentences, I can only make out a few words. As incoherent as they may sound to me, I can still make out the fact that Isabella is always proud to talk about her creative vision. I watch her from a small distance.

Isabella's voice rings out, "...embracing new perspectives...pushing boundaries...artistic journey..."

Then, an unidentified voice, perhaps the host says "...captivating...stunning design...true visionary..."

"Isabella, how do you manage to consistently redefine fashion?"

"...inspiration from unexpected places... collaborative spirit...challenging norms..."

"Your designs are a breath of fresh air in the industry."

"...expressing individuality...empowering through fashion..."

"Over here, Isabella! Can we get a shot?"

"...sure, of course... thank you all..."

Her interaction with the media doesn't surprise me much. I've seen how her departure from Maxwell & Co. marked a shift in her approach, a departure from the familiar, and the world has responded with enthusiasm.

Once we settle into our seats, the ceremony begins to unfold. I watch as Isabella takes the stage to receive her Global Women's Designer award. The applause is thunderous, and I join in. It's a genuine celebration of her achievements. Moments later, she's called to the podium again, this time for the American Womenswear award. I can tell that these accolades, while appreciated, are not the ones she's been waiting for.

She returns to her seat beside me, her excitement and confidence contagious. The moment we've all been waiting for arrives—the Brand of the Year award. The anticipation is almost palpable as the host teases the crowd. My jaw tightens, and I clench my fist, feeling the weight of the competition bearing down on me. The host draws out the announcement, relishing the suspense as the tension in the room reaches a crescendo.

And then it happens. The host says her name.

"Isabella Rivera."

A roar of applause erupts, and I release my clenched fist, my heart swelling with pride. Isabella turns to me, her eyes shining with happiness, and kisses my cheek. I can't help but smile, genuinely thrilled for her. She's come so far, and her success is well-deserved.

She stands up, waving to the crowd. She's come a long way from when she first joined us. She's a lot more confident now. As she climbs the stage, time seems to slow down. I clap along with the audience, my smile a mix of pride and a twinge of bittersweetness. I'm proud of her, there's no doubt about that. But beneath the surface, a part of me grapples with the reality of my own desires. I hate losing at anything.

I watch as she climbs on stage. She takes the award and starts a small speech that I have seen her practice around the house. She even practiced it with me. She asked me what speech I'd give. I told her that I'm not really a good speaker, that I'd just make something up on the go.

"Thank you, everyone. This is truly an incredible honor, and I am humbled to be standing here tonight. It's amazing to see so many familiar faces in the crowd—friends, mentors, fellow designers who have inspired me on this journey."

Her voice is steady, projecting a sense of confidence that belies any nervousness she might be feeling. As she speaks, her words flow with a well-rehearsed rhythm.

"Creating Bella Sogno has been a journey of passion, innovation, and a tireless pursuit of artistic expression. I want to extend my deepest gratitude to every individual who believed in this dream: my team, my collaborators, and my family. Your unwavering support has been the driving force behind this brand's success."

There's a heartfelt sincerity in her voice, an acknowledgment of the collective effort that has brought her to this moment. Her gaze flickers to me in the audience, a brief connection that carries volumes of shared memories and unspoken understanding. I smile back at her.

"Fashion, to me, is more than just fabric and design. It's a language through which we communicate our identities, beliefs, and aspirations. Bella Sogno is a reflection of my commitment to pushing boundaries, embracing diversity, and celebrating individuality."

As she continues, her speech transitions seamlessly, her words reflecting the core values of her brand. Her passion for creativity and her dedication to making a meaningful impact on the fashion landscape shine through.

"Tonight, as I stand here, I'm reminded of the transformative power of fashion. Let us continue to challenge conventions, to create art that resonates with our souls, and to uplift each other as a community united by a shared love for creativity."

I glance to the right and catch Daniel Stanton's smile, a smile that's directed not just at her success but at our rivalry. In that fleeting moment, I see the stark contrast between Isabella and me as a couple.

By the time we get home, we go straight to the backyard, by the pool. Spring breeze greets us, and we are here to soak in the night and maybe even celebrate Isabella's win. We are still both dressed in our outfits, though my shirt is unbuttoned.

"Let's stay here," I say as I sink into the reclining chair on the lawn.

Isabella doesn't hesitate. She sinks into the other. We sit there for a few minutes before I jump on my feet again to pull her up.

"Let's dance," I say with a smile on my face.

"What dance?" Isabella is smiling just as hard too.

"Salsa."

We spend the next twenty minutes dancing barefoot on the lawn. The soft sharpness of the grass tickles my feet as we move.

Isabella pulls away from me and says, "There's something I need to show you." She turns to leave, and I try to follow her. She turns briefly and says, "No, stay," before disappearing into the house.

She comes back to the courtyard with an expensive-looking wine. The label reads "**Leroy Domaine d'Auvenay Criots-Bâtard-Montrachet Grand Cru.**"

"How much is this?" I ask, brandishing the bottle in my hand.

"Guess?" She's smiling while searching my eyes.

"A stack?" I say, still checking the bottle as I'd find the price somewhere on it.

"Not even close." She laughs a little.

"Tell me then."

"A little over twenty thousand dollars," she says.

"Give me an accurate figure," I say as I squint again, still checking the bottle.

"I can't remember. I got it a while ago for tonight."

I'm rubbing off well on her. There was a time Isabella would tell me I'm spending too much on wine. Now, she drinks as much as I do. Maybe even more.

"You know, Isabella," I start after a moment of silence, "growing up was a bit of a struggle for me because I didn't really have a clear idea what or who I wanted to be. Despite my parents' fashion background, I never felt that creative spark. Fashion, designing, they just weren't in my realm of interest."

A chuckle escapes me as I add, "Though I have this odd fascination with baking."

Isabella's laughter joins mine. "Baking, huh? How come you haven't ever whipped up something for me?"

I smile, shaking my head. " I haven't baked in years. It was more of a fleeting hobby."

My gaze drifts over to her, and I continue, "It was kind of written in stone that I'd inherit my father's company. An only child, you know? So, off to university for business administration, then back to the company's development department. I wasn't exactly thrilled with my job, but I was good at it."

As I take a sip of the wine, I confess, "After my father's retirement, I found myself at the helm as the CEO."

Isabella listens intently, her glass held with a solemn air. I can't help but notice the contrast between her poised elegance and the informality of the outdoor setting.

Taking a breath, I admit, "But, truth be told, I've always been more about the business side of things. Profit margins, sales strategies, those are my forte. I don't possess that creative flair you do."

I continue, a trace of conviction in my tone, "My focus has been on building a successful business. And I believe, at the end of the day, we're all working towards a financial end goal."

Her voice interjects, sincere and unwavering, "Not for me, Sebastian."

I nod, acknowledging her perspective. "I get it. Your speech tonight spoke volumes about your commitment to creativity. It's almost a curse, isn't it? You'd choose creativity over profits any day."

A silence falls between us, and I sense her scrutiny, her gaze like a searching light. When she speaks, her voice is measured, "You seem to forget, though, that my designs saved Maxwell & Co. when we were spiraling downward."

I respond, perhaps more defensively than intended, "We would have found a way, Isabella."

Her laughter follows, sharp and tinged with sarcasm. "Would we, now? I distinctly remember how we clashed in the beginning, our opposing viewpoints on fashion."

The edge in her tone doesn't escape me, and I push forward, "Our differences eventually blended, Isabella. But you left. You decided to pursue your own path."

The air between us thickens with unspoken sentiments. She counters, her voice firm, "You speak as if there's no room for creativity in the fashion industry, as if it's all about profits."

I lift my hand mockingly, conceding, "I never said that. But creatives prioritize the 'creative lane' only when it's profitable."

A hint of challenge flashes in her eyes, and she retorts, "And you think that's my motivation? To choose passion over profit?"

I meet her gaze, a mixture of honesty and hesitation in my expression. "You've always been driven by creativity, Isabella. It's your essence."

Her next question takes me off guard. "How do you feel about the award, Sebastian? Be honest."

The question hangs in the air, and before I can respond, she throws another curveball, "Are you jealous?"

Of course I am, but it's more complex than mere jealousy. But I'd rather have my cheeks peeled with graters than admit it to her right now and right here. Before I can say anything, Isabella rises abruptly.

"I'm tired. We've had a long night. I'm going to sleep." She leaves to head inside without me.

We always get into bed together after we shower. But tonight, she's not in the mood for all of that. Perhaps I should rush after her and…I don't know. Perhaps just follow behind her.

I do not.

Instead, I just sit there and watch her disappear into the house, leaving the bottle and the two glasses behind, her heels hanging out of her hand by their straps.

I sit there for another hour, replaying everything that happened between us. The award show. The drive back home. The following conversation, and Isabella walking out on me.

Eventually, I retreat indoors, closing the doors behind me and heading upstairs. The room is empty, and I exhale a sigh.

She's upset.

— Chapter 36 —
Mutual Interests

They say the first year of a brand is either a hit or a miss. Bella Sogno was a hit in the first two years. My first year, I took in Emily as my business development associate, and I won Brand of the Year at the CFDA.

But not even I, with all my fantasies and delusions, make the mistake of thinking it would just be a smooth ride.

So, here I am, sitting in my office at Bella Sogno, a name that once held so much promise, now mired in the harsh realities of the fashion industry. My sister, Emily, now my right-hand woman in business, is across from me, her face a mirror of concern. Edward, our financial manager, has just joined us, his usually composed demeanor marred by a somber expression.

I'm leaning against my desk, my fingers tapping the surface restlessly, as Emily speaks, her words punctuated by a furrowed brow, "Bella, we have a problem."

I exhale sharply, a mixture of annoyance and anticipation mingling in the air. "Tell me."

She straightens in her chair, her fingers tracing patterns on the edge of a paper. "The trends are shifting so quickly, Bella. What was in vogue a few months ago is now considered outdated."

I close my eyes for a moment, as if hoping that when I open them, this would be some sort of bad dream. "So, we're losing our grip on the market?"

She nods solemnly, her voice tinged with frustration when she says, "Consumers are gravitating toward those minimalistic, edgier designs, the ones that have that 'Instagramable' look."

Edward chimes in, his voice carrying a note of caution, "We have a considerable amount of unsold inventory. The pieces we put so much heart into creating are now gathering dust."

I rub my temples, my thoughts whirling in a tumultuous storm. "So, what's the solution? Do we just change our entire aesthetic to follow these trends?"

Emily hesitates, her eyes searching mine for understanding. "Well, I think we need to adapt, Bella. Move with the industry's tempo, incorporate some of these trends into our designs. After all, fashion is about change, right?"

I shoot her a look that's a mix of disbelief and frustration. "So, you're suggesting we compromise our creativity?" I sigh. Everyone is beginning to sound like Sebastian these days.

She winces, her expression tinged with apology. "I know how much Bella Sogno means to you, Bella. I just want us to survive in this competitive market."

As much as I value her input, this doesn't sit well with me. It's like a *déjà vu* of the argument I had with Sebastian, a man I love dearly but whose business philosophy often clashes with mine.

Just then, Murphy, Edward's assistant, hurriedly enters the room. His presence adds to the palpable tension. He whispers some words to Edward, and Edward frowns a bit, as if they've just received news that's far from pleasant.

Emily turns to him, her voice expectant as she asks, "Murphy, what's going on?"

He lets out a heavy sigh, and drops the bombshell, "We're experiencing a significant decline in profits."

The words hang in the air, heavy and ominous. It's like a punch in the gut, a harsh reminder that success in this industry is fleeting, and it's not enough to simply create beautiful designs. The financial aspect is a beast of its own, and right now, it's roaring in our faces.

My gaze flickers between Emily and Edward, my mind grappling with the magnitude of the situation. Emily's eyes reflect a mixture of worry and determination, while Murphy's features betray a hint of guilt, as if he carries the weight of our brand's financial struggles on his shoulders.

"The investors are selling their shares," Murphy continues, his voice bearing the weight of the bad news, "and our stock price is dropping."

I slump back in my chair, a swirl of emotions overwhelming me. I started Bella Sogno to create beautiful, meaningful designs that resonated with people, to bring art into fashion. But now, it seems like I'm standing at a crossroads where art and commerce collide.

Emily's voice breaks through my thoughts. "Bella, we need to take action, and fast. We can't let this situation escalate."

I lean forward, my palms pressing against the cool surface of my desk. "But what action, Emily? We can't just change our entire identity overnight."

She nods, her gaze unwavering. "I know. But we need to find a way to strike a balance. Maybe there's a middle ground where we can adapt to some trends without losing our core essence."

It's a tough pill to swallow, the idea of compromising on something that I've poured my heart and soul into. But the truth is, the world of fashion is ever-evolving, and standing still is synonymous with falling behind.

I close my eyes for a moment, trying to steady my racing thoughts. "Alright, let's brainstorm some ideas. We'll need to assess our options and find a way to navigate this."

Emily's face brightens with determination. "We've faced challenges before, Bella, and we've always come out stronger."

Edward's eyes meet mine, his expression holding a glimmer of hope. "We can strategize, reevaluate our financial plans, and explore potential partnerships."

***

I spend the next few weeks fixing a mistake that has been brewing underneath the surface like a boiling volcano before it finally erupts. Reality is starting to press down on me, the fear of failure gripping my throat, pushing me to work harder than I normally would. I find myself at the office until well past midnight, running business errands and navigating countless meetings.

Tonight is no exception. I walk through the door of our home with the weariness of the day clinging to me like a second skin. The exhaustion is etched across my face, visible in my eyes that feel heavy with fatigue. The living room is dimly lit, a cozy haven that's a stark contrast to the high-paced world I've just stepped out of.

Sebastian's gaze lifts from the TV as I enter, his smile blossoming upon seeing me. Yet, it fades as he takes in the sight of my weary form. He rises from the couch, the show on the TV momentarily forgotten. His footsteps close the gap between us, and he cups my face gently, planting a soft kiss on my forehead before his lips meet mine.

"You're back late," he observes, concern lacing his tone.

I offer a tired smile, feeling the warmth of his lips against my skin. "Yeah, had some things to sort out with Emily and Edward."

His eyes search mine, an unspoken question lingering in the air. "You look worn out. Is everything alright?"

The inquiry lingers for a moment, inviting me to share the burdens of the day. But even though he's my husband, there's a part of me that hesitates, reluctant to dive into the depths of my professional struggles, especially when he's at the helm of another colossal corporation.

I brush off his concern gently, my voice a reassuring murmur, "It's nothing, Seb. Just a bit busier than usual."

His gaze holds mine for a moment longer, as if gauging my sincerity. He doesn't push, respecting the boundary I've drawn. Instead, he takes a step back, giving me space to breathe.

Even in the dim light of our living room, I can see his genuine worry, and I'm grateful for his understanding. Our worlds, though intertwined, carry their own complexities, and it's sometimes challenging to bridge the gap between our business lives and being life partners.

As I slip off my shoes and move to join him on the couch, his smile returns, a silent reminder that he's here, ready to share whatever weight I'm willing to share. The baking show on the TV continues its sweet display, filling the room with a sense of domestic tranquility.

The fatigue from the day starts to catch up with me, my body craving rest. Leaning into Sebastian's side, I allow myself to relax for the first time in hours. The TV show becomes background noise as his presence wraps around me like a comforting embrace.

With a sigh, I finally admit, "It's been a hectic day, Seb. There's just a lot on my plate right now."

He nods in understanding, his fingers gently brushing a strand of hair from my face. "You know you can always talk to me, right?"

I manage a small smile, appreciating his offer even if I'm not quite ready to accept it fully. "I know. I will. Just need to get through this phase."

He nods again, his eyes filled with unwavering support. "I believe in you, Bella."

His belief feels like a lifeline in this whirlwind of challenges. It's reassuring to know that even when the lines between our personal and professional lives blur, Sebastian is here, a steady presence amidst the chaos.

As the baking show on TV continues to play, casting a soft glow across the room, I find myself easing into his embrace. In this dimly lit haven, fatigue and worries start to melt away, replaced by a comforting sense of home.

***

When I hear that Daniel Stanton is here to see me, I wonder what he's in New York for. He's hardly ever here in New York. He sends people. But today, he's decided to grace my office with his presence. The distinctive British accent that defines him echoes in my ears as he walks in, the CEO of Craig Stanton's taking a seat in front of my desk.

A smile plays on his lips at first, a mask that quickly fades. He unbuttons his suit, settling back into my chair with an air of familiarity.. "Last time I was in New York was about six months ago," he begins. "Lovely place, but I must admit, I dread coming here."

I raise an eyebrow, both intrigued and perplexed by his presence. "So, what brings you here all of a sudden, Daniel, if you have such strong feelings about the city?"

He leans back, his fingers steepled in front of him. Before he can answer, I cut to the chase, addressing the elephant in the room. "Is it about the fact that Craig Stanton's has been making some moves that directly sabotages my business?"

The smile returns to his lips, a faint shadow of amusement dancing in his eyes. "Ah, Isabella, always one to get straight to the point." His words carry that unmistakable British charm, a cadence that's both captivating and unnerving.

He doesn't deny it; instead, he offers a cryptic smile. "One cannot keep a lot of investors at bay forever," he says, his tone measured. "Many have voted for Craig Stanton's to break our partnership with you."

The news hits me like a punch to the gut. I knew this day would come eventually, but the stark reality of it sends a jolt through me. My carefully constructed world, the partnership I believed in, is unraveling before my eyes.

Leaning in, he explains with a casual tone, "In simpler terms, they have chosen to pursue their interests individually now. This development means that we cannot collaborate anymore as co-brands."

I struggle to process this information. It's as if the ground beneath me has shifted, leaving me grappling for balance. My mind races, searching for a response that adequately encapsulates the whirlwind of emotions swirling within me.

Daniel's words, that veneer of casual indifference, start to sink in. I nod slowly, a heavy sigh escaping my lips. "I see," I manage to say, though my voice wavers slightly.

He rises from his seat, ready to leave, his parting words leaving a bittersweet taste in the air. "Have a good day, Isabella."

Before he reaches the door, a surge of emotion pushes me to speak, to grasp onto some semblance of understanding. "I thought we were friends, Daniel," I say, my voice tinged with a mix of confusion and disappointment.

He pauses, turning back to me, his gaze meeting mine. "We are still friends, Isabella. But there are no friends in business, only mutual interests."

— Chapter 37 —
The Reunion

Isabella's birthday is around the corner. It's in a week's time, but the way her schedule has been lately, I don't think she has the time to celebrate her thirtieth birthday. Bella Sogno is crashing down, and I know how much it means to her. Her business partner, Daniel, has pulled his company from their partnership, and her stocks have been dropping since then.

Although she has failed to mention any of these events to me, probably too embarrassed to let me know, it's evident in her exhaustion. She comes back late from work, leaves early, spends weekends doing work and running around. I can't even have my wife to myself anymore. The demands of her struggling business are consuming her.

Tonight, I am by the fireplace, watching the fire crackle and dance with breaking twigs. The weather is getting bleak as autumn is ending, giving way to the approaching winter. It's a few minutes past 11 when Isabella walks through the door, looking tired and worn out, much like the past few nights.

She walks over to me, and without a word, sinks into the couch right beside me. I place a gentle kiss on her head, and we sit there in the quiet, the crackling fire providing a comforting backdrop. The silence lingers, broken only when Isabella softly utters, "I'm tired."

Her words are soft, barely audible, and they carry a weight that seems to encompass more than just her physical fatigue. I turn towards her, my gaze gentle, and kiss her head again.

Isabella manages a small, tired smile, the corners of her lips lifting ever so slightly. The fatigue in her eyes, however, remains unchanged.

I turn my gaze towards Isabella, and as I lean in, my lips brush against her forehead in a tender kiss. It's a simple gesture, a silent reassurance of my presence by her side. She's tired, and I can see it in the way her shoulders slump, the way her eyes carry the weight of long days and sleepless nights. She sinks into the couch beside me, and though we don't exchange words immediately, the warmth of her presence is enough.

As the fire crackles and dances before us, casting flickering shadows on the walls, I choose the right moment to speak, to gently acknowledge the approaching milestone that is her birthday. I clear my throat softly and break the quietude, "You know, your birthday is in a week."

Isabella's lips curl up, just a little, into a small, tired smile. It's as though my mention of her birthday has managed to coax a faint glimmer of happiness from within her exhaustion. I find solace in that smile, a reminder that even in the midst of challenges, there's room for a moment of lightness.

The weight of her burdens isn't lost on me, and as our eyes meet, I decide to pose a question, a simple query about her birthday wishes. "So, what do you want for your birthday?" I ask, my tone gentle and curious.

Her gaze remains fixed on the fire, as if she's seeking answers within the dancing flames. Then, her voice soft but laden with the weight of her struggles, she begins to share her thoughts. She talks about her business, the challenges it's facing, and the feeling that everything is slipping through her fingers. I can't help but glance at her as she speaks, my heart aching for her.

And then, her words take a turn that catches me off guard. "Maybe I shouldn't be doing this," she murmurs, her voice tinged with doubt. "Perhaps I should have stopped at being just a designer. Maybe that's all I'm ever good for. Maybe I shouldn't have done this."

I feel a pang in my chest as I listen to her doubts spill into the quiet space between us. It's as if her struggles have begun to chip away at her self-belief, leaving her questioning the path she's chosen. My instinct is to gather her closer, to envelop her in my support and reassurance.

With a deep breath, I wrap my arm around her shoulders and pull her gently against my side. "Isabella," I begin softly, my voice a soothing murmur, "you're far more than just a designer. You're a visionary, a trailblazer, someone who's capable of turning dreams into reality." I turn my gaze towards the fire as well, our eyes following the same dance of flames. "And yes, times are tough now, but that doesn't define your worth or your potential."

My heart aches for her as I pull her into a reassuring embrace. I hold her close, trying to offer comfort as her tears begin to fall. My words are gentle and soothing, an attempt to counter her doubts. "This is a sign that you're making progress as a CEO and a founder. Remember, my father was only a tailor and a fashion designer when he built Maxwell & Co. He faced his own challenges, too."

She listens, her sobs slowly quieting as my words seep in. But when the room falls silent once more, she finally opens up about the extent of the turmoil Bella Sogno is facing.

"Sebastian, we're drowning in debt. More than we can handle," she admits, her voice carrying the weight of her worries. "Investors are pulling out, stocks are plummeting. We have products we can't sell because there's no market. We can't even afford to produce another collection that fits the market. We're running on a loss."

A heavy silence hangs between us as the weight of her confession settles in. Without saying a word, I hold her tighter, offering her a space to release her emotions. She cries softly, and I hold her close, my fingers brushing away her tears as I whisper soothing words.

And then, after a minute of her tears and my quiet comfort, I find my voice again, my heart heavy with the desire to ease her burden. "What if I help you?"

Isabella's tears begin to subside, and she looks at me, her eyes a mix of surprise and curiosity. She asks me how, her voice carrying a glimmer of hope amidst the shadows of her worries.

I get up from the couch, my steps purposeful as I walk over to the wine racks. I select a bottle of whiskey, two glasses, and some ice. As I return to her side, I pour the whiskey into the glasses and hand her one. Our fingers brush as I pass her the glass, and then I say it, my voice carrying a promise that holds our love and partnership.

"I'm going to help you. We are going to be partners, Isabella. Not just employees anymore, but true partners. I'd do anything to make you happy, even if it means going against the board for you."

Isabella stammers as she begins to speak, her astonishment clear. She starts to question logistics, the uncertainties, the risks. But before doubt can take hold, I interrupt gently, ensuring she understands the depth of my commitment.

"Don't worry about the details right now. You're my wife, and the least I can do is carve out a slice of our success for you."

***

I've never been in a court of law before. But I know how it works, at least the basics of it. The defense attorney, the prosecutor, the judge, and the jury.

And right here, it's almost like the court of law. Me as the defense attorney, Robert breathing down my neck like a relentless state prosecutor. The rest of the board, the jury. It's the first day of the board deliberation, and the tension in the room is palpable. The air is thick with anticipation, as if we're awaiting a verdict that could reshape the future of our company.

I stand before the board, my palms slightly sweaty as I begin to speak. My words come out in measured tones, each sentence carefully constructed to build a case for collaborating with Isabella and her brand, Bella Sogno.

"I appreciate everyone's attention today," I start, my voice steady and my gaze meeting the eyes of the board members. "We're here to discuss an opportunity that I believe holds immense potential for our company's future."

I talk about Isabella's talent, her track record, and the potential for a unique partnership that can rejuvenate our brand.

"Isabella Rivera is not just a designer; she's a visionary who has consistently pushed the boundaries of fashion," I assert. "Her designs have garnered accolades, and her innovative approach has captured the attention of the industry."

I emphasize the need for innovation and fresh perspectives, all the while feeling Robert's gaze on me like a laser, scrutinizing my every word.

"We are living in a dynamic, ever-evolving industry," I continue, my gaze sweeping the room. "To remain relevant and captivating, we must embrace new ideas and perspectives. Isabella's brand represents precisely that."

As I lay out my argument, Robert doesn't hold back. He's ready to challenge every point I make.

"Sebastian, I respect your enthusiasm, but we must consider the potential risks here," Robert interjects, his voice measured yet skeptical. "Bella Sogno's recent setbacks raise concerns about their stability and whether they can truly contribute to our growth."

"I understand your concerns," I respond, my tone remaining composed. "But challenges are a part of any business journey. It's how we navigate and overcome these challenges that define our success."

He questions the viability of collaborating with a brand that he views as struggling, citing the departure of Bella Sogno's previous partner and the decline in stocks.

I defend my stance with conviction, countering his arguments with facts and anecdotes.

"While it's true that Bella Sogno has faced challenges," I counter, "we also have evidence of the impact Isabella's designs had when she was with us. Our sales, our visibility—it all saw a significant boost."

I speak about the successes we've had when Isabella was with us, how her creativity breathed new life into our brand.

"Isabella's designs elevated our brand to new heights," I emphasize, my voice unwavering. "Her creativity drew attention and admiration, not only from our customers, but also from the industry at large."

I argue that the current challenges Bella Sogno faces are temporary, and that by joining forces, we can leverage our strengths to create a stronger, more vibrant brand.

"While they are facing challenges now, I firmly believe that they have the potential to overcome them," I assert. "And if we collaborate, we can combine our strengths to create a brand that's innovative, resilient, and appealing to a broader audience."

Robert's argument is mostly about my marriage with Isabella and how he thinks I want to compromise the company's interests for my wife's. It offends me that he thinks that way. He didn't explicitly say it, but with riddles and so much subtlety, he implies it.

Days turn into nights as the deliberations continue, each session marked by spirited discussions and passionate arguments. The walls of the boardroom have heard more than their fair share of passionate pleas, rational justifications, and calculated risks.

On the morning of the resolution, I leave the house after kissing Isabella's forehead. The upcoming decision weighs on my mind as I head to work. Tomorrow is her birthday, and I've promised her a collaboration as her gift. The thought adds to my sense of urgency.

We're all gathered in the same conference room, the atmosphere heavy with the weight of the decision we're about to make. I can feel Robert's presence, his skepticism like a looming shadow. The tension in the room is so thick that you could cut it with a knife.

And then, it's time to vote. The board members cast their ballots, and we wait with bated breath. Each tick of the clock feels like an eternity as we wait for the results.

When the votes are counted, I barely beat Robert by a tiny margin. Relief washes over me like a wave. I can hardly believe it, we did it. The collaboration is approved. I can feel a weight lifting off my shoulders, and I can't help but jump out of my seat in excitement.

Later that night, I walk into the house with a brown envelope of documents in my hand, my face lit up with excitement. Isabella is in the sitting room, her voice still raspy from her cold. I hand her the document, watching as she opens it, confusion mingling with curiosity in her eyes.

"What is it?" She smiles as she fiddles with the envelope.

"Go ahead," I say. "Open it." I pause. Then, I remember the champagne I got on my way here. "Give me a moment," I say. "I have to go get something from my car." I rush back outside to the driveway to retrieve the bottle. As I return, Isabella has already opened the envelope, her eyes teary and her smile uncertain. She looks at me, her gaze seeking answers.

"Happy birthday, my love," I say. "The board approved our collaboration."

Her eyes widen, and as the realization sinks in, she battles with the tears wanting to run down her face. She moves close to me, her emotions overwhelming her. As she leans in, I shut my eyes in anticipation for the kiss. And then, her lips touch mine, and her hand moves smoothly over to the back of my head.

"Now you are gonna catch my cold," she teases through laughter, her voice slightly hoarse. I chuckle, setting the champagne bottle on the table, my excitement bubbling over.

"How about I catch you right now?" I reply, a mischievous glint in my eyes as I sweep her off her feet and start towards our room.

Isabella's laughter fills the room.

— Chapter 38 —
Love, Tradition & Legacy

One evening while we're visiting Sebastian's parents, and I'm sitting in the living room with his mother, she asks me about Bella Sogno, and I shrug, letting out a sigh. "It's been difficult, honestly."

She looks at me with that wise, knowing smile of hers. The kind that says she understands more than she lets on. "You know, Isabella, starting a business is like raising a child."

I chuckle softly, shaking my head. "It's funny you say that. But really, how can starting a business be compared to raising a child?"

She leans back, her eyes softening as she speaks, "Think about it. Both demand your time, your energy, your dedication. They keep you up at night, making you worry about their well-being. But at the end of the day, the reward is worth all the challenges."

Her words resonate with me, and I can't help but think back to the sleepless nights, the endless meetings, the countless decisions that came with running Bella Sogno. Just like a child, nurturing a business requires patience, resilience, and a lot of love.

I find myself nodding slowly, a smile tugging at my lips. "I guess you're right. There's a parallel there."

Sebastian's mother chuckles softly, her eyes sparkling with a hint of mischief. "And just like a child, you watch your business grow and blossom. You see it take its first steps, stumble a little, and then find its stride."

I can't help but laugh at her choice of words, a knowing glance exchanged between us. It's as if she's hinting at something more, something beyond just business.

"You're quite the storyteller," I remark, a teasing tone in my voice.

She smiles, a glint of pride in her eyes. "I've seen a few things in my time."

As we sit there, the warmth of the living room embracing us, I realize that Sebastian's mother is right. Just as a child's journey doesn't end with their first steps, a business's journey doesn't end with its launch. It evolves, it faces challenges, and it grows.

I think about how Bella Sogno has taken its own journey. The ups and downs, the moments of doubt and triumph. And then, just like a child growing up, here we are, on the verge of something even bigger.

I smile once more. "You know, you were right about something else, too. Just like a child finding love, I think our business has found its place, too."

She chuckles, her eyes warm and knowing. "Ah, love. It has a funny way of weaving itself into everything, doesn't it?"

***

The first three weeks of our launch together is a success. I almost forgot what success tastes like, that sweet blend of hard work, determination, and a bit of luck. But as I stand here, gazing at the bustling city lights from my penthouse window, I can't help but reflect on the journey that led me here.

From a young dreamer with a sketchbook full of designs, I've come a long way. Back then, the world of fashion felt like an unattainable fantasy, a distant realm reserved for the chosen few. I wondered if I'd ever step foot into that world, if my creations would ever see the light of day beyond my sketchbook.

And then, by some twist of fate, I stumbled upon that job listing from Maxwell & Co. A chance to work as an intern, to be a part of something bigger than myself. Little did I know that this opportunity would be the spark that ignited my path, setting me on a course that would change everything.

If I hadn't taken that leap, if I hadn't stepped into that office on that fateful day, I wonder where I'd be now. Would I have found my way into the industry on my own? Would I have fought my way up the ladder, clinging to the edge with every setback? Would I have discovered the joy of collaboration, the thrill of creating something beyond my wildest dreams?

And then, there's Sebastian. Ah, Sebastian, whom I hated in the beginning. I often wonder if we hadn't clashed, would we have ever recognized each other and even fallen in love?

Our journey has been anything but smooth. The challenges we faced were immense: the doubts, the naysayers, the sleepless nights. But each obstacle we overcame, every triumph we celebrated, brought us closer. We built something together that was more than just a brand, more than just a business. We built a bond, an unbreakable connection forged in the fires of perseverance.

And now, as I stand at the helm of Bella Sogno, my own brand, my heart swells with a mix of pride and gratitude. The journey to this point wasn't easy; it required sacrifices, late nights, and unwavering dedication. But here I am, a successful businesswoman with a brand that bears my name, my creativity, and my passion.

Sebastian is still by my side, his support unwavering. He's not just my partner, he's my rock, my confidant, my love. The truth is, I couldn't have done this alone. His guidance, his wisdom, his unwavering belief in me, they've all played a crucial role in shaping the path I'm on today.

As I look back on all that's transpired, I can't help but feel a sense of awe. The young dreamer with a sketchbook full of designs has become a woman who's made her mark in the world of fashion. And as I stand here, overlooking the city that's witnessed my journey, I can't help but smile.

***

I've learnt that it's easier to take risks when you have something to fall back on. Like a safety net, some feet above ground level when you take that dive from a ten-story building.

It's a leap of faith. A plunge into uncertainty, hoping that your wings will catch the wind and carry you, not drop you. But sometimes, just sometimes, those wings are designed not just to keep you afloat, but to let you soar. That's what I've realized in this whirlwind journey of fashion, collaboration, and love.

Now, as I stand backstage at our first collaborative fashion exhibition show, the culmination of hard work, creativity, and an unexpected love story, the chaos of the moment doesn't shake me. Models rush by, their elegance forms a blur of fabrics and designs. Conversations blend into a symphony of anticipation and excitement. The air is charged with energy, the kind that accompanies a grand reveal.

Sebastian is somewhere nearby, a calm presence amidst the frenzy. I catch glimpses of him at the corner of my eye, his demeanor composed, unmovable. I don't know what he's sipping from that flask of his, but it's his anchor in this sea of activity. My eyes dart to him from time to time, drawing a sense of comfort from his mere presence.

As the models begin to walk the runway, showcasing the fusion of Bella Sogno and Maxwell & Co., I follow behind them, a small run that's both triumphant and exhilarating. The audience erupts in applause, their enthusiasm like a warm embrace. It's a moment of validation, a reminder that even in the face of challenges, our creations resonate.

As I make my way back, I almost collide first-first with Sebastian's chest. A smile forms on his lips, but it fades as he sees the exhaustion in my eyes. He steps closer, his fingers brushing against my cheek before his lips press against my forehead, then my lips.

"You look beautiful," he observes, concern in his voice.

I offer a tired smile, a mixture of gratitude and weariness. "Thank you, my love."

His eyes search mine, reading between the lines. I expect him to ask if I'm okay.

Instead, he takes my hand gently and starts leading me away from the backstage chaos. We navigate through corridors like a pair of conspirators, escaping the hubbub that's still in full swing.

Finally, we reach the underground parking lot. My breath comes in ragged gasps, and I try to steady myself against the wall. "Why did you pull me away?" I ask in between breaths.

He doesn't offer an answer in words. Instead, he leans in, and the world around us blurs as his lips find mine. Protest and hesitation melt away as I lose myself in the kiss.

When he pulls away, his eyes meet mine, a mixture of desire and tenderness. "I saw you there, weaving through the crowd, and I couldn't stand sharing your attention with everyone else," he admits, his voice husky.

I laugh softly, that mixture of bashfulness and amusement dancing in my eyes. "Sebastian, the show isn't over yet."

He grins, mischief dancing in his eyes. "They don't need us anymore."

With his hand in mine, we move through the labyrinth of the parking lot until we reach a sleek, familiar BMW. I can see why he picked a car no one would associate with him. It's the perfect decoy. He unlocks the door and pulls me into the passenger seat. The engine purrs to life, and we wheel out into the night.

As we pass a sea of paparazzi, they're too preoccupied to notice our inconspicuous car. It's a thrilling sensation, sneaking away from the spotlight, leaving the clamor of success behind.

Sebastian's laughter fills the car, infectious and carefree. I grab both our phones and turn them off, a mischievous glint in my eye. He chuckles, and the atmosphere is light, unburdened.

"Instincts of a fugitive," he teases, his hand finding mine on the center console.

I laugh along with him, the tension of the day slowly ebbing away. There's something beautifully exhilarating about escaping the predictable narrative, about breaking free from expectations.

Leaning back against the seat, I let out a content sigh. "You know, in another world, even after all of this, I'd love to fall in love with you again."

— Epilogue —

I've been to a lot of award shows. The ones I've won. The ones I've lost. But one thing remains clear; I've never really gotten used to award shows. Sometimes, I wonder if I'll ever get used to the glamor.

Sebastian thinks otherwise, though. He thinks I was made for the spotlight. He thinks *we* were made for the spotlight.

Tonight, we sit here at the CFDA awards, his hand resting gently on my thigh.

The evening has been a whirlwind of flashing cameras, stylish gowns, and the heavy glamorous energy of the industry's best. Sebastian has already won two awards tonight, and his success is infectious. I find myself smiling a lot, not just for the camera, but because I'm genuinely relishing in the instant success of our collaboration. Especially when the host at the red carpet from earlier called us the "power couple of the industry."

As the award show progresses, the moment I've been waiting for arrives: the Brand of the Year category is called. My heart races as they announce the nominees. And then, the words I've been longing to hear: "And the winner is...Isabella Rivera for Bella Sogno."

I feel a surge of emotions as I hear my name. My heart skips a beat, and I glance at Sebastian, who's smiling hard, his eyes beaming with pride. He's no longer competing against me. He's standing by my side, helping me compete now.

I stand up, my hand reaching for Sebastian's as he helps me up the short flight of stairs. His touch is reassuring, and I feel a sense of calm wash over me. As he steps back to his seat, I take a deep breath and accept the award.

The applause is thunderous, and as I hold the award in my hands, I can't help but stare straight into Sebastian's eyes. It's like everything around me fades away, and it's just the two of us in this moment. He's beaming, and that pride in his eyes is all I need.

I raise the award, my voice steady as I give my short, two-line speech. "I'm grateful to everyone who made this possible. The sleepless nights from my team and the team at Maxwell & Co. made this all possible," I say, my words genuine and heartfelt. "And especially my husband, Sebastian, who believed in me when it wasn't popular to. This is for him."

The crowd erupts in applause once again, and as I step away from the podium, I can feel the weight of the award in my hands. It's not just a glorious object; it's a symbol of dedication, hard work, and the belief that together, we can achieve greatness.